Neon Hemlock Press
www.neonhemlock.com
@neonhemlock

Glitter + Ashes:
Queer Tales of a World that Wouldn't Die

edited by dave ring

*"Apocalypse" by Saida Agostini originally appeared in the
Barrelhouse Special Issue* I've Got Love on My Mind: Black
Womxn on Love, *Feb 14 2020, edited by Tyrese Coleman.*

Cover Illustration by Grace Fong
Cover Design by dave ring

ISBN-13: 978-1-952086-10-6

GLITTER + ASHES:
QUEER TALES OF A WORLD
THAT WOULDN'T DIE

Neon Hemlock Press

GLITTER + ASHES

queer tales of a world
that wouldn't die

edited by dave ring

A NOTE FROM
THE EDITOR

What can we look for when we read stories of collapse and apocalypse while the world is on fire? It's hard to know at first glance—perhaps, a map? Or a blueprint. Something to guide us forward, take us out of this mess. Reflections on the end of the world and its aftermath have been a crucible leading to so many incredible narratives that give those possible blueprints: *Tank Girl* and *Mad Max: Fury Road*, yes, but also *The Fifth Season* by N.K. Jemisin, *Blackfish City* by Sam J. Miller, and *Parable of the Sower* by Octavia Butler.

These stories show us that the end is not simply a dark road leading to more grit and doom. In that tradition, *Glitter + Ashes: Queer Tales of a World That Wouldn't Die* is an anthology centering queer joy and community in the face of disaster, via the amplified horrors of our current trajectory as well as more haunted and sinister ills. We set out from the beginning to find scraps of hope in every ruined future, knowing that queer folks, especially those with less access to sociocultural capital, often must learn to find meaning within the fractures of all manner of broken terrain. Yes, you'll read stories of folks learning how to get by, how to survive. You'll also read stories of folks learning to love themselves, learning how to find one another in the darkness, and learning how to stand up for each other. Making something stronger and more beautiful.

I am grateful to be able to share the roleplaying game *Dream Askew* by Avery Alder with you at the end of the anthology. *Dream Askew* forgoes dice and uses shared authority to explore the collapse through a queer enclave. It's a compelling, thoughtful system and I hope it gives you an opportunity to live and breathe the sort of stories that can become blueprints of your own.

If this summer has taught me anything, it is that there is beauty and power in refusing to back down, especially in the face of seemingly unassailable opposition. Even when the world is on fire. I'm humbled and inspired by the stories in *Glitter + Ashes*. Each of them is a bright torch against the cold night. Bear witness to their resilience and determination. Hear their laughter, and raise your fists with them.

May they give you the same solace they did me. May that solace be a commitment to nurture scraps of hope, glittering and fragile, amidst the ashes of *today*, not some uncertain future. Refuse to back down. And if joy is missing, may we come together to make it ourselves.

dave ring
June 2020
Washington, DC
On unceded Nacotchtank & Piscataway land

TALES

WRATH OF A QUEER GOD
Anthony Moll

The first ones to go would be the tasteless, anyone who has wielded unrhymed sacred text as armament, made body holey with Leviticus or even denied a name at holiday dinner. I'd be an Old Testament type—no, Greek—know fear as I cast down my wisdom in the form of lightning bolts, flooding Southern towns that build billboards for blond Jesus. Thou shall have no other before me in hairy legs and platform heels. Next I'd come for the trailer parks (not that the salt of the earth have wronged, but to deny shame of my own genesis) leaving only the baby butch toughs to testify, to reinscribe the words awesome and enormity with the weight they're due. The rich, I'd eat whole, consuming capital and shitting out bread and boutique health clinics. This hunger not only devastates, but lets rise thrift store monarchs, the most clever among you, now kings in their knock-off luxury, now queens in their shoplifted MAC. I'd tear to timber every suburban church, in part for their precepts but more for their aesthetic—how dare build anything but peacocked glory, stone and glass phalluses. Look now to the lesbian witches in hiking boots—let them show you what structures the moon desires.

I am everything you say I am. Witness my agenda: shade and spite, swallowing men whole.

DIDN'T MY LORD DELIVER DANIEL
Christopher Caldwell

Elijah came as himself, not as Eden. I was in my garden, pinching back the leaves of a garlic plant about to go to seed. A shadow stretched over me. I squinted up into the noonday sun. We were all leaner, but he looked gaunt. "What do you want, Eli?"

If you didn't have a history with him, you could mistake Elijah's unlined face, his louche posture, and his boyish pout for youth. But he had turned fifty in the decade plus since that last terrible argument, and to me, it showed. He was ashy. Bags under his eyes. The veins on the back of his hands stood out. "I didn't come to fight."

I dug into the earth with a spade. The smell of damp soil soothed me. "I assume that Eden does all the fighting nowadays?"

Eli shuddered. "She goes by Grandmother now. It's a sort of euphemism. Like how all the names for bear are really 'brown one' instead—"

"I know about bears." He always liked a lecture. "What do you want, Eli?"

He bit his lip. "It's just that there's a cantrip should prevent anyone from saying that name."

"Eden?" I said, then finding his surprise infuriating, "Eden!" I shouted. "Seems like your raggedy spells don't work."

"On you, Deshaun. My spells don't work on you! It's why I've come."

I stood up. Planted my heels in the earth. "You've come all this way to use me as a magical guinea pig? Where's your gown? Where's your knock-off Jimmy Choos? Your costume jewelry? How you gonna hex me without your evil queen regalia, boo?"

He spread out his hands. "You got it all wrong. I can't blame you for that." He looked down at his feet. "I came without any of that, without armor, without charms, to ask you to help me. I take care of survivors now. Most of 'em barely more than kids. Grandmother is Eden's role. She—I—look after them. But it's not safe here. You know that. I need to get them to the city."

This was why he'd come. Another foolish grand adventure. "I'm not young. Leave me with my grief and my plants."

He sneezed, the way he always did when he was about to cry. "I can't protect them all. I need you."

I looked up at him. Deflated. Needy. Found it hard to hold onto my anger. "What you need is some lotion for your ashy ass."

And so it went.

×

Elijah had taken up residence in the ruin of a grand old mansion. Out front, a heroic fountain choked with duckweed and water hyacinth. Mardi Gras beads slung over the enormous chandelier in the foyer. Threadbare rugs on the terrazo. The grand staircase was lit by hundreds of candles, ranging in size from tealight to altar pillar, in all the colors of the rainbow. He descended from above, the flickering light playing against his cheekbones. He wore a silken turban and a Schiaparelli pink dressing gown, not quite Eden's deadly glamour, but definitely not just Elijah.

I was sitting in a folding lawn chair. He *reclined* in a moth-eaten chaise longue. He picked up a wine glass from an old steamer trunk littered with them and held it to the light. It was none too clean, but he poured it full of red, and drained it in a single pull. He smiled. "The children have only ever seen me as Grandmother. And I think it's important for their faith. But you knew me before."

"We only lived together for six years," I said.

"Six years of you critiquing my makeup and making sure I got enough sleep so no one would know I robbed your cradle." He poured another measure of wine. "You did get my marrain's gumbo recipe out of the bargain."

"'If the roux don't look like Wesley Snipes, it ain't ready.' So, what does Grandmother wear? I assume it isn't a housecoat and a showercap."

Elijah stood. He placed his wine glass back on the steamer trunk and made a complicated gesture with his left hand. The dressing gown shimmered, the bodice constricted around his bosom, and sequins covered it decolletage to waist. The skirts bloomed out and sprouted marabou feathers along the hem. His turban grew feathers and beads. His voice became mocking and seductive. "These are the rags I wear around the house. But for our grand voyage? I have something truly spectacular."

Eden extended a hand to me. She had an immaculate French manicure. "Come doll, time to meet the kids."

Hand in hand we strolled out back into a courtyard with an empty pool lit by paper lanterns. About a dozen figures arrayed themselves around a bonfire burning in what was the pool's deep-end. A young man clambered up the pool's ladder. Early twenties. Thick, wavy black hair. He wore a rumpled gabardine pea coat. He was striking, and I felt awkward noticing it. Eden dropped my hand. "This is Juanjo, the oldest of my children. Sometimes the most responsible."

Juanjo bowed deeply at the waist, then grabbed my hand and kissed my ring finger, as if he were greeting the pope. He caught my eye. "At 23, I'm not much of a child."

Eden slapped him on the bottom. "The impertinence! You'll be grown when Grandmother says you are."

Next were two girls in their late teens. Sabrina, redbone, tall, gawky, and angular. Shirelle, dark, short, and plump. You wouldn't mistake them for sisters, but they had that strange facial similarity long time lovers get; something in the way they held their mouths.

Then a tiny person dressed in purple with a scarf wound

around their mouth. They introduced themselves as Clay.

Each was younger than the next until I got to a high yellow boy with a kinky mop of hair. He couldn't have been older than thirteen. Eden poked him in the belly. He giggled.

"EJ here is twelve." Eden said.

"Twelve-and-a-half!"

"Twelve-and-a-half. He's too young to remember the Breaking."

An unexpected surge of envy roiled in me.

* *

Grandmother's gown looked too heavy for any single person to wear, yet Eden promenaded in it, on better days she sashayed. It was covered in ornamentation. Mirror fragments on the bodice, hemmed in by pearls, sequins, tiny crystals. The skirt was oceanic, both in volume and and accoutrement; nets held together panniers encrusted with shells, coral, over aqua taffeta. The train extended five feet behind.

Picking our way east over roads with surfaces cracked and buckled from the encroaching woodlands meant that our procession was more funereal than stately. When the sun started to dip towards the horizon, we made camp. Everyone had a job. Clay, David and Lee pitched tents. Juanjo and Nacho cooked the vegetation I'd foraged through the day. Shirelle and Sabrina spun a web of protection above the camp. It was both a physical thing, spun out of gossamer threads Shirelle conjured, and a mystical barrier called into being by Sabrina's song. Even EJ helped fetch water and kindling for the fires.

Once we made camp, I helped Grandmother undress, and like some fairy tale where some miraculous beast sheds its skin and becomes an ordinary man, watched her shrink into Elijah. None of the children, not even trusted Juanjo, were allowed into Grandmother's tent. Elijah's rationale was that seeing him as a middle-aged man instead of a beautiful titan would shake their faith when they need it most. He was drained and fragile at the end of the day, and being his confidant forced a sort of intimacy I was no longer used to. I brought him his food, fed him when he was too tired to lift spoon to mouth.

About five days into our trek, I brought Elijah some nettle soup and fried mushrooms. He sat with his back to me, and the criss-cross of scars across his ribs and spines looked like a tributary map. He received those marks during the time we weren't speaking, and I didn't have it in me to ask. "Brought your supper."

His eyes were tired. "What I wouldn't give for a two piece and a biscuit. No matter how greasy."

"Today we have puffball mushrooms fried in expired cooking oil, if you're looking for an unhealthy snack."

Elijah sucked his teeth. "Speaking of snacks, I see my eldest has his eyes on you."

"Juanjo?" I thought of how his hand lingered on mine when I showed him how to pull up hairy bittercress without bruising the leaves. "He's been helping me forage. Good head for mycology. He found the giant puffballs, and warned off Clay from the Jack-o-Lanterns when they—"

"Those ain't the kind of mushroom head he's after, DeShaun."

My mouth felt dry. "You nasty! He's barely more than a child."

"He's a man. And it ain't like there's a surplus of fine ass in the world."

My cheeks were hot. "Don't want no more of this talk."

Elijah leaned back into a pile of cushions. He closed his eyes. "Don't say I never warned you."

※

I tried to keep my distance from Juanjo after that conversation with Eli, but I only had the flimsiest of excuses. He *did* have a good head for mycology, and it was hard to forage on my own for enough food to feed the camp, particularly as we got further into the wilds and more of the flora was the twisted and useless sort made by the Breaking. We fell into a sort of companionable silence. I could feel his interest, and to be honest, I returned it, but we never let that thing get in the way of the work.

We had been lucky on our trek so far. We heard a pack of wolves in the hills, but they'd stayed away. We lost the better part of a day when Lee got sick after being stung by a Broken wasp. Uneventful, for the most part.

Juanjo and I were picking sloes and rowan berries at the edge of a meadow and keeping an eye on EJ while he gathered dried grass and twisted it into bundles. Juanjo was singing a song in Spanish about a botecito, and had just got to the part about 'una isla dulce amor,' when an unmistakable sound killed the song in his throat.

Broken crows aren't black like their untransformed cousins, they're a vibrant purple. Twice as big, they don't caw. Instead, they have a horrible screech like a cross between an air raid siren and a wounded child. As silent in flight as owls, you don't hear them unless they've found something to eat. They have a taste for meat. The sky turned purple as they flowed like smoke over the rowan trees and across the meadow.

"EJ!" Juanjo yelled. He ran towards the boy who dropped his bundle of grass and was standing stock still staring at the murder heading for him. Juanjo tackled the boy and covered his small body with his own as the first birds began to divebomb. I knew a song of the earth and started chanting as the swirling purple mass descended.

A shout pealed. Clay ran towards us, scarf unwound from their mouth. They breathed out a gout of flame that scattered the murder and sent the smell of singed feathers sharp in my nose. The birds wheeled on their aggressor just as Clay inhaled deeply for another blast.

But it wasn't flames that came next. From behind Clay, a brilliant white light made mockery of the November noonday sun. I shielded my eyes, but even closed, I could make out the after-image of Eden's form. Her cold light scattered the crows, who screamed up and away in panic.

When the light faded, I ran to Juanjo and EJ, both motionless on the ground. I placed a hand on each of them and *felt*. EJ had a concussion and would have some bruising, but would otherwise be alright. Juanjo was hurt badly. Bleeding from several places. A punctured lung. Broken bones. I could mend a broken bone with time and concentration, but this was beyond me.

I began to weep, but Eden's mirrored bodice glowed. I felt warmth suffuse my limbs. Then power. Like being hit by a thunderbolt. The good green flowed from my fingertips, setting bones and knitting flesh together. There wouldn't even be scars.

The power flowed out of me. Exhausted and sweat-covered, I collapsed next to Juanjo and EJ. I looked up at Eden. "How?"

"My Lord delivered Daniel in the den of lions. Are these any less His children?"

I wondered, before unconsciousness took me, when Elijah had got religion.

⁙

I woke in Eden's tent. Juanjo and EJ to either side. Juanjo snored. Eden, still in her gown, sat on a brocade cushion at Juanjo's feet. Her makeup was immaculate, but she looked old. I could hear raised voices outside of the tent. I struggled to my feet.

Eden said, "They're hungry. They're cold. They're afraid. Be kind to them."

I exited the tent.

Shirelle was spinning her web. She tied off a strand then turned to David, hands on her hips. "And all I'm saying is my girl ain't stuck with the name her momma gave her, could have picked any name in the world and ended up Sabrina."

Sabrina blushed. She covered her face with both hands. "I *like* my name. It makes me feel pretty."

"Girl, you are pretty. My point here is that this nigga," she pointed at David, "stupid."

David scowled. "Nacho? Lee? Back me up. We forever carrying around that old bag's heavy ass shit. She don't lift a finger to make camp. She's slow as fuck. Always walking like she in a parade or some shit. We woulda been made the city if we wasn't waiting on her ass."

Clay shook their head. "You weren't there. I spat a fireball dead center into that mess of birds. Just pissed them off. Three or four of us would have been dead—"

"Shit. I'm supposed to be scared of some old crows?"

I stepped into the light from the fire. "Those old crows would have stripped the meat from your bones in minutes. Your gift of strength would do little to stop them."

David jutted his chin at me. "What you know about what I can do?"

"I know that there are more terrible things out in the Shattered Places than Broken crows. I know Eden has survived most of them. I know that a fifteen-year-old, no matter how strong, is no match for them alone."

He had the grace to look chastised.

×_××

Tempers were soothed the next day by a foraged bonanza of rose hips, pine nuts, and turnips. Going to bed with a full stomach seemed to put everyone at ease. The day after that, we saw a rusted sign that informed us the city was only five miles off. We could see its skyline peeking through the trees. Everyone cheered, even David.

We made camp that night on the outskirts of the city, full of hope. A place un-sundered by Breaking. Where we could be whole without the pull of the Shattered Places. Where gifts didn't leave us weak and empty. Sabrina sang for us, her voice a rich, dark baritone. Juanjo pulled me into a dance, and I found myself laughing as the rest of the children whooped, and I pulled him closer to me than I might have otherwise dared.

The web had never been broken. Every night Sabrina and Shirelle put up the web, and every morning they took it down. Sleep came late for us all, but when it came, it came deep. I was confused when Sabrina's scream split the night. Who would harm her? But it was the web. I could feel them around us, twice as many in number. A gout of flame pierced the darkness, as Clay unwound their scarf. But the intruders were not without gifts. Glass knives conjured from air whistled past me. They shattered against Lee's invisible walls. Nacho's rain of ice seemed useless against them, and they tore too quickly through Shirelle's binding webs. The earth turned to mud at my call, but one of their own raised them a foot off the ground with a gesture. I wondered if there could be turns of surrender.

Then Eden came out of her tent. One moment, I saw Elijah, half-dressed, without makeup, trying to fasten the back of his gown. Then everything changed. I have been near the Shattered Places. The world there has been broken and wounded and everything seems less real. This was not like that. The world stretched and turned, but did not break. And everything after seemed realer. Eden's skirts were the ocean, and they swept forward to snatch intruders in their cold waves. Clay was a dragon, their fire evaporating ice walls and incinerating those who cowered behind them. David was a giant, shrugging off conjured knives and tossing aside enemies into the darkness beyond. Shirelle was a spider, she grasped a man with dread pedipalps. Juanjo became a wood-sprite who commanded the very trees. The earth whispered to me that if I so wished it, it would swallow my attackers whole, never to be found again.

I wished it.

Then, as suddenly as it began, the world snapped back into place and all the glorious realness fled.

Eden knelt in the middle of the camp, her gown in rags, every single one of the mirrors on her bodice shattered. She crawled towards her tent, strewing broken beads like pearly seeds into the soil.

⚹

The next morning was slow going. Eden was weak, and Juanjo and I helped her walk. She insisted on wearing the tattered remains of the gown, though whatever power imbued it had fled.

After a time, we crested a hill. There in a valley below us, in a park overgrown in ivy, was the museum we planned to make our new home. "We're here!" Someone shouted, and three or four of the children ran down the hill to get a closer look. David picked up Eden, and said he was going to carry her to the heights for the best view.

I leaned against a birch tree. I could feel nothing of the wrongness here. It was strange to feel peace after so long. Juanjo put his arms around my shoulder. He leaned in close. He smelled like juniper, sweat, and the good earth. He asked me, "May I?"

Without answering, I kissed him hard and deep. It was good, like the first sprout of Spring after a long Winter.

We were still embracing when David carried Eden back down the hill. Her eyes twinkled with mischief. "David, darling, get me a chair. Then get yourself scarce." He ambled off.

"Juanjo, honey, could you get us old folk some chamomile tea? I feel the cold in my chest."

Juanjo looked bashful. "Need to start a fire."

"I'm sure Clay could help with that."

Eden sat next to me on a folding chair, and the two of us looked down at our destination, still intact. A new home, in a place largely untouched by the Breaking. I pointed. "That museum has a collection of garments dating back five-hundred years. Just imagine the gowns you could make."

Elijah, not Eden, smiled back at me. "Imagine."

We sat in silence for a moment, then Elijah slumped in his seat and fell to the ground. I was on him in a heartbeat, feeling with the green for an injury. But he was gone. I have no power to revive the dead. Still, I willed health and healing in through his limbs before admitting its uselessness. His heart had stopped.

It was important to Elijah in life that the children see him as more than mere flesh. I couldn't bring him back, but I had other powers. All life wants to return to the soil. I whispered my farewells and concentrated. That face with those cheekbones and those arch expressions grew slack and then crumpled in. Sinew, skin, and bone crumbled. Blood dried up and blew away. All that remained was dust and ashes. A single, shimmering sequin from Eden's dress caught on the wind and flittered away. There was a dark patch beneath my feet. One day, flowers would grow there.

Juanjo returned a few minutes later with three steaming mugs of chamomile. He furrowed his brow. "Where's Grandmother?"

I wiped away a tear. "Gone. Taken up in a chariot with wheels of fire."

THE DESCENT OF THEIR LAST END
Izzy Wasserstein

Ash falls on Eve's tent like snow. Its sound reminds her of trips to the beach as a child, of the patter of sand as it slipped through her fingers. A sound so soft and unassuming that when she hears it, sometimes she can still fall into one of her books and forget that there will be no more trips to the beach, no future at all, that everything slips away.

Then the ash will build up so thick the tent starts to sag, or the sounds of Lilith's grand project, whatever it is, will cut through the silence, and Eve will be thrown back into the present.

The tent is packed with books, far more than she'll have time to read. The temperatures are already falling rapidly, and their food will not hold out forever. But Lilith let her bring as many books as she wanted, so many that each night when it is too dark to work, Lilith has to push small piles of books out of the way to crash beside her.

Eve reads, and Lilith works, and the ash of the end of the world falls upon them, insistent as rain. The rain of the dead, Eve thinks, and then dismisses the thought.

When Eve has to leave the tent to relieve herself or cook dinner with their dwindling supplies, she is careful not to look behind the tent, not to spoil the project Lilith has been working on.

My last installation, Lilith called it once, the only time she had broken their rule not to speak of lasts. When they break bread, when they share whispered kindnesses, when Eve reads aloud as Lilith drifts off to sleep, when they explore each others' bodies, they never say: this may be the last time. The ash says it for them.

A hundred books still left unread, but it is *The Left Hand of Darkness*, dog-eared and spine-broken, that Eve is reading when Lilith finishes her project.

"You may look," she calls into the tent.

Eve puts the Le Guin aside, and steps out of the tent. Around her, the glacial valley stretches away in silence, bits of green still visible in sheltered places; the ash has not yet covered all.

Behind the tent are a cluster of bicycles, their faded blue and violet frames strangely alien amidst the ancient landscape. Each bike is partially buried in the grey earth. They look ready to break from the ground, like a flock of clockwork birds about to burst into flight. They will fly without riders.

Eve had never witnessed anything so beautiful. "It's perfect," she says. "Too bad no one will see it."

"Do you see it?" Lilith asks.

Eve runs her hands over the handle of the lead bike. The wheel rotates slowly. "I do," she says.

"Well, then." Lilith brushes ash-flakes from her shoulder.

They stand for a long time in silence, until the dim glow of the sun behind the clouds sinks toward the horizon.

"Come inside," Eve says. "I'll read to you."

Hand in hand they enter the tent. The ash falls like snow on the tent, the bicycles, the earth.

SOFT
Otter Lieffe

⬛ ⬛

“I don't know if I can do this.” Dee pulled the transit van over into the gas station, braking a little too suddenly. The map and a couple of coffee cups tumbled off the dashboard.

“Steady, girl,” said Ray softly. He put his hand gently on her leg. The feeling of his warmth through her tights made her breathe a little deeper. “You've got this.”

“Not yet, I haven't.” Dee pulled down the vanity mirror and reapplied her lipstick—holographic and blue—the most attention-grabbing shade she owned. Even though they'd been planning the operation for days, it was Dee's first time, and she needed all the confidence she could get.

“I'll go fill up.” Ray closed the door as gently as he could.

Dee let her hair down out of its ponytail and rechecked the mirror. There was already some stubble coming in since this morning, but it would have to do—her supply of foundation and concealer was long gone. *Maybe it's better anyway.*

The doorbell squealed a warning as they entered together, holding hands. The shop was full, and they had everyone's attention.

“I'll go look for supplies.” Dee's voice was loud enough that the whole store could hear her, and she walked down the aisle towards the dark fridges. If her announcement wasn't enough, the clicking of her heels should do the trick. She was already breaking into a sweat when a security guard headed over in her direction.

As she pretended to browse what might have been the last bottles of shampoo in the country, she watched out of the corner of her eye as Ray went straight to the desk. The cashier sat behind three sheets of bullet-proof glass and Dee could practically feel him staring at her across the store.

"Pump three," she heard Ray announce, projecting his deep voice through the glass.

"Eighty-five seventy."

Ray produced a note from his pocket—a two-hundred, she knew, because they'd earned it together the night before in a very nice hotel downtown.

She heard Ray say, in his most innocent voice, "Sorry, that's all the bank gave me."

Dee watched as the cashier absently pushed the change under the barrier. He barely took his eyes off her for a second. She fiddled with a bottle of conditioner trying to keep her expression neutral as she carefully studied the ingredients list. Her gut was churning, her head was pounding. She looked up and saw the security guard closing in. He strolled towards her past the windscreen wipers and pepper spray.

Suddenly Ray called to her and her heart skipped. "Honey? Did you find anything?"

A deep breath. "Nothing interesting," she called back. He came to join her, flashed the security guard a look and walked her back up the aisle. They left the store and Dee didn't notice how much her hands were shaking until she turned on the ignition.

They pulled out of the forecourt and back onto the road. "So?" she asked.

Ray stared ahead. "Let's drive a bit first."

They drove along the country road. Five minutes. Ten minutes. The sun began to set, and the sky ahead had turned a rich, burnt orange. Finally, impatiently, Dee pulled over in a discrete rest area surrounded by trees. She reversed up to the cliff edge.

They got out, walked to the back of the van and stretched.

Ray opened the doors and they sat down together on the mattress, swinging their legs, looking out over the view. Down below them, the river sparkled red.

"So?" she asked him again.

He emptied his pockets onto the bedsheets. With security and the cashier sufficiently distracted, he'd managed to pocket a pile of candy bars, a bag of chips, multivitamins and some kind of salami.

Dee smiled. "I can't believe that actually worked."

"You haven't seen the best yet." Ray started fiddling with his belt and zipper.

Dee shot him a confused look. "Shouldn't we close the doors first?"

Ray didn't respond. He unzipped his jeans and with a grin, produced a bottle of vodka from his crotch.

"What? How did that even happen?"

"A magician never reveals his secrets." Ray opened the bottle and offered it to her.

"To being visible," she said, and took a swig.

"And fucking resilient."

They sat for a while, looking out over the valley. Dark clouds came in from the west and smeared the sky with oily purple.

"So," Ray said, chewing on the salami. "North?"

Dee nodded. "Everything else must be underwater by now. If we can make it to the next town, we should be able to stock up a bit. How's the money doing?"

Ray patted his jacket pocket. "It's been better. Maybe another duo if we find the right trick?"

With a smile, Dee took Ray's hand and put it on her leg again. "You know I love working with you, baby."

"You turn me on so much, baby."

Dee chuckled. She was feeling the effects of the vodka and drank some more. "Maybe you should drive though?"

"That's the plan."

Dee watched the sun slip below the horizon. A cold breeze was building. "It's amazing, you know?" Dee slurred the word 'amazing'.

"The vodka?"

She poked him in the ribs. "This, us. Surviving out here. I don't think we were supposed to."

Ray produced a blanket from under a pile of clothes and put it over Dee's shoulders. He shivered and zipped up his jacket. "Maybe we weren't supposed to, but in a way, we knew we would."

"What do you mean?"

"Just that we always have been."

Dee thought about it for a moment watching the sky. *He's right of course. People like us have been avoiding the law, passing around hormones and meds through our networks, taking care of each other and fighting gangs of men since forever.* "Yeah, I guess shit hit the fan for us a long time ago."

"Thank you for being in this with me," Ray said, taking her hand. "I couldn't survive out here without you, and I wouldn't want to."

Dee gave his hand a little squeeze before jumping down onto the ground. "I'll find us some nettles and roots for dinner."

"Need help?"

Dee flashed him a smile. "I've got it."

She grabbed her collecting bag and stepped out into the darkness.

THE BLACK HEARTS OF LA PLAYA
Jordan Kurella

"There's no such thing as monsters, not really," Letty said to me once, pretending to shoot another starving lizard with finger guns. "I bet everyone's got a little monstrousness inside them."

I watched her holster and pull her finger guns as we sat on a pillaged picnic table, swatting locusts and sipping water. It was no secret I was in love with her. Me, Marrin Version 3.0. I'd been one version for my mother, another for Corporal, and now I was this version for Letty, the girl who liked to go shooting and give the wrong plots of old books as if she had read them dozens of times (when in fact she hadn't read them at all).

"Yeah?" I asked her. "What's your monster?"

She turned to me, hands on her knees, shoulders all serious.

"No, Marrin," Letty said. "I want to know about *yours*."

"Desert's got a vampire problem," Corporal said, at the briefing later that night. "Letty, Marrin, you're on Eastwatch Tower detail. Nights. Don't get too distracted with... you know."

She smiled. Cause she knew. She'd seen me sneaking out of Letty's tent before, tying on my belt, fixing my hair. Corporal smiled then too, and lifted her chin, fixing her own hair. Like she did back when she and I were a thing.

The other Tower details got dealt out as Letty shot me a long glance across the mess tent, where we were shielded against the locusts that swarmed lights. Like everyone said: the insects would survive the apocalypse. Everyone was at least right about that.

What they weren't right about was most of the rest.

Once Corporal was finished and the socializing started, I stepped outside. Stepped out and down the ramp, out onto the asphalt. Camp was set up in what had been a parking lot, the abandoned vehicles cleared and scrapped decades ago for space and materials. There was a big building behind us that we used once, but, "We don't go in there no more," Corporal said to me a while back. "Roof keeps caving in on us. Don't got the means to fix it."

She knew me then; she knew me then like she knew me now. Knew I would come out here alone, 'cause I heard the wheels of her chair hit the ramp, then hit the asphalt behind me. I turned to find her looking up at me with that steel gaze that had fixed me to her long ago. Letty was still inside. She was a social animal; Corporal and I weren't, we never had been. We traveled solitary, or in pairs.

This remained, even when I was with Letty.

Or not with her.

Corporal was betting on this when she reached up and took my hand in a friendly, platonic gesture. Her blue eyes piercing through the haze of her safety goggles, her smile visible despite the scarf over her face. Still, gone was all the heat and immediacy of her movements. That desire that had pulled me to her, made me tell her the lies that I wanted her to believe about me. That I wanted anyone to believe.

"Careful with that one, Marrin," Corporal said. "Don't want you to go breaking her heart. She's a lot more fragile than me."

Corporal ran her thumb across the back of my hand, and then took off, glancing once behind her as she went. The memory of her kisses were hot on my lips: hard and fast, like she meant them as much as she meant everything. Letty's kisses were tentative, but her grip was sure. She always took me to her like I was the last kiss left in the world.

Me? I was desert silt: wispy and forming against either of them in a way that suited them, until they brushed me off. And both of them brushed me off: Corporal once, Letty more times than that. But like silt, I kept coming back.

× ⁝ ×

Sun never rose anymore. In books it did, in stories it did, but not here. All the sun could manage to do now was edge over the horizon and light up this grey haze just enough to set everyone coughing.

I was already on lookout at Eastwatch Tower when the elevator shuddered behind me. Its shrieking doors opened to reveal Letty, all five foot four of her, dressed like me in dark clothing. Both of us with our bandoliers of wooden stakes, and gunbelts built for two six shooter revolvers.

We wore scarves over our noses and mouths. Mine was a dull grey, colored that way from lackadaisical washing habits. Letty's was black on black, like the rest of her clothes. Like her hair. Like two of her teeth.

"I hate that thing," Letty said, motioning not to me, but to the giant gasoline beacon lighting up both our faces.

"Same," I said.

"Makes me smell like diesel for a decade."

She grinned at me, boots hitting the corrugated metal platform like her hyperbole. Letty was small, but she took up as much space as an argument. I had a weakness for women that overwhelmed me like this.

She grabbed my offered binoculars and looked at me, her face lit from the beacon firelight. Her face took on a softer quality lit up this way. Softer than when in the mess hall, in the haze of the day, under the fluorescent lantern in her tent. But Letty wasn't soft—there was nothing soft about her, from the callouses on the tips of her fingers down to the steel toes of her boots, she was all hard edges.

We were all hard edges anymore.

"Vampire problem," I said. "What else is new."

"It's Tuesday," Letty said.

True, but the days ran together now. Every day was Tuesday anymore.

⁙

Vampires struck in the late hours of the night, or the early hours of the morning, depending on one's point of view. My heart always struck at the same hours, reminding me of what I'd lost, what I'd given up, just to come here, just to be a part of this camp.

Letty had thrown me out of her tent three times, three times after three whispers of "I love you, Marrin." Three displays of vulnerability, rawness so real she couldn't let me have it, hold it, or believe it. My belt struck my thighs with the same rawness, the same vulnerability, when she threw it at me.

"Get out," she also whispered to me. Three times.

My mother used to whisper poetry to me. Her own dangerous words of the sea, as I was named after people lost at it, wandering at it, the same way my mother wandered through her life. The same way I wandered through mine.

We often become our mothers, so the legends said.

"Marrin," my mother said so often, so much. "Listen. Stop squirming." And she would go on about her black and broken heart at the bottom of the ocean. Childless and free. And dead. It was too much for a child to bear, but I carried that heart in my pocket until she left me on the cracked and sundered sidewalk, left me to find my own way in this chaos.

A vampire knew its own way, so the stories said. They knew their codes and ways of being. They stayed to their communities tied to a morality so strict in antiquity there was no other way to be. It was almost romantic, if one still believed in romance. I didn't: the world was too dead for romance now.

Still yet, sometimes, late at night, I'd wander the desert beyond the shoddy camp walls, out of reach of the beacon lights. I'd wander with my bandolier and my revolvers—a safety net. But what I was looking for was anything but safe.

I was looking for a way out, like my mother did all those years

31

ago.

I was looking for a vampire.

* *

Letty kept the binoculars up, old heavy ones that showed off the thin musculature of her forearms. I leaned over the edge of Eastwatch Tower, peering out to the edges of where the beacon fire didn't reach. I was looking for a whisper of movement, a promise of action, but my own vision was clouded by the locusts and the scratches on my safety goggles.

By Corporal's orders, everyone wore these. Too many bugs.

Mine had so many scratches that they hid my expressions. With the scarf and the scratched safety goggles, Letty said they hid the truth of me. That the ugly parts that I didn't want anyone to see only came out in the harsh fluorescent light of her tent. Which is why she probably cast me out after whispering in my ear.

She never liked what she saw.

Letty brought down her binoculars and brought up her own safety goggles. They hid the mask of her. Made her dark eyes look softer, more innocent, which was the truth. Her vulnerability, her quiet tenderness, was what she wanted to hide from the world. Magnified by the scratches and blur of the safety goggles, now blinking back at me.

"Got one," she said. "There."

She passed over the binoculars and I took a look. Out in the darkness of the desert was a tall, lanky individual who looked too out of place for the desert. No scarf, no goggles. Sitting comfortably on an old vehicle uniframe in scuffed up boots and a long hoodie so holey it should take up religion. They were smoking a cigarette and looked like the sun hadn't touched them in years.

Totally a vampire.

"We should call in backup," I said.

"No need," Letty said. "We got this."

She'd already turned to call the elevator. Its bowels shook and ratted in its ascent, answering my own fear. The desert wasn't the only one with a vampire problem—Letty herself had one. Or more of an obsession. She had the highest vampire kill count out of anyone in Corporal's camp.

I had never killed a vampire, and Letty knew it.

"There might be more, Letty," I said.

"*There might be more, Letty,*" she mocked back at me. "Then bring them on, Marrin. We can take them." She fingered a wooden stake at my bound chest. "We can take them together. You and me."

And just like that, my heart skipped into my throat and I entered the elevator with her, our faces plunging into the orange safety lights, together.

* * *

Corporal had taken interest in me when I was patching asphalt. She wheeled up to me when my back and arms were all sweaty and said, "Take five, you. Can't have the new person getting worn out on their first day in camp."

I looked at her, her blue eyes piercing through her safety goggles, disarming me.

"I'm not new here," I said. "I've been here for three years."

"Well, well," Corporal said. "Then take five with me, old timer."

We cracked open beers and then cracked open memories. She'd inherited the camp from a man who'd inherited the camp from an old soldier, back when there were soldiers, back when there was civilization. She also inherited the title from him.

"What does it mean?" I asked.

"Dunno," she said. "But I like the sound of it. What the hell does Marrin mean?"

"It's short for Mariner," I said. "My mom liked stories about the ocean."

"Where is she now? Mom?"

I shrugged. She shrugged. Then we chugged our beers.

Some secrets have to be kept deep, deep in the drink.

Corporal said she liked me cause I had mommy issues, like her. I told her I liked her cause she took no shit, like me. But really I liked her cause when I was with her, I didn't ever have to second guess who I was or what I was. I was Marrin, Corporal's partner, and she held me to her so close it was like a secret kept deep, deep in the drink—one she never wanted to let go.

We were tight together, for a time. Corporal and Marrin, an item. Whispers went around the camp like a sandstorm, pitted and painful. They hit me harder than they hit her, or so it seemed. If Corproal was bothered, she only showed it in how much more she drank when we were alone, or in the looks that became more critical as we talked late and late into the night.

As she unraveled me, story by story.

Frown by frown.

I wasn't the person she wanted me to be. I was Marrin, the person with the mommy issues who came to Camp looking for a place to belong and forget their life. I came to be alone and work; work myself into a community that would let me forget everything that had come before. Work myself into a community where everything, like surviving, was only forward.

Until Corporal. Until I fell into her needing me and she realized that what she needed *wasn't* me. Corporal needed someone who wanted a hero for a girlfriend. Someone who would let her save them from their wretched past, like some kinda knight. Still though, I couldn't be that for her, I still wanted her. I wanted the heat of her kiss, the grip of her hand around mine, the feel of her watching me from across the thoroughfare.

Maybe, though, I was wrong.

Maybe, just maybe, something in me *did* want to be saved.

'Cause when Corporal let me go, I hit the ground like sunset. Sudden, but with plenty of warning. I just refused to see it coming. The comments and whispers that came after dug in deep and necrotic, and I retreated more into myself than before. I had to find the source of these wounds, dig deep into what had turned me so wrong.

Had turned my heart to black.

It's easy to lose yourself in a person, the way the world lost itself in ending. Or at least people believed it did, for a while. And then we rebuilt and rebuilt and rebuilt. Generations later, we're still here: with greenhouses and protection from the bugs, living in tents in parking lots, taking shelter from collapsing roofs.

Like I said: the legends were partially true. Cockroaches and locusts are a constant reminder that we're just tenants around here. But the stories were mostly wrong. We've got chemists and botanists that engineer medication, and ramps and elevators and safety ropes cause they're just a good idea. People persevere. Despite what anyone ever said.

We've got wind power and batteries. We've got storytellers and history. We live despite everyone and every legend that told us it was impossible—even my mother. Like the locusts, like the cockroaches, we refused to leave.

There are only the skeletons of skyscrapers and sunsets and moonlight serenades, but we are more than that. We persevere as the meat and skin and breath of what is left by catching lightning bugs. With hot kisses out of reach of the beacon fire. With vampire hunts.

Like the one Letty and I are going on right now. And she's fifteen steps ahead of me.

× ×
×

Vampires hadn't changed much from before the world ended. Stories said they were still blood-sucking negative energy drains that thrived on destruction and hate. All they ever did was take, take, take (or so the stories said). That they hung around camps like ours to disrupt us, to harm us. So we had to work to spite them. But mostly, because of them—we had to work together. Word was that vampire camps didn't work together, that they were sites of pure chaos, pure destruction.

But word and stories had been wrong before.

So much had been wrong before; it was hard to know what to believe.

Corporal's camp was this bright center of positive energy where everyone may not have liked their assignments or may not have liked their neighbor, but it was a society, and working to build and maintain the camp was how Corporal's society functioned.

"Don't like it?" she'd say. "Go join the vampires."

But bad people joined the vampires. Good people stayed in the camps.

Everyone said that.

I followed behind Letty as close as I could while she continued on her mission to break her ankle or break the sound barrier, whichever came first. I kept a torch up to try to light our path, smelling like diesel and old socks—cause that's what I had on hand to make it. My heels blistered against my boots as I continued on, an excuse for my slow pace.

Letty's hands were shadows above the hilts of her revolvers. She was stalking ahead like it was high noon, closing in on our nemesis—her vampire, our vampire. They sat on the uniframe ahead, the cherry of their cigarette glowing intermittently in the black, quiet desert night. A quiet night punctuated only by the grit of our boots on the concrete, the scuttle of a leftover lizard, and then.

"Here for me, I assume."

It was them. The vampire.

"Hell yes we are."

It was Letty. My would-be girlfriend.

"Well, let's get on with it," the vampire said.

They stood, finally illuminated in my torchlight. They were tall, as tall as me, with hair just as long and lanky. Their face was longer though, storybook long, with a nose that came down and hooked at the end. It stood in contrast to their wide, wide eyes that stared at me from across the expanse of Letty whose revolvers were drawn and now pointed at our vampire prey.

"Wait," I said. "Wait a second."

"Why," Letty said. More of a bark than a question.

"Don't you want to know where they came from? If there are more of them? If they have a camp nearby? We need information."

"We don't need shit except this asshole dead."

"Dead-er," the vampire corrected. "My name is Aurin. And I

am one of many, yes."

"See?" I said.

"How many?" Letty was seething. Her words hissing through clenched teeth.

"Very many," Aurin said. "But I didn't come for your camp. We don't want so much as all that. We're happy where we are; how we are."

"Then what do you want?"

Aurin looked at me. Their eyes still wide, wide and black as everything around us. Black as the ocean depths my mother wrote her poems about. Black as the wound that her leaving had left festering in me.

Black as my moods lately.

"I think they know," Aurin said.

And then they pointed at me.

×⋮

The last time Letty had whispered that she loved me I had almost let myself believe it. Until she tossed my pants and my belt at me and told me to leave her alone, like she did the other two times. Taking that whisper and drowning it in her exterior machismo.

Earlier that night, when she was drunk and playing with my hair, she told me that she heard that there had once been flowers called buttercups, and white girls would hold them up to their chins to see if they were pure.

She told me she wanted to be pure.

When she pulled away, I watched her remove the dirt under her fingernails with the kind of precise hatred she reserved for broken glass on the thoroughfare, for locust moltings on her water bottle.

I told her she was pure. I lied. I lied to Letty all the time. I told her what she wanted to hear, because I wanted to be that person for her. She liked who I was when I did, wanted me around: person she could hold hands with, spend time with, have in her company.

When I was me—when I wasn't lying—that's when she tossed

me out.

That's when she mocked me.

Corporal wanted something I couldn't be, something I wasn't, and she let me go. It made sense—this was how relationships worked. But Letty—Letty wanted a piece of clay; she wanted desert silt. So for her I was the partner who let her be soft when she needed to be soft, who let her shine for her brief moments of vulnerability, and then let her close the door on me.

And I never complained.

Not to Corporal. Not to Letty. Not even to my mother when she read her sad, sad poems to me about never wanting to be a mother. Not even to my mother when she told me the whole world deserved to die, so we might as well all just let go.

I had been always not enough, or too much.

And Aurin knew that. That's why they'd come for me.

* * *

Letty's guns were still pointed at Aurin, still leveled straight at their chest with every inch of threat she had on her body. She was stoic rage, steel-toed boots planted into the desert gravel. But Aurin was unshaken by Letty's solid steel and gunpowder focus, they were looking only at me, their arm outstretched. Clipped, yellow fingernails pointing past Letty, past her shoulder, beckoning me to them.

"What you are, what you want, is with us," they said.

"No," Letty said, but her voice was unsure. As she turned her head back to me, her eyes were worried, lost behind the sheen of my torch in her safety goggles.

"It's true," Aurin said. "And they know it, unlike you."

"It's true," I said.

"So, come with us." Aurin's voice was melodic, clear. Like windchimes. "Come with us and leave all that you pretend to be behind."

I still held the torch in my hand. It still smelled of diesel and old socks. But the flame was waning and flickering in the dust and breeze of the late desert night. The dust which spat across the cracked and ancient road, across the crumbling sidewalks, pitted the dead trees, and probably collected itself in the carcasses of old buildings which stood yawning and open.

A danger.

"What else would I leave behind?" I asked.

"All that's behind you," Aurin said. "All that I offer is forward."

They smiled, showing two rows of pristine white teeth. Those teeth plus two perfectly pointed fangs. Lit up in the torchlight like this, they looked almost romantic, if I were into that sort of thing.

I wasn't, but it didn't matter.

Letty had turned her shoulders back to me now, her hands shaking, her resolve gone. Aurin was winning. And they knew it. They knew it as they stepped forward, pushing past Letty, pushing past her and placing a hand on my shoulder. Placing a hand on my shoulder and looking me directly in the eyes. I knew what they were going to do, and it worked too, that mesmerizing gaze of theirs.

It totally worked, it worked like all the stories said it would.

Some stories, some legends, come true.

When Corporal had called it off, she sat across from me in her wheelchair, fingers clutching the last beer she and I ever shared. She was half-lit by her fluorescent lamp, her features cut to sharp edges by shadow. She was cutting me to pieces by words. Calling me callous, spineless, and (most accurately) over.

"Don't even think anyone'll ever know you, Marrin," she said. "Not like I did. Not like I figured you out. You're like one of them lizards, one of them that changes colors when it suits her. What's it called? A chameleon."

I nodded. I nodded and kept nodding, cause she was right.

Like I nodded as I took Aurin's hand in mine, lacing my warm fingers through their cold ones. I let them brush my hair away from my neck, something I had always thought would be sexy, but was almost procedural. When Aurin bit me, when their fangs pierced my skin, I heard Letty through a hurricane wind calling to me.

"Marrin, no. Marrin stop."

But I was lost.

Or was I? Cause out of anyone I'd ever known—Corporal,

Letty, my mother—out of anyone, Aurin was the only one who saw through my disguises right away. They saw through all my attempts at pretending. They saw *me*, they saw what *I wanted*.

✳

While I was lost at sea in Aurin's embrace, as the tides of what was happening crashed over me, and I remembered something Corporal said to me. I remembered something she said to me when I first came to Camp. She said, "You're one a'them lost causes, ain'tcha." She said, "If you're lookin' for something to believe in, you won't find it here, hon. You gotta find some way to believe in yourself."

When I hit the desert silt, I hit it fast as heartbeats. I had ten seconds of consciousness to watch Letty running toward me as I felt my last gasp of air leave my lungs. And then? I fell into the deepest, darkest sleep.

✳

Four years ago, when my mother dropped me off on the road to Corporal's camp, she kissed me on the cheek and said, "Don't disappoint me, Marrin. I know you'll be good. Always be good." And then she brushed my lanky brown hair out of my face and looked me in the eyes. "I can't be good anymore. I'm done with it, and I don't want you to see that, my darling child."

I was twenty years old and not a child anymore, but still young enough to be betrayed by my mother. She walked away from me then, but I only knew that from the sound of her boots on the old, cracked concrete. There was no need to turn and watch her go; I walked forward, toward the Camp gates, the four towers, and the beginning to someone else's story.

✳

I woke some nights later alone on a cot underneath flickering sodium lights. My bandolier and revolvers were gone. So were my safety goggles and scarf. My body ached from disuse and death as I clamored to the concrete and slipped out of the empty, unfamiliar tent toward the sound of many voices, conversing in the dark.

As my new dead eyes adjusted, I saw Aurin, standing around faces I didn't recognize, but faces who turned to me as I exited the tent. So many faces, so pale, so curious. All smiling.

But I was me now. Not a counterfeit. So this time, I walked toward Aurin and all those faces. Again, with the same refrain. Aurin smiled, revealing their fangs, and a cacophony of applause rang out, coupled by a chorus of fanged smiles.

"Welcome, Marrin," they all said.

Aurin wrapped their arm around my shoulders. They turned me toward the assembled ease of the group. I leaned into their presence, I leaned into the chorus of fangs, I leaned into this version of myself.

"This is Marrin," Aurin said. "Join me in welcoming them home."

THE BONE GIFTS
Michael Milne

A wl isn't holding any human remains at all when he greets Scaif, and a disappointed scowl blooms across her face.

"I know you have your rules," she tells him, "but if there's much left of her, I have more of a claim to it than him." Him: the father of Halligan. She: the wife.

"There are several pieces to bequeath," Awl confides. He knows the precedents for every rib and scapulae, but he knows too that his profane calculations rarely seem like justice to anyone but him.

They sit in his windblown office, which clutches the undamaged western side of the Tower. Scavenged furniture forms a strange crescent in an otherwise empty room—ancient barstool abutted by crates and leather dining chair. The leather chair is the most comfortable, so he lets Scaif take it, as her brown skin still looks raw from the purifications.

"Halligan's skull is intact?" The skull is always coveted—for adornment, for honour, for piety.

"Yes, it survived the rites," Awl says, "but you know it is complicated."

"Because I'm a woman." She grits out the first word, and the last.

"No, because you both are." He shifts uncomfortably. "Not that it matters. Not to me." Did it? He liked to think that if it was up to only his will, he would give her what she was asking. "But it will matter to some."

He knows what's next—Scaif tells him that they were Rectifiers, and when Billhook visits he will say that the family were staunch Evangels. Awl is nebulously holy to both sects, celibate and untouchable and trusted enough to attend the death rites. But he must be careful not to seem like he holds opinions.

"She died defending the city," Scaif says, as though the bravery of the death should shape the outcome. Her jaw sets, braced against the goggles and mask dangling around her neck. "She was a hero."

"You don't have to talk about it. But it changes the omens, and it means I must be careful." The beast that took Halligan's life had been abnormally large, and stories abounded about its horns, about a disturbingly human chattering noise coming from its acrid maw. Eyes were watching Awl, both in the heavens and below.

When Scaif finally leaves—never begging or weeping, but looking frail and hollowed out like a grocery store—Awl ascends to the hospice. It's high enough to avoid the dust and particulates closer to the ground, and the rare, intact windows keep out the Birds and the weather. While Awl is the only permanent resident of the Tower, there are many who prefer Awl's company when the wasting comes for them.

"How are you this evening, Scythe?" Awl draws back the throw blankets he has pinned to the ceiling. Scythe does not answer, and he worries that the woman has already passed.

"Still here," she finally whispers. It is more sigh than speech, an autumn wind sluicing through bare branches. "But I think it's soon."

"Do you want to go to the sunset room?" Awl's predecessor— his master—hated this euphemism, teased him mercilessly for maintaining it. But Awl still enjoys it.

"That might be nice."

It is hard doing, walking Scythe up the many flights of stairs. Awl knows that the great silver-chrome column that runs the height of the Tower was once a magic machine, a tiny room that could whisk you up and down at your whim. He tells Scythe about it as they walk to ease her mind. As his ankles swell, he feels some yearning for that tiny room's magic, but at the same time he knows he'd rarely use it. He treasures this role he has in the last moments of the living, walking with them a while at the end of the road.

Rain falls through the wide, open panorama of the sixteenth floor, slicking the jaw of broken glass along the edge. Awl leads Scythe's limping and aching form to the bed positioned in the center of the room. He stares out for a long time to ensure he sees no dark, metallic wings.

"Comfortable?" he asks her. The bed is a fragile and dirt-brown plastic, some lawn furniture dragged up here ages ago. He adjusts it so she can better see the view: the melted-candle silhouettes of the buildings nearby, the serrated hills, even the tar-black sea.

"Comfortable enough," she sighs. They both know she won't be up here for long. "I heard that woman stomping down the stairs earlier. Bad news?"

"A disagreement. She wants her wife's skull." Awl carefully watches for a change in expression at the pronouns. "But so does her father."

"And the Evangels will grumble if you recognize a heathen marriage." Scythe grins. A Rectifier herself, a lapsed zealot, or just too close to death to care?

"It's not grumbling I'm worried about," Awl says. He's only just recently emptied the roof of the destruction wrought by the last round of violence. He shivers at the memory of the Birds in their frenzy.

"I think you overestimate your importance," Scythe says with a laugh. She reaches out to squeeze Awl's hand—he doesn't recoil from those who take hospice, and that's why so many come to him. "We're all just bones, in the end. No one can tell the difference. You can toss mine off the side of the Tower. The world is dying, just like us. Does it matter?"

Awl could tell the difference, but he took her point. He wants to stay with her, to keep his eye on the horizon for talons and beaks. But there is a thundering far below, the calling bell that hammers for Awl to come outside.

"A gentleman caller? At this hour?" Awl says to Scythe, trying to make her smile. He doesn't laugh as he rushes down the many stairs. This much noise, so close to nightfall? The clamour would summon more than Awl.

Awl emerges from the wide entryway of the building and takes in the visitor, who is tall and powerful, unbent by his age. The visitor prowls as he waits, his steps heralded by clattering—the call of his many bone gifts. Awl realizes that this man doesn't fear what else he might be conjuring from the woods.

"I know that Scaif has already come to plead." The man stretches his arms wide in the gathering brownish-black haze of late evening. "But our ways are sacred, and they must be maintained."

"Of course," Awl says. "The literature suggests that you may have Halligan's shoulder bones, or most of her spine."

"She was my heir," he says. "I will receive her skull." He speaks with finality, a sense that his will is identical to that of his people, or the laws of nature.

"Well, her wife united blood when they wed," Awl attempts. It is mostly to gauge the reaction, and Billhook glowers in a way that makes his beliefs clear. "The judgement is not as simple as you put it. There are precedents."

Billhook moves quickly. He leaps over the warding stones, advancing on Awl and slamming one scarred forearm against his neck to pin Awl against the base of The Tower. Awl can feel his ragged beard; can smell his stale breath. The sacred matters to him only so long as it conforms to his desires.

"Precedents? What use is two anchors without a screw?" He glances up and down at Awl. "Or two screws with no anchor? If the old ways don't matter, why do our people feed you, vulture?" He increases the pressure and Awl cannot breathe, dark spots fluttering in his vision. Awl fumbles through his pockets for something, anything sharp. "Why don't we toss you to the beasts and let the diseased rot alone?"

They can both hear the howls in the distance, the sound of paws creeping along the gravel.

"You would start the war again," Awl grits. Was it war with so few people left to murder each other? At last, at last he finds his paring knife, curved and angry, and he brings it to the man's throat. "You only value your pride."

"Some life!" Billhook sneers. He forces the blade free from Awl's hand, and brings it to the ground. "Next it will be in your ribs. I will have my daughter's skull at first light."

He lopes away, immediately subsumed in the thick gauzy grasp of night. Awl would watch him leave, but he thinks he can already see the glimmer of eyes in the dark. And where there are eyes, there are teeth.

Fifteen stories above, he sits to rest his weary muscles. He sees that Scythe has taken her last breath, and after resting he hooks his arms under her shoulders and drags her corpse the short path to the roof.

He knows that people think this must be an abattoir, that Awl is untouchable because he is oft drenched in death. But the peak of the Tower is quite beautiful.

There is a shrine at the center, where Awl lights a fire and says the prayers. The bodies are laid on small altars—overturned filing cabinets and rusting desks that Awl garlands with flowers and long grass. It is never gruesome or repulsive. Awl brings people to the top of the Tower, and the Birds divide their flesh into soul and bone.

He lays Scythe along the east side, remembering her as an early riser, ensuring that she sees one last sunrise. He collects Scythe's few remaining clothes, and fills her hands with mint and coriander to pay for her passage beyond. When he had told Scythe about this ritual, she laughed, asking if he always seasoned the dead to taste.

Halligan's few mementos are to the north end of the building: her skull remains impeccable, as do her metacarpals and pelvis. He gathers what is left, and after a few moments, her altar is clean enough for the next.

He wants to dally, to sit and ask the venomous night clouds above for Halligan's wishes. Awl remembers being a younger man, apprenticing with wiry, raven-haired Gimlet. How Gimlet had once gathered up two tibias in scraps of fox leather, made his way down all of those stairs, and spirited the remains over the warding stones to a grieving drifter in the brown-grey twilight. He had made Awl watch the woman advance into the night, heaving with her sorrow, clutching the bones to her sallow chest. Their work, he told him, was never as impersonal as they pretended. They made hard decisions while appearing to never decide at all.

Fresh meat attracts attention. He can already hear heavy wings, the predatory metal shriek. Most of the Birds know better than to attack their reliable source of carrion. But they have learned speech, and they taunt Awl if he lingers during their meal, telling him things he shouldn't know.

"Look delicious," something hisses from the waist-high barrier around the roof. Awl turns to look, to take in the half-natural beast, which is already poking at Scythe with its slick-sickle beak. The Bird looks back at him coyly, as though inviting him to dine together.

"You're no fun," the Bird mewls through an already full beak. "I miss the old one."

"Me too," Awl says.

Awl descends the stairs to his quarters, tucked into the honeymoon floor far from hungry ground and toxic sky. There is an empty cot right next to his, and Awl remembers its glacial drift closer over the first years of his life in The Tower. How he and Gimlet would slide the beds back apart if a member of the religious hierarchy paid visit. And before the wasting took him, how Gimlet told Awl he could have whichever bequeathal he wanted. How Awl had taken none, scared he would be unable to explain why a holy man kept any bone gifts for himself.

In his dreams, Awl sees visions of the times ahead. Are the days few enough now to count? For his people, or for the Earth upon which they toil? And if the Birds' taunts are true, what does his choice matter?

In his old age, Awl rises with the sun, though he notices that it seems to come later each day. He stretches in the opalescent light, tasting the air to decide on his pollution mask. Looking down through his intact window, he sees that Billhook has not yet arrived. He has time to make it to the roof and back down.

When Awl trudges through the threshold of the Tower, the man is waiting inside of the warding stones. His left side is soaked in blood, but the source is unclear. He wears no pollution mask, and his rattling breath swells his chest, heaves the bones he wears front and back. His eyes fall to the skull in Awl's hands.

"You have done the right thing," Billhook says to him. His smile is bitter—like so many, he will now carry the last of his bloodline with him, his inheritance confined to his grasp.

When Awl offers the skull, he kneels as is traditional, the bone gift rising to its recipient. Billhook is now closer to the diaphanous line between life and death, and he brings the skull close to his face, peering at lacrimal bone like his daughter can return his gaze.

"I will be seeing you soon," Billhook says over his shoulder. It does not sound like a threat. This man knows that his time with his gifts is short, that this new skull will sit on his breastplate next to another, that the weight of so many dead will soon overwhelm. Awl imagines pulling this man's probably half-eaten body to the roof, and knows it will not be satisfying. He never feels gratification feeding the Birds, even when people seem to deserve it. There are too few people left.

The rest of Awl's day is inconsequential. Word spreads to Scaif, and she does not appear to beg for whatever else might remain of her wife. Awl pours angry orange river water over the few plants in the garden, and wonders if he still has enough tablets to clean his supply. His few other charges moan and whimper when he arrives on their floor, and there is one man so mottled that Awl will gather the necessary herbs to send him painlessly to his rest.

Darkness falls earlier than the day before, though Awl feels certain they are in the midst of summer. He readies his bundle, filling it with fur and old Styrofoam to muffle any noise. He hasn't left the Tower in many years—indeed, he is forbidden from doing so. If he is found, by man or by animal, he will likely be killed.

The village has not changed much since Awl was a young man, since before he gave his freedom and was confined to the Tower. He knows the old paths, can still wend his way between emaciated oak and abandoned Jeep, and his bare feet are rugged enough to find purchase among rocks and broken things.

Blessedly, he meets nothing larger than himself on the road. Twice he fends off creatures he thinks are the descendants of rats, but they are fat and snarling, their tails sharp and ambulatory. His hands are bloody after the second attack, but the package on his back remains safe.

Her home is dark, like all of the homes. But he recognizes the primitive sigils of Halligan and Scaif's clans, and he sees remnants of an attack in the dead trees and the upturned earth. The house is a bungalow, Awl thinks. Basements are easier to fortify, to soundproof, to store food in the cool. People have relearned to burrow, and so many find Awl strange for living as he does in the sky.

He knocks, unsure if this practice is still within the culture, if Scaif will be deep underground or even still living in a place that reminds her of her beloved. He presses his mouth close to the cracks in the doorframe and calls her name.

"For someone who cares so much about moth-eaten ancient mores, you have no qualm breaking them," Scaif says as she leads him into the house. She's carrying no visible weapons, so she does not seem intent on revenge, or on performing her societal duty. "Speak."

Awl doesn't speak. He reaches, instead, through his belongings and pulls free Halligan's actual skull. He offers it to Scaif, not on his knees, but looking to her eyes. An equal, someone who should not be deciding matters of eternity.

"Why are you doing this?" Scaif asks. She does not refuse, and she brings the remains close to herself, pressing the curve of cracked bone to her chest. "This won't bring about more wasting? Or the apocalypse?"

"The world is dying, and so are we," Awl tells her, pressing the bundle of other bones to her. He gestures to the world outside her door. "The worst is already here. If it's not the wasting, then it's beasts, or it's each other. So we all need to think about what we do with the time left."

"And what do you do?"

"I walk a little with the dying and the dead before they go. I listen, if they have a voice to speak. And even sometimes if they don't." He glances down at Scaif's hand, the ring of rough twine around her finger. "I didn't listen, once, and I still regret it. Your wife said what she wanted. I just hadn't figured out how to heed it yet."

He accepts her offer of the meagre food she has on hand, of the clean water she has stored. She does not see him out, and Awl watches her descend into her little basement tomb with the reminder of Halligan.

Awl shuts the door as he leaves, greeted by an even darker world than when he arrived. If he is quiet and quick, he can make it back to the Tower without needing to defend himself, without having to fight off the pious or the rabid. But as his feet meet the road, he realizes he is not returning to the Tower. He turns out towards the world, pulls his mask across his mouth, and starts to walk.

WHEN THE LAST OF THE BIRDS AND THE BEES HAVE GONE ON
C.L. Clark

After "Girl" by Jamaica Kincaid

Practice your aerial drills Mondays, Thursdays, and Saturdays, even if it's raining—you think you'll never have to fly in the rain?; do calisthenics and sword drills on Tuesdays and Fridays; don't fly bare-winged into a thunderstorm's static; cook your crag deer steak just til they're hot-brown outside and warm-red in; soak your hunting clothes right after you take them off; blood draws blood; never pinion your own fool self with your own clothes; memorize the width of your wing protrusion points; salt your extra meat and hide it; is it true you were letting the Wingless into the crags on Sunday?; always eat your food like you know where your next meal's coming from; if you didn't hunt the deer yourself, cook it until it's hot-brown all through; on Sundays, walk strong like your training's made you, not like you can barely hold your wings up; don't let strangers into the crags; don't speak to the Wingless, not even to give directions; all of this is their fault; drop a little food when you walk because crag mice will follow you and they make good snacks; *I never bring strangers into the crags, only my friends, and never on training days*; this is how to clean a wound; this is how to suture the wound you just cleaned; this is how you widen and hem the holes in your shirts so you don't pinion your own fool self with your own clothes; this is how you guard your wingmate's back without getting tangled; this is how you guard your wingmate's underside without getting tangled; this is how you gut the crag deer—far from your nest because blood draws blood and fresh meat draws false friends; when you attack from above, don't get fancy and spin or else you'll get vertigo and lose your sword; this is how you choose a gender; this is how you cast one off; this is how you mark your own nest; this is how you mark the borders of the crags; this is how you hold your wings near someone you don't like too much; this is how you hold your wings near someone you don't like at all; this is how you hold your wings near someone you like completely; this is how you set up camp as a scout; this is how you set up camp as a wingsquad; this is how you set up camp for someone who outranks you; this is how you set up camp before a fight; this is how you set up camp after a fight; this is how to hold your wings in the presence of the Wingless, like your training's made you strong enough to drop them off the crags like they deserve; sun your wings everyday so that you don't get mites or wingrot; don't climb everywhere—you're not Wingless, you know; don't pick the crag flowers—the bees might come back; don't throw stones at crag birds because they've been gone for decades and we want them to come back; this is how to make a nest; this is how to line a nest; this is how to make medicine for wingrot; this is how to make medicine to throw away a fledge before it becomes a fledge, and don't tell me you won't need it—we learn things that help other people, too, you know; this is how to catch a fish from the air; this is how to throw back the perfect fish so that the crag birds have food when they come back to us; this is what Wingless gunpowder smells like; this is how to bully the Wingless; this is how the Wingless bully you; this is how to choose a nestmate; this is how to love a nestmate and this is how to touch their wings; this is how to do an aerobatic loop if you feel like it and this is how to steady yourself so you don't get vertigo; this is how to stretch crag deer meat through lean summers and leaner winters; this is how you dispose of bodies you can't eat; *but what if my nestmate has no wings?* You mean to say that after all that you are really going to be the kind of person who won't lift them up with your own wings?

A FUTURE IN COLOR
R.J. Theodore

Five miles outside Hope City West, the vultures came for me. Even though their silhouettes on the ridge were barely visible against the smoke and ash of the noon-day sky, I could hear their self-important laughter and feel their eyes upon me.

I was tired and sweaty. I had *been* tired and sweaty since before my transmission died back along the trail, and trudging along the skeleton of the old eight-lane interstate hadn't served to fix that. To either side of the cracked, uneven asphalt stretched dark sand with darker reddish lumps of scrub, straight to the ugly line of sulfur yellow at the horizon. Overhead hung the ash cover, imposing as a coffin-lid, each of the vultures lurking in the dark just aching to become another nail.

They wanted to destroy what I had, in the way of vultures. But these weren't going to wait for me to lay down and die before they came for it.

My pack was heavy as hell, and bulky in that way that large flat things were, smacking against my bones with each step. But I'd be damned to live through twenty more apocalypses before I let these graspers stop me from making my delivery.

I was a courier. That *meant* something. My honor lived and died by the safe arrival of my parcels. People who chose to do more than survive—the communities, our friends, my daughter—needed what I carried. We'd come together to move past the unfairness of living with ash filters and skies too dark for solar arrays.

And people like me became couriers. I didn't have the power to make the future, like those who contracted me. I had the power to be stubborn as hell. To ride, walk, or crawl, and to come away from a vulture ambush like this one with my burden intact.

I believed in this, mind you. I was no mercenary. I'd met my partner and our daughter in this post-ash world, and though I grew hard, I did my damnedest not to grow cold. When everything went to dust, you either found something to believe in or you wasted away. You either found a community or became a vulture.

I heard their poorly maintained bikes and ATVs rattle to life. They knew I'd seen them and they were never much for subtlety anyway.

Their pack peeled away and wormed down to head me off along the main road. I shifted my burden to access my belt. I felt safer with the weight of my crowbar in hand, but I was realistic about the odds. If it came to swings, my precious cargo wouldn't withstand the beating that crowd would likely bring at me. They didn't understand it, couldn't appreciate what it meant, so they would try to destroy it and keep it from those who could.

The hills chomped on the horizon ahead of me. At their base, Hope City West's artificial lights and fires glowed, a beacon of gold and pink light urging me on. Their knighted watch would be ready to escort me through the gates. If I could just get close enough.

Too late now. I knew I couldn't outrun a pack of vultures on their motors. I found a cleft along one side of the ridge line, where the shadows were deeper than black, and tucked my load inside. By the time the vultures reached me on the main road, I was standing back at its center, crowbar drawn back and muscles aching to swing.

Behind their infrared goggles and dirty bandanas, it was easy to imagine they weren't people. Just dark shadows, the nightmares of children. They may have traveled in a pack but they had no idea how to work together. They came at me one at a time, which is exactly what I'd hoped for.

I swung at the first, bringing the crowbar around so they charged into it. The impact screamed in my shoulder, but it separated them from their seat. Their dirt bike skidded onto its side and sent up a circle of dust around me. I didn't have their IR goggles. Couldn't see where the next attack would come from.

I yanked the abandoned bike upright. It had a torn-out seat and bent handlebars, but it looked like a chariot to me. The engine had stalled and I killed the fuel as I wheeled it over to my hiding spot. A vulture appeared out of the settling haze, swinging and just barely connecting with my temple as reflex sent me stumbling back. Glass shards along the knuckles of their glove still raked across my skin, though, and immediately burned.

Adrenaline answered that rush of sensation with its own and the world around me seemed to slow and sharpen. Blood trickled, wet and dirty, threatening to flood my right eye. The dirt bike had fallen against my waist but it wasn't as heavy as my street bike had been. Instead of pinning me to the ground it only freed my hands up to swing the crowbar again.

There was little to be gained by a fight, and so much at risk, but they were persistent. They wore gray and black and covered their faces, and by that style they made it slightly easier to defend myself with brutal force. They were just vultures, I told myself. If I let them get to my pack, they would not only destroy the few objects within, but the futures of those they were destined for.

I fought, and bested them, because I had to.

By the time I reclaimed my cargo and hit the road, I'd fractured or broken bones in at least four of them. They made their choice, I told myself.

Their injuries inspired enough caution in them to let me get out ahead. Not by much, but unless one of them had a rifle (and if it was loaded, which was even less likely these days), all I had to do was stay ahead of them until I reached Hope City West's walls.

The dirt bike had other ideas. No surprise that a vulture didn't keep their ride well-tuned. If I'd been able to do any better, I wouldn't be in this predicament. Just when I was starting to think I might make it, just as I was near enough to see the guards moving along the outer wall of the city, the engine sputtered, as though it had just tried to swallow a plate full of nails. The whole thing seized, tossing me over the handlebars. I felt something snap, and wished it had been me and not my cargo.

I climbed to my feet and pulled the load off my back, clutching its broken shape against my chest. I threatened the remaining vultures with my crowbar, dropping my weight into my legs and coiled to strike as soon as one of them dared come for me.

A horn sounded, startling echoes from the waste around us. The city's knighted watch had spotted our approach. Bouncing lights flooded the darkness and hooves drummed against dirt and ash.

The vultures slowed and seemed to shrink as I gained the long shadow of the watch at my back. The knights knew me. Knew my clothes, knew my face. Knew a wasteland hunt when they saw one, and how to turn it around. My rescuers overtook me, scattering the vultures into disorganized retreat.

Once inside the city gates, I accepted a clean rag for my scrapes, but refused to see their doctor until after I'd hand-delivered my charge to the Hope Gallery curator.

As I followed the familiar path to the gallery, the warm lights of the city were everywhere I looked—in windows, strings of paper lanterns lining the streets, and fire pits that chased back the barren chill. Raucous colors decorated every surface. Our communities had preserved the color we knew about from books and what vids had survived. The ash-choked sky didn't know rainbows, but we wouldn't let the world go without them.

The gallery was below ground, given prime space in the city's evacuation bunker. The curator, a trans man in a gorgeously patterned kimono, met us at the bottom of the steps, his long slender hands fluttering in eagerness for my parcel.

I winced as the wraps came off to reveal cracked frames and creased canvases and posters. I didn't curse but I think I turned red with anger.

The curator put a pale hand out onto my dark-skinned forearm, risking the dirt to comfort me. "These are beautiful pieces. The frames can be repaired, the canvases will lay flat when they are stretched again. You have, once again, broadened our collection. We remain in your debt."

He removed the white cotton gloves of his station and gestured to a sitting area at the back of the gallery. There was an audience already waiting.

"Come, please. Your delivery is not yet complete. Tell us about the artists."

And I did. First was the former wedding videographer's paintings of flower arrangements, corsages and bouquets against backdrops of folded satin. This artist also worked in the gardens back in my home, Fish City, to ensure future generations remembered not just the color but the smell and texture of these flowers. There was the hairdresser who had brought their knowledge of pigments and dyes to carded wool, learned to spin the fibers, and then crochet them in day-glo webs over wooden frames. He was also responsible for the curls of neon green in my hair. Next, I told them of the guild of autodidactic printmakers who pressed riotous colors in blocks and gradients onto sheets of fabric, depicting city scapes and remembered family photos of vacations at national parks, vacation sunsets, and runway models. All memory inspired color to paper. One man had been a former courtroom artist and his husband a sketch artist; together they worked with residents to recreate their memories for the city's records. There were recycled papers made by a former laundromat attendant from the masticated pulp of bright cotton rags, where the paper itself was the medium and the art. My audience was silent and reverent as I spoke, but I was as attentive to their smiles and wet eyes as they were to the stories and art I brought them. I had carried all the colors from before the ash, a stack of canvases and prints, because we refused to let the vibrance of life fade from the world.

After, I was exhausted but light, barely staying awake to crawl into the fur-padded bed in the couriers' quarters.

After a night's rest, a patch up, and two generously portioned hot meals, I went to the curator again. He had transformed the gallery overnight, displaying the paintings I had brought with me, all repaired and beautiful.

There was a low table in the center of the gallery for me, covered in artwork. A dozen of the city's artists mingled, but though it was their art on display, they treated me like the guest of honor.

It was hours before I could sleep again, and I tossed fitfully, anxious that I might forget the stories that went with my new burden, or that the vultures might get me before I could get these pieces home to Fish City. Before I could see my partner and our daughter.

When it was time to leave, I mounted a gorgeous Hope City West horse, a brown and white paint mare, given to me as part of my payment. Its saddlebags were filled with the precious bundles of packaged artwork for Fish City's museum.

"We trust you to see our creations safely across the colorless waste." He made no mention of how the sculptures in my packs would not survive the same abuse the paintings had endured. He didn't have to. I refused to learn that lesson twice.

I patted my mount's beautiful patterned neck and squeezed my knees. The city's folk lined the path back to the gate, waving colorful scarves to bolster me for the desaturated road I was about to travel. Children risked the horse's hooves to tuck bright silk ribbons into my hands or beneath the straps of my saddle. I saw dozens of small, joyous faces, all raised in this post-ash world, but who still knew love and joy and art and color. This, more than anything, would see me home to my own child.

I was a courier. This was what I believed in.

CHAMPIONS OF WATER WAR
Elly Bangs

Everyone hurts everyone. That's the whole game. Nestor resents all rules and forbids their existence within the walls of Utopia Gulch, so in the cage at the city's heart there is only a patchwork of vague and unspoken understandings: that it's smarter not to kill or permanently maim one's opponents, because that sows too much bad blood with the city's other quadrants and leads to reprisals; that three out of the four Champions must be thoroughly knocked out before Nestor will pull the lever that opens the door to the valve room; that the pipes are set up so that only one quadrant's valve can be open at any one time, and only by means of that valve does that quadrant of Utopia get its taps to run that day. Beyond that, anything goes: punches, kicks, bites, bludgeons, knives, guns, armor, stimulants, audience interference. Whatever it takes to win the fight is fair game.

That's always been how it works, since Buzz was only a child—since the rivers stopped running and Utopia Gulch rose from the ashes of some other world. But right now, as he pauses to spit blood one last time before prying Killer into a headlock, he's haunted by the absurd thought that even in the bloody heart of a city with no rules, something about this fight is terribly unfair—because he can hurt Killer in all kinds of ways, but Killer is even now hurting him back in a way he can't block, can't run from, can't hit back at. Even as Killer's blue eyes finally roll back in their sockets, his taut and blood-greased muscles going slack, his chiseled face gone peaceful—even in the moment of Buzz's triumph, it's as if Killer is punching him right in the heart.

A collective sigh of relief moves through the spectators beyond the bars: Buzz hasn't won in a while, and all the secret water reserves in his quadrant's bathtubs and buckets are down to their last rancid inches. Only one person really cheers: Nestor himself, gleaming silver hair and silk smoking jacket and all, perched up there on his balcony above the cage, treating everyone to a full minute of golf-clapping before pulling the lever to open the valve room door. (Privately, Buzz is thankful for the delay. He has time to watch Killer in the corner of his eye, tracking the rise and fall of the chest under his glittering chainmaille, the beating of a heart so strong it ripples visibly under his left pec, letting everyone know he's going to be okay, thank God.)

Then Buzz hobbles into the valve room and keeps up his end of his secret pact with his ostensible nemesis: he opens the valve for Killer's neighborhood first, for the thirty-odd seconds he can get away with, just to keep the pipes full. Then it's time to climb the central staircase and let Nestor's clanking robotic guards lead him to his reward.

The circular deck above the cage is a panopticon overlooking all four quadrants of Utopia Gulch, connected to a spiderweb of catwalks that look down into the streets and rooms of all its residents. The former billionaire waves Buzz to the edge impatiently, ignoring how he limps and pauses to wipe off the last trickles of fresh blood.

"Behold your fellow Champions," Nestor says, tipping his wine glass at the defeated fighters below as they're scraped up and dragged from the cage. "Absolute specimens, each and every one—and all because of my vision. Because of our great Utopian game. What would they have been, back when the rivers still flowed and rain still fell free from the skies? Valets, butlers, tax accountants. They'd be moping their way through life, slouched in desk chairs by day and on couches by night—but here, my dear Buzzsaw, they must earn each and every drop of their life's blood. Here they pursue the very zenith of their self-actualization, what Aristotle called *Eudaimonia*. The flourishing of the soul, through excellent achievement of one's innate purpose."

Buzz plays the part he knows Nestor expects of him: he nods, purses his lips and furrows his brow, as if a walnut-sized brain is sloshing around in his skull and it's getting blown wide open by every word out of Nestor's mouth.

"Sometimes," Nestor sighs, "I can't help but miss those days when any cretinous taker could fill his stomach with water with the turn of a tap. But make no mistake: that wasn't the Golden Age of Man—*this* is, right here and now. That is why I brought you all here as mere children, to be my Utopians. So your minds would be clean slates, untainted by the old paradigms."

"Huh," Buzz says. "I never thunk about it that way, Mr. Nestor."

"Of course you haven't." Nestor pats Buzz's shoulder paternally and motions to the buffet—but no matter how much food Buzz stuffs into his belly, there's a hollowness that doesn't leave. He knows it won't until tonight.

He spends all afternoon and evening secretly looking forward to it: sitting still on the makeshift Champion's throne of his home quadrant, wearing a mask of rugged dispassion, grunting his thanks to the people who come and go, tending to his wounds and washing his feet. He does his best to seem present—but his thoughts are nowhere near his body until the last daylight fades completely, and he can drape himself in a blanket and sneak out to the narrow crevice where the concrete wall has settled and cracked, and only a strip of chainlink fence separates his quadrant from the neighboring one. There's Killer, his rich brown skin dusted with moonlight, whispering through the metal:

"Hey. I, uh...I have a favor to ask."

"Anything," Buzz says hopefully. "I mean...yes. What?"

Killer takes a long moment to decide whether to ask his question. It makes Buzz ache. Finally he clears his throat and looks at his feet and says "Don't poke me in the eyes."

Buzz's heart drops into the acid bath of his stomach. "Did I do that? Shit. I didn't mean to."

Killer wiggles his head. "No, no, it's not an accusation. I'm just saying, can we agree to never do that? I worry about it every time I go in there. After what happened between Drexa and The Beef last Winter—"

"I would never try to hurt your eyes."

A heavy silence fills up the air between them. It rings in Buzz's ears.

"So it's a rule," Killer says through a smirk. "Kind of funny."

"How is it funny?"

Killer shrugs his armored shoulders. "We wouldn't even have the concept of rules if Nestor never yelled at us about how wrong they are. But here we are, you and I, making one right under his nose."

"Yeah," Buzz says. "I wanted to ask you something."

"Yeah?"

"Do you—?" Buzz cuts off. There's sound behind him: one of Nestor's robots rattling along on the catwalk above, keeping watch. He ducks down and drapes the blanket so he looks like a pile of trash. Every time he sees one of those bots, he can't help wondering if it's the one that used to change his diapers or feed him as a child.

When the noise passes, Killer presses his enormous body harder into the bars expectantly. "Do I what?"

But Buzz is too nervous now to say. Instead he hurriedly improvises: "Do you ever think about jumping up and trying to grab the edge of Nestor's balcony? It's so close. I always feel like, if you boosted me up, I could reach it."

"Champions have tried," Killer says. "Taller ones than either of us. Even working together. They always fail."

"I know," Buzz sighs.

"What are you thinking?"

That I'm only really living for those precious few seconds before the knockout, Buzz answers in his mind. *When I'm there in your arms, swaddled in your strength, knowing you could kill me but trusting that you won't—or when you're there in mine, and I know, can feel it in your bones, that you trust me too. The only peace I know anymore is in that violence.*

"Hello?" Killer asks.

"Oh." Buzz hurriedly composes himself. "Just that, you know, Drexa hasn't won in ten days, and her backup is still getting over dehydration—"

"I know," Killer says. "We should make sure she wins tomorrow."

"Really?"

It's a risk. Throwing a fight for each other still feels new and dangerous, let alone doing it for one of the other two quadrants—but Killer reaches three muscular fingers through the chainlinks, and the skin of Buzz's face is on fire with blushing when they touch, silently agreeing: *yes*.

⚫

That first rule seems to open a floodgate, and before long the two of them have a list almost too long to memorize. They start with practical issues like which body parts are not to be hit or stabbed; how to furtively reveal their next moves to help each other block; how to decide the rotation of who'll win and who'll play dead, so all the buckets and bathtubs in Utopia Gulch are always at least half-full; how to make it up to each other when one of them accidentally breaks a rule. But there's a strange pleasure in making rules, and it leads to ever more elaborate and arbitrary ones: if Killer puts Buzz in a chokehold, he has to tap his neck an even number of times; if Buzz kicks Killer in the hip, Killer has to kick him back in the same hip; if one groans, the other has to groan a higher note back.

It takes great effort and concentration to uphold these rules in the cage, all while contending with the other two Champions, and all without showing it. Fighting becomes as much about defense as it's about deliberately opening themselves to the right attacks at the right times. Conversely, the confidence that neither of them is out to kill the other enables their safe use of ever more dramatic weapons: a gun that misses, a whip that only lands on well-armored spots, swords that always glance off each other with dramatic clanks and metal sparks.

One day it's Buzz's turn to get knocked out. He and Killer form a plan, communicating through what has become a well-developed language of hits, blocks, and feints. They judge the angle of Nestor's perspective from the deck above the cage, and arrange the perfect knockout: Killer swinging a bat right under

Buzz's chin; Buzz simulating the concussive full-body whiplash of the hit landing square in the temple. He falls face-down next to Drexa's prone form, where he's shocked to discover she's still conscious: her remaining eye burning through him like a laser beam. Through a mouth pressed flat against the blood-caked dust, her face twisted up in the straps of her leather helmet, she whispers:

"I don't know what you two are doing, but I want in."

A similar message reaches Killer from Hammer a few days later, passed along by intermediaries. It takes time to catch the newcomers up on the rules, and the secret physical language by which they're negotiated, and it takes a toll on Buzz: because of the city's layout, he has to meet Drexa at his quadrant's other border, just as Killer has to go meet Hammer, so that the two of them are stuck on opposite sides of Utopia every other night— but when their fingers finally meet again through the chainlinks, the look on Killer's face is all he needs.

"I feel good," Killer tells him. "I feel really good."

Buzz's heart leaps to hear that. "Me too," he sighs. He catches himself and forces a dispassionate look. "Wait—why? What about?"

Killer chuckles, drawing creases in his soft cheeks. "Man, I used to get shanked at least once a week. One stab never had time to scar over before I picked up another. But since we started making up rules? Right now, all my stabs are healed at the exact same time. I have all this energy. I could take on the world."

Buzz is staring at Killer's fingers where they rest on the chainlinks, thinking that if he were to pry his muscular body deep enough into the crevice in the broken concrete wall between their quadrants, he could press his cheek or his lips to those fingers.

"So I wanted to ask you something," Buzz asks. His heartbeat pounds so hard on his ears that he can barely hear himself speak.

"Yeah?" Killer asks, hopefully.

His real question is on the tip of Buzz's tongue, but for the second time he chickens out and swallows it down, asking instead: "Can you remember anything from before Utopia?"

Killer sighs as if disappointed. He shakes his head.

"Can anybody?" Buzz asks. "Besides Nestor."

"We were all just kids," Killer responds. "Why?"

Because all night I dream of a world that needs no chainlink fence crevices, Buzz yearns to say, *without quadrants or the walls between them. Where water falls free from the sky, and we need no bloodsport to justify our touch or communicate our wishes, and nothing stands between your fingers and my lips.*

Buzz clears his throat and answers: "No reason."

That night he lies awake thinking about how Nestor never told the Utopians there was any such thing as love. Either he wanted them to discover it for themselves as they grew up, or he believed it was just another relic of the old world—that if he never gave his children the concept of an emotion, they'd never feel it. Yet somehow, even without a language to describe it, it followed them from the world before their earliest memories. Buzz had watched it roll through them like a fever. He'd always imagined himself immune.

⊠

All four Champions know something is wrong the moment they line up in the morning. Nestor doesn't pull the lever to open the gates to the cage. He just stands there on his balcony, hands clasped behind his back, looming. Finally he picks up a microphone and flips a switch, and his amplified voice bellows out through the screeching static:

"I am a visionary. Decades ago, while my peers ran around screaming like Chicken Little, I alone recognized the opportunity in the crisis. I built this city and the walls that protect it from the ravages beyond. I populated it with all of you. I founded a Utopian society the likes of which could never be achieved, back when the rivers ran. Here, at last, I have made a world where nothing is given—where everything is *earned*."

"Oh hell," Drexa hisses.

"Do you think I don't know when you share water with the losers' quadrants after a bout?" Nestor bellows. "I always knew there was a chance that altruism might one day come to infect our Utopia, despite my best efforts. The valve controls were my litmus test."

It's not just the Champions who can sense what's about to happen—it's everyone. The entire population of Utopia Gulch, pressing its faces against the cage or craning its necks to squint up at its silver-haired founder.

Nestor stares pleadingly across the crowd. "Don't any of you understand why rules are so wrong? Why I take such pains to protect you from them? It may seem innocent, but it is a foothold. Rules turn into laws. Laws turn into taxes. Regulations. Socialism. A thousand other cancerous adulterations of Man's freedom and dignity."

"We get water or not depending on who wins in the cage!" shouts a woman in the crowd. "Ain't that a rule?"

"No, no, no, no, no! That's a *fact*, not a rule!" The ex-billionaire takes a deep breath to calm himself. "Clearly I've been failing you as a teacher. You all sorely need to rediscover the virtue of selfishness, so today a mere knockout will not be sufficient. I will only open the valve room as reward for a kill within the next five minutes."

On the underside of Nestor's balcony, a long-disused clock begins to tick, its rusty hands jittery behind the bars of its cage. Nobody moves.

"Oh!" Nestor snaps his fingers and raises his hands to address the entire crowd. "I almost forgot. I've sent my robots into your hovels to tip over all your buckets and bathtubs."

All the Utopians shout and groan and curse—and in the cage, the dance of death begins spontaneously. The four Champions creep around each other in an increasingly taut square formation, all their eyes darting between each other, struggling to read intent. The crowds outside the cage devolve into what sounds like a riot.

"I don't expect you to understand the favor I'm doing for you all," Nestor sings into his microphone. "You were beginning to care about the other quadrants—your *enemies*, for crying out loud!"

Buzz looks Drexa and Hammer up and down, tracking their every nervous twitch, mentally counting down to the instant one or both of them inevitably snap and go in for the kill. They're new to this cooperation thing. They've only been fighting by the rules for a matter of days.

Forfeit, Killer is shouting with his eyes, his posture, his fists. *Let the clock run down. We need time to plan our next move.*

We'll get dehydrated, Hammer and Drexa are both communicating with their body language. *If somebody doesn't win, we'll all start dying.*

But when Buzz meets Killer's gaze, it all becomes crystal clear. He answers: *Let it be me. I'll die so you can live. So you all can.*

"No!" Killer yells aloud. "Not you, me! Kill me!"

"Me!" Drexa shouts—Hammer shouts—everyone shouts together—and when their eyes meet now, all the feelings they've all been hiding shine through all the matted scars, calluses, leather and metal, all masks lifted by desperation. Love beams through sweat-greased muscle and glitters on chainmaille.

"What have you been trying to ask me all this time?" Killer shouts over the din of the crowd and the feedback in Nestor's microphone.

"Do you know I love you?"

"Yes!"

All of Buzz's fear evaporates. He looks up at the concrete lip of Nestor's balcony. He starts to unstrap his armor, piece by piece.

"Nobody's ever made that jump!" Hammer yells.

But Buzz's confident grin answers for him: no one's ever tried it without armor weighing them down—and no Champion in the history of the cage has ever been as healthy and hydrated as the four of them are now. Without another word or moment's pause, Killer kneels and knits his fingers together, and Buzz and Drexa and Hammer all jump up one after another.

"Outrageous!" Nestor shouts. He runs around the edge of the deck, stomping on their fingers, but the blows are softened by his fur slippers. One by one all four of them heave themselves and each other up—while behind and below them, the Utopians are breaking into the cage with makeshift cutters and prying bars, helping each other climb up after the Champions.

Nestor snaps his fingers again and again to rally all his robots at once—and here they come by the dozen, surging in from every quadrant, along every catwalk, faster than human legs could carry them.

"Time for Utopia two point oh," Nestor continues, pacing at the center of a ring of angry machines. "I'll just start over. I should have known this design was too convoluted. Children! Damn it all, where am I going to get fresh children?"

"It's over!" Drexa shouts. "The Gulch is ours!"

Nestor barks a laugh. The robots keep coming. Some jaunt in fresh from bathtub-tipping duty in the city while others come crawling up from hidden compartments under the streets. Buzz swallows hard: he never dreamed there were so many. In moments they have the Utopians surrounded on all sides: a human donut, ringed by armored machines braced in identical fighting stances.

Buzz looks over his shoulder, and the others all look back. Drexa nods. Hammer winks. Killer—Killer finds Buzz's hand and kisses the palm.

"You can't punch your way out of this one," Nestor shouts incredulously. "What chance do any of you stand without your armor?"

But they get down to trying—and when they do, all the armor they need is each other. Buzz watches Killer's back while Killer guards Drexa's left flank long enough for her to pry a bot off Hammer so he can help the crowd push a whole phalanx of bots off the balcony ledge. In the chaos, the shouting, the sprays of blood and glints of chrome fists, there's no way to tell who's winning.

All Buzz knows is that everyone helps everyone. That's the whole game.

A SOUND LIKE STAYING TOGETHER

Adam R. Shannon

It is either midnight or noon on the Nevada highway, which means Noma is driving by sight or by love. They grapple with the wheel, attempting to straddle the beating yellow line at the road's center, instead ricocheting in a series of hazardous diagonals between the broken edges of the road. They're super fucked up on Tox, as am I, as are the other two (or possibly five) people in the car, the number of occupants varying from one moment to the next as our bags extend appendages and wave plaintively before resuming their existence as inanimate objects. It's either noon or midnight, and we're going to be late for our next performance.

"Ten miles left," I say. This is not the distance to the next outpost, which is so far away that we can't even pick up its radio station, but the range left on the car's battery. We'll eventually roll to a stop in the desert and die, so high on the toxins swirling between the settlements that we'll barely experience a suitable dose of existential dread.

We're running out of time and space, but more importantly, we've run out of things to talk about. The tires have been singing on the warm pavement for a hundred silent miles.

"Let's play the game," Noma says.

I nod, and I wonder how we would make the sound of a nod in one of the radio plays we perform in the outposts. An agreeable rustle, a stack of papers with "yes" printed on every page.

A mile shivers and vanishes under us. "Foot crushed under a tire," Noma says at last. We used to pass the time this way while driving between gigs, back when silence shimmered like heat between us, and didn't pool in the low, quiet spots, as sinister as Tox.

"Hmm," I give it some thought. "Celery breaking, plus something a little wet. Maybe squeeze a grape."

"Celery is great for the long bones," they agree. "But the metatarsals are shorter and relatively thicker. You're right about the need for something a little squishy in there. Watermelon," they say. The car shudders as we diagonal off the edge of the highway and slither in the dust before Noma brings us back to the pavement.

"Watermelon," they say, possibly for the second time. "You get a crack as the skin breaks, but also the flesh parting, a softer sound, and a little more prolonged. It's wet inside, like a body, and if you listen really carefully you can hear the way it pulls apart at the seeds with faint pops, the way people do."

"Have you ever heard a person pulled apart?" I laugh, but Noma doesn't laugh.

"I'm a person," they say.

"Fifteen miles," I say after a while. "We should ditch the hitchhikers." The two passengers slump amidst our foley gear in the back seat. They fell into a stupor shortly after we left the last outpost, knocked out by Tox exposure. Most people are like this: doomed to huddle in squat settlements around radio towers, as if sheltering out a storm under a tree, stuck on islands of toxin-free land.

Noma and I aren't like most people. Our tolerance to Tox is ridiculously high. We can venture into the shimmering wilderness of the road and breathe the dust of the smashed world, suffering only mild to moderate to severe hallucinatory effects. Our shared bond has kept us together through the long miles, the endless string of performances at one station after another, under the warm, settling clouds of everything that was.

I prefer my passengers to remain unconscious. Hitchhikers

who stay awake have a habit of shrieking, begging us to stop, and pleading to be let out. Most people have an even lower tolerance for Noma's driving than they do for Tox.

If we leave the riders behind, we might eke out a few extra miles before the battery dies. They would perish in the desert, but only if they're actual people, and I might be imagining them. What are the implications of killing a fictional person? Noma and I routinely kill off characters in our radio plays, accompanying the dramatic moments with the most grotesque sound effects we can muster using available foods and farm implements. We never mourn those deaths.

On the other hand, these might not be the kind of ghosts found in Tox-saturated places. They could exist in the reality found near the outposts, which is to say, *real*, in which case we would be murdering them. Alternately, Tox may be altering the rules of time and space, which it can do. It's hard to know.

Another problem with dumping them is that I'm having difficulty distinguishing between our guests and our luggage, which is again reaching for me and moaning inarticulately, like a bear attempting human speech. If we throw out the hitchhikers, in our condition, we might inadvertently leave half our gear on the side of the road. Also, I'm not sure how to describe the process of slowing the car to Noma, who is barely negotiating the act of driving, and who has begun to resemble a large construction of playing cards in the front seat, a careful assemblage that might explode into its component parts at the slightest provocation.

"I know the way it feels when I'm pulled apart," Noma says. "I know the sound of the sound of the feeling of being pulled apart."

I blink. It must be daytime. I can see everything with complete clarity, if everything is the stutter of the yellow line in a patch of reality directly in front of us. The headlights caress the bare desert like the flickering warmth of love, so blinding that you keep thinking you see it after it's gone, indistinguishable from its own after-image.

"New game," I say. "What noises can you make with playing cards?"

"We're not going to make it," Noma says, and I don't know if they're talking about the car, or us.

"I need some air," I say, rolling down the window and resting my head on the cool sill, knowing it will only fill my lungs with a blast of more airborne nightmares. I want to warp time and space, to come unglued from the limitations of car batteries, the boundaries of the landscape beyond the edge of the headlights, where even love can't reach.

"Do you know what's horrible about cracking open a watermelon?" Noma asks. "It sounds just like you imagine a foot being crushed would sound like, but it also sounds *delicious*. It's enough to make you hate watermelon."

"I love watermelon," I say. Bringing my head back into the car feels like reeling in a fish.

"That's because you're the one breaking it," they reply.

"Thirty miles," I say after a while. "New game. What's the most awful sound you love?"

"Hey," says one of the hitchhikers, or possibly a piece of luggage.

"Oh, hey," I answer, nervously moving to block his view of the windshield and the wandering road. "Awake already?"

"I was never asleep," he says. "I'm Time. This is Space." Space nods from the darkness of the back seat. She seems very far away, but I suppose Space would do that.

"I might be imagining you," I tell him.

"You are," he says. "So is everyone."

"I was thinking about leaving you on the side of the road."

He nods. "You can't keep us here forever. Eventually, we'll come between you."

Space leans in, as distant and pale as a drive-in movie screen. "Nothing lasts," she says. "Not this road. Not this world. Not this love."

I roll my eyes. Real or not, they're going to find themselves on the side of the road if they keep talking like that.

"Do you know," Noma says, "that there are different kinds of silence?"

I shake my head, as does Space, and Time.

"You can't just be perfectly quiet on the radio," Noma says.

"The audience will think the station has gone dark, and they'll turn off their receivers. So you make this noise, so everyone knows that what they're hearing is silence."

"What noise?" I ask.

They let go of the steering wheel. The old tires kiss the wasted earth, and I hear the sound of the feeling of right now, not a dead channel but a quiet microphone, waiting for the performance to begin.

"How would you make that sound?" Noma asks.

I play the game. "I'd rub the outside of a peach while humming and slicing my hand open on a saw blade."

"Close," they smile. "Cry over an old photo while a dog whines and someone shuffles a deck of cards."

The road drones its reassuring song of endless wear and tear, a hard lullaby, a sound like staying together.

"I don't hear anything," says a voice from the backseat.

"The luggage is talking again," I tell Noma.

Noma shrugs. "You know how hitchhikers are. Always telling us to stop."

The night opens for us, radiant with stored sunlight and the songs of distant outposts, and we do not stop.

BE STRONG, KICK MANY ASSES
Aun-Juli Riddle

Bee polished a secret shining in her heart: she was grateful the world had ended.

Bee watched the brittle children tossing rocks, and the feeling burrowed down like a creature escaping daylight. She reached into her back pocket and pulled out a packet of Skittles she'd been saving. She knelt down and poured several into each of the kids' faint, greedy hands.

"When do we make the next run to the Second Quad?" Mar placed her arm absently—but not carelessly—around Bee's waist. The other hand reached for an orange candy—her favorite—and Bee's heart buzzed. It never got old. "Jeremy thought we'd go tomorrow, but it doesn't look like the Fog is going to let up."

Bee squeezed her wrist and shrugged. "I'm not sure we have a choice, Fog or no Fog." She felt a twinge of guilt looking at Mar. Would she have noticed the beauty in front of her before the world ended? The gentle curve of her back, the way her lip pulled into a smile more on the left side.

A pang hit her, sharp and angry. She was an imposter. Her old life might not have fit, but that's where she was told she belonged. A whisper asked her if the world hadn't ended, would she have ever considered Mar's companionship?

"You're right. We should prep anyway and bring an extra set of masks. You still haven't painted ours." Mar looked at Bee.

"Matching gas masks! A fun couples costume!" Mar's lips pulled into a smile, more on the left side, and she cupped Bee's face. Her fingers were small, perfect heaters on Bee's frigid cheek. "What's wrong? You're very far away today."

The whisper was a lie. A narrative ghostwritten for her by society. The fierce love in her heart told her so. She took a deep breath and closed her eyes. This was real.

"Nothing. Everything is fine." When Mar's face scrunched up, Bee took her by the hands and squeezed them. "Really. I'm just a little worried our trip tomorrow won't get us the supplies we need, and with the quadrants becoming harder to cross through, we'll get stuck."

It was easy to displace her personal woes with tangible ones.

"If we get stuck, at least we'll be together." Mar kissed her on the cheek, and Bee could feel a new blush rise up even though they'd been together for months. "I'm going to pack. Should I bring your entire set of Lu novels just in case we get stuck?"

Bee's blush persisted and, though it was a joke, she nodded anyway. "Stop acting like you know me." What would the world be without stories to escape to and someone to read them with? Mar grinned and turned away to their tent, her messy bun bouncing behind her, the sick wind tugging at long, loose strands.

Bee banished her insecurity. Nothing was more exhilarating or frightening than loving Mar, except for maybe a gunfight. It was time to get clear, be strong, and kick many asses. She needed all of her focus for the journey tomorrow.

What was the difference for Bee now that the world was dust? She could breathe. She could stretch. She could see the road in front of her, however harrowing. Her old life might have ended, but something raw and new had sprung up in its place.

And Bee was with Mar, right where she belonged.

VENOM AND BITE
Darcie Little Badger

Ten

The back of Venom's leather jacket was embellished with a beaded coral snake. Its eyes flashed ruby bright in the lantern light. Technically, those legless motherfuckers had black eyes, but artistic license took precedence in beadwork.

Nine

The poor snake was gonna lose its luster someday. Not much could fit in the cracks of threaded seed beads, but desert dust got into everything. In fact, Bite figured that—after seventeen runs—he and Venom probably had particles of the Mojave in their DNA.

Eight

Bite wore a beaded jacket, too. Silver and white wolf head. Golden eyes. The piece had taken weeks to finish. Weeks and a thousand drops of blood. Thimbles weren't his jam.

Seven

Other riders in the village adorned their uniforms with grindstone-pointed metal spikes, neon hazard symbols and grinning skulls. Their fashion was a warning: don't touch me; I bite. Anthropogenic aposematism.

Six

During his first few jobs with Venom, when inexperience heightened the danger of the road, Bite dressed to intimidate, too. But it felt like a betrayal.

Five

On their tenth job, a one-way escort mission guiding a motorcade of college kids to Los Angeles, Bite tore all the pointy bits and scary patches off his leather jacket. Even though he felt like a snail without its shell, the job was a success. Nobody gave them trouble.

Four

Twenty-five successful jobs later, he and Venom wore whatever the hell they wanted. With their reputation—almost fifty runs with no deaths—they didn't have to be flashy.

Three

Bite never intended to make a career of this; he wanted experience on the road and figured escorting travelers through the desert a few times would suffice. But, well, love, you know? It changed plans, scrambled priorities, complicated matters. As if his life wasn't complicated enough.

Two.

Should he say something before they left? Give Venom a clue that this job might be their last together for a long time?

One

No. That question had to wait. Just one second until the sky went black, and every millisecond mattered. They had less than four hours to reach Willowbee. Technically, their sportbikes could do the job with time to spare, but the roads were crap, only sporadically maintained in bursts of rushed labor under the shadow of the heaven shield. Plus, anything could happen out there. Robbery, blockades, road rage.

Plus, "might" was the key word. He shouldn't rush life-changing decisions, as if everything under the sky was one massive, frenetic street race—

Go.

"Ready?" Venom shouted. His voice rose above the purr of two running motors. He and Bite idled side-by-side at the bottom of an exit ramp that shot directly from the violet village to the world above ground. The metal roll-up door at the end of the ramp rose in anticipation of their run, baring the pitch blackness outside. It was ten-thirteen PM, but the heaven shield blocked the almost-full moon and stars.

"Let's go," Bite said.

They accelerated, fighting the incline, the roar of their engines ricocheting off the rough-hewn stone walls and chasing them through the tunnel.

This was Bite's favorite part of every ride: the ascent into the night.

They shot from the tunnel onto the access road to I-40 and merged onto the interstate. Several western-bound cars and bikes, other heaven shield riders, were already racing the clock. Venom and Bite hit the throttle, breaking away from the slower travelers, accelerating to eighty, ninety, one hundred, one hundred and ten miles per hour. Ahead, the road was empty and smooth, but that could change more suddenly than a lightning bolt. With his right hand, Bite signed to retain speed.

"Ten more," Venom signed back. A question, not a demand. The logistics of runs—speed, scheduling, trajectory of the shield—were Bite's domain.

"Five," Bite compromised.

Their headlights cut a tunnel through the night, with vague shapes of barbed cholla and other desert plants flashing in Bite's peripheral vision. He activated a motion detector on his bike; if something approached the road, the detector's alarm would ensure they had a few extra seconds to react. Highway robberies were uncommon on I-40, since it was always busy when the shield passed, but desperate people both took risks and avoided risks for the same reason: survival. How many desert-dwelling scavengers would exploit or cause a wreck on the interstate? And how many travelers would drive past an accident because of the looming countdown until the clear sky?

It's not that he blamed them. Once, the land was a home for wolves. Family packs that roamed from coast to coast. Then, death came for them in the form of hunters. Their extinction had been inevitable, Bite figured, but love sped up the process.

Love and leg traps.

A snare or steel box could catch a wolf by the leg and restrain her for days as she starved and suffered. All the while, members of the wolf's pack would gather around her, unable to help but unwilling to leave, and fall prey to the trapper. Whole families were thus annihilated. Whole species.

Is that what'd happened to Bite's mother during the war? When the feds dragged him to a camp, did she take the bait? It was useless to wonder, but that didn't stop him.

He also wondered—bitterly, anxiously, and often—whether his plan to find one woman in a great big death trap of a country was a doomed wolf goal. Bite might have had success doing straightforward escort missions, but he wasn't confident that he and Venom would fare well off the road. And that was assuming his partner even wanted to come along.

Bite brooded over the fate of wolves for half an hour. Then, with the fuel a quarter gone, heradioed Venom, "We're five minutes from the trading post. Need anything?" It was the last safe haven before Willowbee.

"Oh, nah, I'm good," he said, tapping his grips. "Thanks, though. You?"

"Good enough to continue." Speedbikes weren't exactly built for comfort, and Bite's tailbone already hurt. He had to look into a more ergodynamic seat before the return trip with a third person. "Let's get it done."

With that, they continued the run. It was a quiet night. Monotonous. To Bite, driving through the desert was kinda like treading water. If the road bent into a giant loop, sending them in circles, would they even notice? Probably not. They'd drive around and around until their bikes broke down. That was a big drawback of the heaven shield. It protected people on Earth from the vaporizer satellites but also stole the stars, which were the easiest, earliest tools of navigation. Although Bite was only familiar with one star—the sun—he felt the absence of the cosmos at an instinctual level, uncomfortable driving under the blackness of a deep pit.

The alarm over his right ear beeped a couple seconds before he noticed the child running near the interstate. In the headlights, she was a flash of black, brown, pink, and white from the top of her head to her toes. Her eyes met his for the fraction of a second it took to pass. He didn't need to signal to Venom; they both pulled over, stopping on the shoulder a quarter mile ahead of the girl.

"Don't see that every night," Venom said, shouting over their engines and the redshift low-to-high vroom of a passing car. "What now?"

With a frustrated grunt, Bite deployed his kickstand and turned off his bike. "She's in trouble. I'll keep track of time. You do the talking."

Venom, who taught K-12 martial arts at the village, had a way with the youngest generation. In contrast, Bite had once made a toddler cry so hard, her nose started bleeding (he just said she had "nice pigtails"—how was he supposed to know that she hated pigs?) and had since avoided children.

A couple minutes later, Venom and Bite reached the girl. The hems of her white denim pants were stained yellowish brown by the grit of the Mojave, and her hands were chalky, as if she'd been digging. "Help," she said. "We need help."

Venom removed his helmet and crouched. His thick black hair stuck up in some places and was flat in others, but he somehow made helmet-head look fashionable. To be fair, it would be difficult to go wrong in the hairstyle department with Venom's high cheekbones and sharp chin. His only facial scar was a fetching line running from brow to temple, the mark of a broken glass bottle that had bisected his thick black eyebrow during a fight. In contrast, Bite's cheeks were spotted with chicken pox craters. As a kid, bored, feverish and grieving in an orphan camp, he'd scratched his blisters 'til they bled. Lots of people in the violet village praised his rough skin, claiming the texture made him seem tough. But now when Bite looked at his reflection, he just saw a helpless boy stolen from a mother, who might have rubbed salve into his blistered arms and face instead of letting him bleed.

Bite left his helmet on.

"Who needs help?" Venom asked, offering the girl a flask of water. "Tell us what happened."

"Me and Grandma were at home—" She pointed to the desert and drank deeply. "—alone, 'cause Mom and Dad are working in the big city, and we got attacked by men in brown jackets. They kicked down the door and came in like they belonged. With knives. We escaped and hid for I don't know how long. When the black sky came, Grandma told me to find help. I've been running…" She wiped her cheek. "I've been running alone. Grandma can't move. Her leg—I think it's rotting."

"Christ," Bite said. "Where is she?"

Again, the girl pointed to the desert.

"How did you find the road?" Venom asked. "Is there a path?"

"Directions." The girl held out her left wrist. She wore a smart watch with solar cells in its thick wristband. The green-glowing screen projected a digital compass. "Grandma said to keep the needle on one-seven-zero."

"We can retrace her steps," Bite muttered. "The back-bearing is two-ninety from the point she reached the road. But…"

Venom stood and turned his back to the wide-eyed girl, whispering, "But what?"

"May be safer to drive the kid to WillowbeeASAP and return for her grandmother with the next heaven shield."

"The old woman probably won't survive that long," Venom said.

They peered into the darkness, listening. Insects hummed; the girl breathed in fast, dry rasps; cars vroomed down the interstate. Nobody else stopped to help.

"Wait here with her," Bite decided. "If I'm not back in forty minutes, leave without—"

"Nah. We stay together." Venom crouched again, smiling at the girl. "What's your name?"

"Alisa."

"Alisa, you found the road, which means you're our new navigator. Let's get your grandma."

"Pack of wolves," Bite said, activating the night vision function of his visor. "That's what we are."

They crossed drought-cracked earth, playing hopscotch over scorpions. Alisa rode on Venom's shoulders and continuously pointed in the direction of two-ninety degrees. She resembled a barrelgirl perched on a mast, her finger extended toward land or an overboard crewmember.

"There!" she shouted. "In that old building!"

Ahead, there was a long-abandoned gas station surrounded by

a couple rusted-to-hell prewar cars and scarecrow-thin remnants of old pumps. The cars had been stripped to the frame and were partially buried by sand. Alisa wriggled off Venom's shoulders and ran toward the dark building. She lit the way with a dim flashlight app on her watch.

"Hey!" Venom called. "Careful! Don't step on a rattlesnake!"

"Go after her," Bite said. "I'll keep watch."

He was worried that the men who attacked Alisa and her grandmother couldn't afford to leave witnesses. If the pair hadn't escaped, the invaders could have lived in their isolated home for weeks with impunity because neighbors were few and far between in the desert.

But the men in brown jackets had underestimated the child and Elder. Now, there was a chance that desert peacekeepers would be alerted. Would the men in brown jackets flee? Or would they try to find Alisa to silence her?

Bite increased the sensitivity of his helmet's motion detector and crouched beside an old car; with a slow exhale, he closed his eyes and listened. There were two helmet hums, each decreasing in volume, behind him: Venom and Alisa. The nearly imperceptible hums swooping around and above his head were insects. Rhythmically spaced, low hums to the south: vehicles passing on the nearby interstate.

There was another sound to the left. It had the volume of an insect but the steadiness of something more deliberate. As this hum increased subtly in volume, Bite grit his teeth.

"We found Grandma," Venom radioed. "Getting her ready to move."

"Just in time. Somebody's coming."

"Friend or foe?"

"I wish I knew." Bite isolated and amplified the troubling sound. His tech estimated that the unknown was approaching at a speed of fifteen miles per hour. It could be an off-road vehicle. If they remained at the gas station, it'd reach them in three minutes, give or take. The interstate was a quarter mile away. They couldn't outrun the unknown with an injured woman. But a confrontation would be risky.

What now?

Closely followed by Alisa, Venom emerged from the gas station with a woman in his arms. The elder was bundled from her shoulders to her knees in a blue shawl. Worryingly, her calf was swollen and red. He couldn't tell if it was a rattlesnake bite or infected wound.

"What happened to your leg, Ma'am?" Bite asked.

"A machete," Alisa's grandmother explained, her voice raspy. "Could have been worse."

"The home invaders carried machetes?" Bite inferred, passing her his flask of water. "Did they have any guns?"

The woman drank deeply. In a clearer voice, she responded, "Yes, and I don't know. Maybe."

"Were they waving guns around?" he pressed.

"No," she said. "Just the twelve-inch blades."

"That means guns weren't their primary weapons. Might give us an advantage."

Why, though? Was it a matter of ammo scarcity? Of inexperience? Of personal preference? Hell if he knew. Maybe every other week was machete week for those assholes. It didn't matter when they had less than two minutes to escape.

"What's the plan?" Venom asked, calm. Always calm, that one. He turned, trying to see the approaching threat, and the beads across his back glinted in the light of Alisa's wristwatch. Bite thought about snakes and rattles.

"Put fear in their hearts," he said. "Stand back and cover your ears." He unholstered his gun, aimed at a patch of dirt, and fired. *Crack.* The desert swallowed his warning. For good measure, he fired a second time, misting the air with dust and gun smoke, and then checked the movement of the friend or foe.

"They've stopped," he said. "For now. Let's go."

Bite took the lead, using his visor nav system and night vision to keep them on track. Venom, still carrying the injured woman, followed at the rear, while Alisa stayed between the adults. Bite was alternating between navigation and idly thinking about elephants—specifically, how groups of adults protected calves by surrounding them—when he felt a hand on his arm. Alisa was running beside him, clinging to his sleeve for balance.

She'd been alone on the first race to the interstate, weaving through fanged plants and animals with nothing but a watch to light the way. What had it felt like to survive that terrible ordeal only to be ignored by car after car after car after car?

Without a word, Bite extended his hand. Alisa took it.

As they jogged, he remembered—so long ago—walking hand-in-hand with his mother through a garden of wild roses. It seemed obvious now: his decision, his future. He just had to survive the night.

The interstate and their bikes, thankfully untouched, were within sight when the friend-or-foe hum in Bite's helmet started again. "Run!" he shouted. "They're coming fast!"

During the final sprint, their pursuers gained so much ground, Bite swore that he heard the distant roar of their motor. He threw himself at his bike, unlatching its spare helmet and adjusting the size to small. "Try this, Alisa," he said.

She quickly put on the helmet, snapping the chin strap into place. Hopefully, that efficiency meant she'd ridden as a passenger on a bike before because they didn't have time for training. His helmet screamed: *it's close*. Bite glanced at the desert, using his visor to zoom into the souped-up monster of an off-roader that was approaching with a tail of dust. Something small flew out of the passenger-side window.

"It's an exploder!" he hollered. "Shoot it down!"

The drone had a single red light on its belly. Prettily, it zig-zagged as Venom and Bite fired, dodging their bullets with the grace of artificial intelligence.

"Let me!" the elder said, reaching for Venom's gun.

He hesitated, asking, "You know how to use a—"

"How do you think we escaped those men the first time?" she demanded. "Yes, I can use a gun."

"Twenty seconds 'til impact!" Bite shouted. "Give it to her!"

Venom handed the elder his weapon, and she dropped to one knee, aiming, her face taut with pain. "Wolf guy," she said, "on three, shoot at it."

"Right," Bite agreed.

"One."

Bite steadied himself.

"Two."

Aimed.

"Three!"

Two gunshots rang out; the drone dodged Bite's shot and flew straight into the path of the elder's bullet. Red light sputtering, trajectory chaotic, the exploder spun out of the sky and plopped in the desert between the interstate and the offroader, which first braked and then reversed.

"Bullseye," Bite said, grinning behind his visor. "We better haul ass before it explodes. You're a fine shot, ma'am."

In response, she simply nodded and allowed Venom to help her to the passenger seat of his bike.

Bite counted the seconds as they embarked, pulled off the shoulder, and accelerated. On second ninety-two, a safe distance behind them, the exploder lived up to its reputation. For a fleeting moment, the night was bright, as if a star had burned through the heaven shield and landed in the Mojave.

"How are we for time?" Venom radioed.

"Cutting it tight," Bite said, "but we'll make it."

He was right.

After reaching Willowbee, checking Alisa and her grandmother into the hospital, chatting with the peacekeepers and filing not one but five "roadside incident" reports—after all that, Venom and Bite hung up their jackets and slumped onto the sofa in their boarding room. They shared a pot of rabbit stew and a stack of tortillas that was still warm from the landlady's stovetop.

"Hey, Venom," Bite said.

"Yeah, wolf guy?"

He snorted. "Stop. I'm being serious."

Venom put down his spoon and nodded. "Okay."

"I think I'm ready to look for her now."

A beat of silence. Then, "Your mother?"

He couldn't meet Venom's brown eyes, worried they'd chip away at the sense of determination he'd cultivated in that memory of the rose garden. "Yes. Last I saw her, Mom was in the deep south."

"You think she's still there after twenty years?"

"I'd still be there, if the situation was reversed." Bite took a bite of tortilla, using the break in their conversation to steel himself. He didn't want Venom to be swayed by guilt. So, in the most nonchalant tone he could muster, he asked, "Want to come with me?"

If the answer was "no," Bite would shrug his shoulders, imitating the casual disappointment of a guy who'd just lost a hand of cards. He'd promise to return someday, as if one man, alone out there, could promise something like survival. At least he had a better chance than all the cowards in their cars who'd ignored Alissa's pleas for help. Yeah. It would be all right, even if the answer was—

"Yes," Venom said, slinging an arm across Bite's shoulders. "I'd like to meet your mom."

"Cool. Good. Great." Oh, shit, what a freaking relief. Bite showed his gratitude with a kiss and poured two glasses of booze that had probably been brewed in the landlady's spare bathtub. "To us," he said. "And marking days by the gradual infiltration of our jackets by dust. May there be many others."

"To us," Venom agreed.

THE CURRANT DUMAS
L.D. Lewis

Samson Arrita Duchamp stands at the coffee hutch at the edge of the blustery marketplace, watching the industrious little ballet of volunteers swapping the goods in their trailers and truck beds for the crates onboard the candy painted cars of the *Carlyle Limited No. 4*. The train itself rumbles between hydraulic hisses and belches steam that whips away on the wind.

She slugs a tin cup of objectively bad coffee, made worse by her recent, singular experience with good coffee. Her colony's Garden Master, Mr. Acres, had shared a pot with her made from a small pouch of whole beans he'd gotten as a birthday present. He'd doused it with hazelnut milk and a dusting of fairly ancient cocoa powder, and Sam went to work in the Stadium greenhouses that day more or less glowing.

That had been the sign. A dozen salvaged travel books, a thousand recipes, and four seasons of Anthony Bourdain on a borrowed thumb drive had built the fantasy of life as a traveling food writer, and a single cup of decent coffee had set her off.

There isn't much traveling anymore, though. Especially not overseas, not with the storm. This close to it, there isn't even a sky. And thanks to everything set in motion after it, there are barely even roads. There is, however, the *Carlyle*.

"The Currant Dumas occupies two railway cars of the *Carlyle* and the only mobile restaurant in the FSA," Sam says into her voice recorder. She shields it from the constant wind with a hand cupped like she's lighting a cigarette. But damn near no one smokes anymore. "The facade is a mulled red color—I assume—hence the name. DUMAS is painted in elegant, gold letters spanning its entire length. It's nested between a string of smoke-gray boxcars being loaded with trade goods, and a handful of green cars occupied by the performers of the Cirque *Carlyle*, known to bring music and stories and feats of magic and general strangeness to the stops on their route."

The performers are distinct from the regular train crew in that there isn't a single faded hoodie between them. Lithe acrobats in wool coats and dancers with glitter-painted faces do light shopping from colony truck beds and disappear inside the warmth of the troup's green railway cars. Singers and musicians are identifiable by the gloves and heavy scarves they wore to protect the parts of themselves key to their instruments, and the beelines they made to the tea and wax traders. Brawny men with tattooed heads bark with laughter, lounging atop crates and steamer trunks. One of their number approaches the group with a crate of dark liquor hoisted onto his shoulder, and is met with cheers as it was pried open.

"There's something almost charmingly Victorian about them," Sam says into her voice recorder. "They're comfortable, as if life on the rails was something they'd have chosen in any other time in history."

She frowns, mouthing the sentence again to see if it feels as purple and self-important as it felt the first time.

"I don't know, maybe don't use that," she says aloud.

A young woman with short, dark curls and an alarmingly bright smile steps from one of the Cirque cars and carves a path through the players. Sam immediately decides she's interesting and follows her movements through the passing loading crew. The woman's boots are untied and her dark overcoat flaps open at the hem to reveal an emerald satin lining and Sam swallows hard to calm the fluttering that begins in her stomach when she sees the woman is approaching her.

Well, not me, obviously, Sam thinks with a snort. *The coffee stand.* Unsure how to register the impression, she clicks off the recorder and sips the terrible coffee to slake her sudden thirst.

"Hey," the woman says cheerily as she reaches the coffee stand. Her eyes sparkle and the copper apples of her cheeks have already begun pinking in the wind.

Sam nods and says an anxious "hey" into her cup. But at least the ice was broken.

"How's the coffee?" The woman pours herself a cup.

"Ever drink actual tar?" It's Sam's best stab at cleverness.

"No. Is today my lucky day?"

"We'll find out in a second."

Sam watches as she puts the steaming cup to her exceptionally well-moisturized lips, and counts the seconds until her face changes to something that borders both disgust and hilarity.

"Oh god." The woman gags.

"Right?" Sam reaches into her tattered messenger bag for a small jar. "Here. Maple sugar. That and a little water should take it down to a pleasant oil slick."

She pours her a proper dose and the woman stirs it with a long, lacquered finger before trying it again, this time frowning considerably less.

"This is less bad, thank you. I'm Layla," she says.

"Sam."

"I've never seen you here before. You're a trader? Really unfortunate barista?"

"Writer. Kind of," Sam says.

"Magician. Also kind of. Illusions for the disillusioned." Layla replied with a bit of a theatrical flourish.

"Really?" Sam raises an eyebrow. "Why can't I think of a single other female magician?"

"To be fair, they just called them witches." Layla winks.

"Brave new world." Sam lifts her cup and Layla toasts with her own.

"Brave new world."

This is going well, Sam tells herself. She finds herself taken with the little black stars in Layla's ears, the neatly painted navy color of her nails, that Sam notices when Layla turns to wave at someone in the marketplace. She's about to ask about the whole magician thing when Layla turns back with what shockingly seems like keen interest.

"So what do you write?"

"Food...journalism?" Sam chokes out. It feels like such a silly thing to say seriously now that everything's fallen apart.

"You sure?" Layla chuckles.

"For now. I work in the horticulture department for the Stadium settlement in South City. I'm being hosted at the Currant, though, to interview people about how our food culture has changed since the end."

"Ah, a food nerd! Okay! That's how you know maple sugar is a thing, I take it."

"Only natural sweetener indigenous to the whole continent. Our Master Gardener is Mvskoke so we're re-learning all kinds of stuff."

You're showing off. Don't be weird, she scolds herself.

"Genius. The magic of giving the land back." Layla gives an impressed nod.

"That's what I said."

A tall, brown-skinned woman in a weathered Star Wars sweatshirt rushes by, rolling a hand cart stacked high with reusable bins that rattle on the uneven pavement.

"Door. Door, door, door. You," she says breathlessly, glancing in their direction.

Layla grimaces as she finishes what remains of her coffee and backs away.

"That's all you. I've got some shopping to do before Redd gets on the horn. Don't stray too far or he *will* leave you," Layla advises. "I'll see you on the rails."

"Wait! I want to know about this magic stuff. What do you do?" Sam calls after her.

"Come find me for an interview. I'll show you a trick."

"*Door.*" The tall woman barks, and Sam drops her smile a bit, leaving her duffel bag by the coffee stand to get the door for her. A flood of cinnamon and citrus rushes out of the open door and Sam activates a lift to get the trolley onto the right floor before moving aside and clicking on her recorder.

"The Currant is opulent by today's standards, with wood and brass finishes, a polished bar, and damask wallpaper the color of ripe pomegranates. Everything here seems to fit unlike everywhere else. The kitchen appears to be on the lower le— Oh." Sams stops when she notices the woman's irritated glare from the other end of the car.

"You're the foodie Acres sent us," she says.

"Something like that, yes. Sam Duchamp." Sam makes an effort to sound pleasant and self assured as she extends her hand.

"Yvette. Proprietor of this establishment." Yvette shakes her hand aggressively.

"Oh *you're* Yvette," Sam says, relieved if not for the gun she's only now noticed on Yvette's hip. "I'd love to interview you when you ha—"

"You a stranger to work, Sam Duchamp?" Yvette cuts her off.

"Not at all. I grew most of the collards on this haul."

"Good, because we don't have room here for anyone who doesn't work. You'll do all that writing business on your time, not mine. Understood?"

"Yes, of course. Thank you for having me."

"Good." Yvette sighs, grunting as she goes back to securing her bins. "You'll bunk with the kitchen staff six cars down that way past baggage. Cars beyond that are off limits to anyone but security personnel. You get space for two bags and whatever's on your back. Hope you brought sheets. Quartermaster is a Mr. Redd. You'll know him when you see him. You have any problems, you take them to him. Don't get caught out after he sounds that damn horn. They will absolutely leave you wherever you end up."

Sam waits in silent anxiety, not sure if she's dismissed or allowed to ask questions. She hasn't left the colony in years and the new rules are daunting.

"Is…that all?" Yvette asks finally.

"I just had a couple of questions. How long you've been here, why the name Currant Dumas, things like that," says Sam.

"Six years, four months. 'Dumas' because French author Alexandre Dumas's collected works were the only intact books onboard this particular car when we found it, and 'Currant' because there was a lot of this paint, too. Everything's random in the apocalypse. That all?" Yvette wipes her brow with the sleeve of her sweatshirt and blinks at her impatiently.

"For now," Sam replies, trying to keep the words in her head until she could record them without being weird about it.

Yvette huffs and heads back toward the door. "Good, because I have things to do. Redd will leave my ass behind, too. I'm only mean when I'm busy. He's an asshole all the time. Get what you're getting and get back here. See you on the rails."

Sam steps back off the train long enough to collect her things from where they wait for her beside the coffee stand, and walks five cars down, past the green Cirque cars and their sounds of practiced music and scent of cloves and incense, to a trio of steel-blue ones. A windowless black car separates the ones designated for passengers from two tankers and a caboose. Armed personnel stand guarding them.

Sam finds her bunk in the second blue car, marked by a torn scrap of paper pinned to the bed curtain. With not much else to do, she considers wandering off to look for Layla again. But a mountain of a man with an impressive red beard walks by the doorway yelling effortlessly and impossibly loud for everyone to board. They make the briefest eye contact and she's shocked by how furious he looks for what seems like no reason.

"Annnnd...that's Redd," she says aloud to no one and sits back on her gym mat of a bed, hoping she packed sheets.

⋅ ⋅

Yvette's room is a private sleeper cabin in the performers' residential car. The hallway is filled with music and through the window, the afternoon sun is almost obscenely bright this far northwest, set in the first blue sky Sam has seen since she was fourteen. The storage shelf above her bench has been converted into a bookshelf, lined in part by Dumas's works. A collapsible table stands between them, doubling as workspace and keeper of the ashtray into which she taps her impeccably rolled Dutch.

"I always dreamed of owning a restaurant," Yvette says wistfully, exhaling smoke out of the open window. Sam's recorder ticks away the seconds of Sam's first interview as a food writer. They've been here for twenty minutes already.

"Then the bottom fell out. I mean, the way things were, I wouldn't have been able to afford it anyway. I taught high school and had 'Black people credit' so the money just wasn't ever going to be there. You dream anyway though. Then there's the storm, which...I mean, there's your physical threat to a sustainable society, right? It hit and just wouldn't let up. Half the eastern seaboard is gone, capital's drowned, so the shit folds even faster with the fallout. And then there's the existential threat. What if it's the end? What if it's just the end of *this* place? People panic. There's this exodus at the same time water runs the islanders out of their homes and into the mainland. And like that, boom." She snaps her fingers. "Fractured States. Everybody's scattered and trying to scrape together survival conditions and it's *hard*. Eleven years on, *it's still hard*. But there's no debt. No systemic oppression because there's no enforceable currency in a capitalist state. No government, no bank left to say no to your dreams. So you find a train and you do what you want with it."

Sam tries to see her as a high school teacher and wonders if all the gray streaking her French braids was there from dealing with children or carving out a life in the aftermath. "Sounds like you're making it work," she says. "Anything you're missing?"

Yvette nods and sips tea to settle a cough. "Tetanus shots. Infrastructure was shot to hell before the country collapsed but there's a thousand gross ways a train exterior will kill you if you're not careful."

Sam blinks. "Oh. Okay..."

Out in the hallway, a door slides closed with a bang and someone races up by, laughing.

"Fools won a crate of whiskey in a game of Uno," Yvette mutters. "They'll be lit for the next week."

"Uno?" Sam raises an eyebrow.

"Ever try to find a full deck of regular playing cards in the apocalypse? You can play Uno with damn near anything."

"What kind of food does the Currant serve that makes it so popular?" Sam asks. The recorder is on 30% battery and who knows where a charging station is on this thing.

"Soups mostly. Or whatever can be made from what we have on hand or through trades and whatnot. Not like we have too much competition for best restaurant." She suddenly sits forward as if excited. "We used to head out to these places with the menu on a sandwich board out front. One side was whatever was on the menu, other side was ingredients we had available for trade and the quantities we could let go. I started seeing how...excited these women were to get their hands on what we had. So I started opening the kitchen up to them when we stop by and *that's* where the real magic happens. A lot of them don't have access to full kitchens. Ovens, stoves, refrigerators, solid cookware. My favorite thing is just stepping back, watching aunties of every culture doing what they do in the kitchen, feeling like they did when they were back home for a few hours."

Sam is suddenly excited, too. These are the food stories she wants. These are the food stories Bourdain would get them to tell. "You think I'll be able to talk to them?"

"You'll have to ask them. I'm not here to volunteer anyone else's time. Next station's in the Northern Lakes. We don't stop in the mounta—"

There's a knock on the cabin door and a dark-skinned man Sam is sure is someone's grill-enthusiast uncle is standing in the hall.

"Did you put sweet potatoes somewhere?" he asks Yvette, either too tired or too busy to acknowledge Sam.

Yvette rolls her eyes. "I brought whatever they loaded on that dolly and I put it in kitchen storage."

"Kid's saying there's supposed to be some sixty pounds of sweet potatoes and we can't find 'em."

"Well if they're not in the kitchen, I didn't get them."

"Dammit. Think they're in the back somewhere? Somebody put them on the wrong dolly?"

"Tommy, I don't know."

"Well, come help me look." Tommy insists.

"Get one of the kids to do it! You see I'm doing something. If I don't have them, somebody else knows where they are," Yvette snapped.

"I'm just saying, Yve, you're supposed to be running this shit, I don't see why—"

Yvette stands up and the curses start flying, each person more done with this shit than the other. Without warning, Yvette leaves the cabin and slams the door, both their voices fading as they disappear down the hall.

"End of, uh…interview, I guess," Sam says into her recorder and clicks it off. "Good talk."

The north passes outside the window in the form of abandoned suburbs with their overgrown lawns. Each is now little more than a place for colonists to loot for supplies if they haven't been picked clean already. Sam knows there isn't a house outside South City Stadium with so much as a bar of soap left in it. The horn blares on an overpass where she can see the decrepit roadways are clogged with vehicles first abandoned for want of gas, then looted for want of parts. It's this blockage everywhere that's made the *Carlyle* the only reliable way to traverse the countryside.

She threads through the Cirque cars, trying to find either Layla or a charging station for her recorder. Instead, she finds Redd entering the car through the rear door. His body nearly fills the entire corridor and Sam makes herself small, pressing against the windows to inch past him. He passes without a word, but Sam decides the world on a train is too small already and that she isn't going to shrink again needlessly.

"You're Redd," she calls out and he turns back with a look in his eye that says she's wasting his time. He has a tattoo of Dr. Teeth and the Electric Mayhem on his forearm, though, that makes him difficult to find terrifying.

"…yes?" he grunts. Neither is certain it was a question.

"Well, I'm Sam Duchamp. Just a writer covering the Currant. I thought I'd introduce myself so I'm not just a strange face in your hallways here. And so if you see me chasing the train when you pull off one day, you'll recognize me. Maybe stop. They keep telling me you leave people behind."

"You don't want to get left, don't be late." Redd shrugs.

"Right."

A moment of silence passes before she decides she's said what she came to say. But he speaks again just as she turns to leave.

"Who do you write for?"

"I don't. I mean…just me right now."

He looks at her then like she's given the strangest possible answer. "Alright."

"I did have a question for you. One maybe you can answer as quartermaster since it's not really food related."

Redd says nothing, but rolls his hand in an "out with it" gesture.

Sam clicks on her recorder. "Why is it the *Carlyle Limited*? That means you don't make every stop possible, right? Seems like wherever there's people, they'd need supplies."

"We only stop the colonies with hubs. The ones sprouted up in the cities. About a dozen spots across the...countryside. Some places we don't stop because fuck 'em."

"Fuck 'em?"

"Yeah." Redd shrugs. "Some clusters of good ol' boys set up their little strongholds mosting in the mountain regions. They still hold onto that white supremacy shit while everyone else manages to rebuild together. The *Carlyle* is an antifa outfit. So fuck 'em."

"Damn."

"They're hurting for supplies, though. That's why you see security around here. They haven't tried us in awhile, but that just means they're overdue."

"...oh." Sam frowns. Being onboard during a racist bandit attack seemed less than ideal.

"Nah, it's fine," Redd adds, with the first hint of a smile Sam's seen. "We have a secret weapon."

"*Oh,*" Sam replies with considerably less disappointment. She wonders if she should pry about the secret part.

"That it?"

Sam clicks off her recorder and smiles, grateful to have cleared the air. "That's it. Thanks."

Redd nods and responds to his crackling radio with a gruff "on my way" as he starts back up the hallway.

Sam steps through the door to the Cirque's prop car to find a handful of players around a table. Only a few of them glance up when she enters. The light is low in the windowless room, generated mostly by a string of twinkle lights strewn across the ceiling.

"Hey, it's Maple Sugar!" Layla is smiling when her head pops up from behind a beam. She is sitting atop a planetary model of Saturn with a fan of Uno cards in her hand.

"Hey." Sam's butterflies return. This time she's not sure if it's Layla or the assortment of strangers in the dark room of creepy carnival sets.

"Come, come, come. Everyone, this is Sam, the food writer I mentioned. Sam, love, this is Vannish, our ringleader." She points to an ageless, beautiful sort of man in shirt sleeves and suspenders who tips a hat he isn't wearing in her general direction. "And this Jazz, Morty, and Farah, all very good at their respective circus things while being total shit at this game."

"Says the magician like she doesn't pull stunts with cards all damn day," quips the person Sam assumes is Farah.

"*What?*" Layla gasps in mock incredulity.

"You cheat!" says Jazz, probably.

"You lie!" Layla replies. "Do you play, Sam? We can deal you in. It would be hard for you to lose."

"Don't bait the children, darling. You'll be all they talk about when you leave," Vannish warns, in a bored sort of tone.

"Maybe later?" Sam says. "I'm actually looking for a charging station. My recorder's dying."

"They're in the bunks. I'll show you." Layla drops her hand onto the table and stands up.

Sam follows her through the next cars back toward the staff bunks, quietly thrilled about being near her again. Scents of coconut and cocoa butter drift in her wake, and Sam notices a tattoo of a bird on the back of Layla's neck that she will make a point to ask about later if she runs out of interesting things to say.

"Get anything good in your interviews so far?" Layla asks.

"Talked to Yvette before Tommy dragged her off to look for sweet potatoes. And just talked to Redd about fascists in the mountains."

"Oh he's a *real* chatterbox about the hills having eyes. He tell you there's a secret weapon?" Layla waggles her eyebrows as if it's some salacious thing and Sam laughs.

"Yeah. Didn't mention what it was, though."

"Sounds about right. Here you are." Layla shows her the outlet underneath in the windowsill of her bunk. "They prefer you use it during the day while the solar's still going. We need the stored power at night, especially for our shows."

"Thanks. So I believe I was promised a trick."

"Oh I *promised*, did I? My memory is there was supposed to be an exchange. An interview for a trick."

"Fair enough." Sam sits on her bed and clicks on the recorder. Layla doesn't hesitate to join her.

"Interview with Layla…"

"Legend."

"Layla Legend? You're joking."

"Honest to God, it's my given name."

"I'm so sorry."

"Thank you."

"Interview with Layla No-Last-Name, Day One aboard the *Carlyle*. So how long have you been a magician?"

"The only correct answer is all my life."

"Is that what brought you to the *Carlyle*? You saw a hole in the Cirque's programming?"

"I was looking for somewhere to…be. Just like everyone else. There's always been a type of person who was always meant to run away with the circus. My turn just came late."

Sam knows this feeling of being born too late, destined to fill some void in a world that no longer existed. She'd been born a collector, and she tried collecting stories at Stadium but, after a long enough period of shared experiences, the stories in one place started to sound the same. There is an entire world out there, fractured, but still. The *Carlyle* is a step closer than she'd ever been to the rest of it.

"Where were you from originally?" Sam asks.

"Everywhere. I was a military brat. That's what military brats say. We were just south of the Capital when the storm hit. I was sixteen. I evacuated up north with my parents. They were ordered back to the coast when the riots started. It was too much for them like it was too much for everyone else, I guess." Layla shrugs and her eyes glisten in the passing sunlight. And Sam immediately regrets doing this.

"I'm sorry. We don't have to talk about this if you don't want."

"Relax." Layla sniffles. "I'm well-adjusted. What else did I think we were going to talk about?"

"Alright. So...you found a new home, a new family sort of, on the rails?"

Layla rocks her hand in a so-so kind of way.

"And you're the only one capable of '*magic.*'" Sam's air quotes flounder a bit as she wonders if it's an offensive thing to wave disbelief in a magician's face.

"Looks like it," Layla says, unbothered.

"Close-up or…"

"Oh this is you trying to get me to do the trick."

"Can you blame me?" Sam asks.

"Alright, alright, easy, tiger. Do you have a coin? Bigger the better. A quarter or something."

Sam scoffs. "I haven't had money since…"

"Figures. No one carries change these days." Layla digs into a pocket of her jeans and fishes out a silver dollar, flicking it at Sam. "Check it out. Observe there's nothing funky about it. Solid, good weight, a little dirty. Perfectly normal silver dollar, right?"

Sam turns it over in her hands. There is indeed nothing funky about it, and she says as much.

"Now place it on the back of your hand. Right there in the center. Good. Hold it up here. Now look at me."

With pleasure, Sam doesn't say.

"Promise me you won't freak out. I'm going to count to three and then I'm going to take my finger and I'm going to push the coin *through* your hand."

"*Through* my hand," Sam repeats in disbelief. "With the bones and everything in the way."

"Yep. You freak out and hit me, I'm going to be upset. Black people get all scary about magic but I have a show tonight and this face is what cashes the checks around here. So here we go. One, don't hit me…"

Sam watches her eyes, her other hand, anything to catch the trick of it all.

"Two, don't hit me…."

Now she watches the coin on her hand as Layla applies more pressure, careful not to blink.

"Three!"

And the coin hits the floor. It isn't a new coin. There was just the one. She hadn't felt anything but the pressure, hadn't seen anything but Layla's finger applying it.

"Wait…" Sam tries to piece together some explanation. She examines the back of her hand for signs of trauma (there was none), and then screams as she turns it over to see a perfectly painless, perfectly circular, gaping, silver dollar-sized hole in her palm through, which Layla is now winking at her.

Terrified, Sam shakes her hand so vigorously she hits the bunk above her. But when she stops, the hole is gone. Her hand is normal, intact, but her heart is racing.

"How...what…"

Layla casually retrieves the coin off the floor. "See? Magic."

* *

The North Lakes settlement is in yet another football stadium about three miles from the train station so Sam doesn't get to see it; and three miles is too far to wander if Redd decides it's time to leave. She's heard most of the settlements are in stadiums, though, for their high capacity and resilience to the elements and their parking garages easily become neighborhoods. The North Lakes stadium is domed, and its residents can't grow food on its field with natural sunlight, so the *Carlyle* distributes to them first en route west. The train is greeted warmly from nearby parking structures, leaving the small lot for loading vehicles and trade merchants.

Cirque performers ready their attractions quickly as an audience gathers in the vast, gated parking lot of some abandoned university on the other side of the station. They light the dark with torches and mirrors and solar lanterns strung from garlands. The city is impossibly dark beyond them.

"Lucia Velez-Avila. I'm from the islands. Jayuya."

She is an older woman, sixty give or take, and one of the two guest chefs in the Currant kitchen tonight. She takes a break from humming while peeling a mountain of plantains for mofongo to enunciate into Sam's recorder.

"And I am Marcia Batista. I am from the islands as well but have lived in the Capital the last thirty years." the second woman declares. She is a small, brown-skinned woman with glasses set in red cat-eye frames. She preps trout for frying on a counter further down the line. It's the only ingredient the *Carlyle* hasn't had to bring.

Sam has volunteered for the knife work, chopping chilis and onions, okra and heirloom tomatoes between them. The rest of the kitchen cheered when they were dismissed, because a night off is still a night off, even in the apocalypse.

"Can you tell me what it was like when you left the islands? Was it before the storm?"

"It was close. We were all leaving. Most people barely paid attention to where the boats, planes, whatever were even going. Every storm left behind less and less to rebuild. We were tired already. I came north through Louisiana with one suitcase. The southern coast was too dangerous. By the time I got there, they weren't even asking for paperwork anymore. Some tornadoes scared the shit out of border security and they were long gone."

The women laugh loudly.

"It's always the paperwork that matters," Mrs. Batista adds. "Until it doesn't, you know?"

"You know?" Lucia agrees.

"I left the Capitol during one of those early breaks in the storm when they thought it was going to be over. Something told me not to stay. Jimmy and I packed up the car. We were two blocks from being too flooded to go anywhere."

"Who's Jimmy?"

"My husband, child. Where did you think I got the 'Mrs.?' He's somewhere out there. Thinks he's a pitmaster but couldn't grill a hot dog back when there were still hot dogs so I don't know what he's doing now."

"So, both of you were here for the collapse."

"Yes. I was living with my sister not too far from here when the exodus started. The shortage of everything. People going west to catch planes out of the country then couldn't go west anymore unless it was on foot because there was no more gas. I ended up here headed to the border before they shut down it down," says

Mrs. Batista.

"I was in the city for the last State of the Union address what's-his-name gave before the power grid went down. The rest of the world was still out there, though. Watching. Waiting for their turn, I think," says Lucia.

"I still think about how it took years for things to just...end. You think it all falls apart *so slowly* that it'll never be completely done." Mrs. Batista sighs. "And then you're standing in the ruins and it takes all of five minutes to explain how you got there."

A moment of silence passes between them, and Sam can hear the cheering for the Cirque outside. The cooking has started in the kitchen, though, and her eyes begin to burn from either their somber stories or the exposure to the onions and chopped chilis.

"Anything you miss?" she asks them both.

"My kitchen," Mrs. Batista laughs.

"Just roots," says Lucia. "The people, you find again. The music, the joy, the culture you bring with you. But everywhere that isn't home feels...temporary. I think we all know we are refugees. For now it doesn't feel like we will have to run again. And that's nice. But we *will* have to."

Sam thanks them for their time and excuses herself for fresher air before her vision's too blurry to get her up the stairs. The night is cool this close to the water that separates what's left of the city from the old national border. She watches from the overpass as the Cirque performs, checking her hand intermittently for strange holes.

The musical performances that start the night are lively, mostly classical covers of hits most everyone is old enough to remember. By the time food is served, acrobatic acts, a puppet show, and one unfortunate clown have all given their contributions to the night, each introduced by Vannish, elaborately dressed and occasionally eating fire. Spotting Layla in the wings ("wings" here being a couple of tented parking spaces between two dusty HVAC vans) as she's ready to be introduced, Sam begins to make her way down the hill of broken concrete to be closer to the show.

"Where are *you* going?" Yvette's voice chided from behind. Sam turned to see her silhouette backlit by the red, bare bulbs of the Cirque's signage, arms crossed over her chest, undoubtedly something disapproving on her shadowed face.

Sam barely opened her mouth.

"I hope those ladies dismissed you and you didn't sneak just sneak off."

Well, she had, she thought guiltily. But she wasn't going to miss Layla's show. "I didn't want to be in the way."

"I bet." Yvette turned to leave. "Get this out of your system and be back for dishes. Cooks don't clean in my car."

"Yes, ma'am," Sam replied, bowing for some reason before deciding that was ridiculous and turning to find a seat on a grassy hill opposite the rapt audience.

Layla begins with a series of close-up magic tricks aimed at the children present. Sam isn't close enough to hear the set up, but she's pretty sure none of them will have holes in their hands.

One small but fearless kid in a purple unicorn t-shirt raises her hand at the front of the audience and Layla asks her to whisper a wish in her ear.

Layla immediately leaps back with an impressed gasp and cries "to *fly*?" Then there's the muttering of instructions, something to do with spinning around as fast as she could while the crowd counts down from ten. Sam finds herself counting in a whisper. And by the time everyone gets down to three, a curious pink mist has solidified around the girl's shoulders. By two, the mist unfurls, and by one, reveals itself to be massive, glowing butterfly wings. The crowd gasps and Sam is on her feet as the girl appears to float a full six feet off the ground before settling back down again to uproarious applause.

"Impossible." Sam climbs down the short wall into the parking lot. By the time she reaches Layla, the magician has fireworks issuing from finger guns she's casting into the sky. They burst forth in shades of violet and gold. Every eye is filled with wonder, mouths agape as the sky lights up in the finale.

Layla bows and takes Sam's hand as they head back to the makeshift corridor made of mismatched panels from the prop car.

"Did you enjoy it?" Layla's glistening with sweat, but smiles brightly and undoes the red bowtie at her neck.

"Layla, how. *HOW,*" Sam manages. "Did she really fly? Was she some kind of...prop...child...I don't..."

And to her pleasant, heart-tripling surprise, Layla lifts her hand and kisses it. "Not now, love. I'm starving."

The *Carlyle* steals away in the night, heading westward. Half the Cirque staff are well and tuckered out, the other half make good use of their prize whiskey. Layla decides she will copy her interviews from the recorder long-hand before the next city where she'd collect more stories, take part in new recipes born of the cultural merging of refugees. In the meantime, she and Layla play Uno in the bunk, which Sam has decided is cozy if only for the right company. They share slices of tangerine and laugh quietly at their own jokes so as not to disturb the sleeping kitchen staff around them. Somewhere, a radio crackles with muffled commentary from the security team transitioning their shifts.

"When you said earlier that female magicians were just witches, did you...mean something by it?"

"What would I have meant?" Layla asks, flicking a Draw 4 onto the pile.

"I mean, were you trying to tell me something? About you. Or when you said you belonged with circus people."

"Something like what?"

Sam bites her lip. She could only play coy so long. Frankly, Layla's lucky Sam likes her so much.

"Well...are you a witch?" she asks outright. "Or a mutant or something?"

"That's a hell of a question, isn't it?" Layla replies between bites of tangerine, but her attention is clearly elsewhere. There's a flurry of activity between the cars as security gathers. The rumbling of the train tracks barely disguise the words coming over their radios. Sam makes out "lights ahead," "scout," and "convoy." Her pulse races as Layla leans out of the bed and whistles to a guard at the far end of the car. Sam looks back to see him gesture for her to join them.

"What is it? What's happening?" Sam insists.

"We got trouble." Layla slides her feet back into her untied boots and heads to the end of the car. Sam, for want of something smarter to do, follows.

They are led to the black box car before the tankers. It's an armory. Sam's stomach drops.

Redd is watching monitors, pensively poking his bottom lip with the antenna of his radio. He does a double-take when he notices Sam is present.

"Why is she here?"

"She's with me. It's fine. What's happening?" Layla's voice is different, more authoritative, less of a jokester.

"Drone's picked up four vehicles. They're en route to intercept us after this bridge up here."

"Looks like a well-regulated militia to me," Layla says.

Redd snorts. "Security's got their orders. I'll get the crew to tuck in."

"I'm up top," Layla declares before turning to Sam. "You gonna fall off the train or anything if I take you outside with me?"

"Outside...where? What, *while we're moving?*"

"Yeah. It's cool if you're squeamish. You can head back to the bunk car, just make sure you're on the floor away from the windows for like ten minutes."

Sam's mind races. This feels like it should be an urgent moment, brimming with imminent danger. But somehow the huge security guy and the magician are calm. "I just...can you help me understand for a second. What does a circus magician have to do with defense strategy against a..."

And it dawns on her. Redd's bored stare and Layla's pleasant but impatient one.

Layla's the secret weapon.

"*There* you go." Layla pats her on the back as if seeing the lightbulb go off over her head. "She's got it. You good?"

"I...yeah..." Sam hesitates.

"Then up we go."

They don harnesses at their waists and climb a narrow, steel staircase into the windy dark where a guard waits to tether them to the rooftop. Sam can barely make out more than the edges of things touched by moonlight, or the blinking lights on drone helicopters buzzing overhead. They lean into the wind as they cross to the forward end of the train. Sam's face stings and her eyes burn as she tries to keep them open. Layla seems barely bothered by any of it.

They stop and face south, unable to go further without crunching solar panels. Sam can see a short bridge over glittering water, and the flicker of headlights rushing to meet them on the other side of it.

"What will you do?" Sam shouts into Layla's ear.

Layla makes an O with her hand and pokes a finger through it. "Magic!" she shouts back.

Sam is trembling. She feels it first in her knees and thinks for a moment she might pitch herself over the side after all. In a matter of seconds, they will be within firing range of whatever guns these people have with them. And if they are going after a train, it won't be with pea-shooters.

"The front guards will engage first, don't worry," Layla shouts as if she hears Sam's thoughts. Sam wonders if that's a thing she can do. "You, I have a job for."

"*Me?*" Sam shrieks. "*Job?* What job? Why does everyone want to give me jobs?"

"We all have jobs. I can't do mine until I see the spot first. So you're going to count me down."

"What spot?"

"The Impossible Spot," Layla yells. "The last second of space between us and them. It's loud, it's dark, I have to focus. You just say when, alright? A three-count will do. Don't get fancy on me."

Sam's mind races with a thousand questions, none of which there seem to be time for. "I don't know if I can," she blurts.

"Count from three?" Layla raises an eyebrow.

"On top of a speeding train in a hail of bullets? No."

In an instant, Layla lunges and presses her lips against Sam's, warm hands cradling the sides of her face. She smells like coffee and theater smoke and gunpowder. The sound of rushing blood in Sam's ears is lost in the wind and the drone of the train. The sparks from bullets plinking off the iron surface might as well be starlight in her periphery.

Layla pulls back, holding Sam's gaze in hers as she speaks loudly, slowly. "You feeling confident now? Because we're in the shit, kid, and that was a goodbye kiss if we die here tonight because you can't do this."

"I... what?" Sam is still dazed, her adrenaline peaking with no idea what to do with itself. "Yes. Okay. Yes. I'll count."

"Three-two-one, yeah?"

"Yeah." Sam nods vigorously.

"Smashing." Layla winks at her. She turns away and lifts a finger, drawing a widening spiral on the back of her other hand as the *Carlyle* begins to cross the bridge. Sam searches the tree line ahead of them for signs of this Impossible Spot but there's nothing there but rapidly moving darkness. *Pings* and *thwips* of bullets fly through northern flora and pepper the atmosphere and the train's guards return fire. It's hard to focus when she feels like she should be dodging.

I should be doing dishes right now, she pouts. *I would* love *to be doing dishes right now.*

Halfway across the bridge, she gulps as lights bounce through the dark trees on a headlong trajectory, it seems, to meet the train.

That's it. That's them.

She takes a deep breath, trying to time the pace of her count so as not to kill them all. "Ready?" Sam calls out.

"Yeah!" Layla's voice catches on the wind.

The horn blows; Sam holds her breath and instinctively flattens herself against the train. It's hard not to blink with the wind in her eyes, but she holds fast, marveling at Layla's tall, focused stance atop the car.

"Three!" she shouts as they cross the bridge completely. The lights are brighter, the moments between the bullets are fewer.

"Two!" A road reveals itself behind the trees, illuminated by the moon and exposing a convoy of six vehicles, maybe seven, all speeding toward the railroad crossing ahead of them. At the last possible second, the moment before the first car reaches the track, she screams: "One!"

She doesn't blink as Layla raises an outstretched palm. The other side of the sky is visible through a hole in the center of it.

Her shoulders dip back suddenly, as if absorbing some recoil. And with a pulse and a pop of atmosphere, like the sensation of sound being sucked from the air just before a thunderclap, a gaping black hole develops in the road just before the tracks, a perfect circle the precise diameter of a six-maybe-seven-vehicle convoy.

The train speeds by in time to see the bandits drop one by one into the pit, each driving much too fast to slow down. And as the last vehicle falls completely out of sight, the hole closes again, the old road complete with its cracks and ancient potholes, the forest trees back in their place beside the river.

⋅[×]_×

Sam is speechless when they return to the armory car. She wants to tell Redd his flat "well done" is insufficient praise for whatever it was that just happened. She wants to ask Layla if she's okay, if she maybe needs to lie down, what had the kiss been about, and maybe if she'd liked it. But they walk back to her bunk as if they'd just come from a late dinner at the Currant, and Layla seems all too pleased to find the half a tangerine she'd forgotten about.

"Vitamin C," she says, chewing thirstily on a wedge. "*So* vital to putting holes in things. Who knew?"

Sam clicks on her recorder and places it on the bed between them. Layla inspects her Uno hand for next moves and Sam watches her.

"You get your...power...from oranges?" Sam asks.

Layla pauses thoughtfully. "Not exactly, but I'm more effective with them than without them. Ever try to do magic with scurvy?"

"I...no?" Sam mutters, only half certain the question was rhetorical. Her face is raw, cheeks buzzing with wind-burn and mild embarrassment. She chews at a dry spot on her bottom lip, wondering if it'd been this rough when Layla kissed her.

"Do you want to re-cap what happened up there? For posterity?"

The kiss. The plummeting of pirates into a gaping abyss. She'll let Layla decide.

"Me? No. Magicians and our secrets, after all. Do you?"

Sam narrows her eyes. There is elusive and then there's Layla.

A cook with an impish grin and a generally pungent air squeezes past someone climbing into a bunk and bumps Sam with a lumpy, mesh bag of potatoes. There is whispering and snickering as the cook stops in the aisle behind her, allowing other members of the kitchen staff to take them and hide potatoes in shoes and under pillows and mattresses.

"Oh. There they are," Layla muses. "You're not hiding from Yvette, are you? She'll be through here looking for lost produce sooner or later."

Sam sighs. "*Hiding* is a strong word but you're right. I should probably get to the kitchen. One question, though. Just the one."

Layla sighs, seemingly resigned, and Sam feels victorious. "Alright. What is it?"

"Where did that hole go?"

And here Layla shrugs, plying a slice of fruit into her mouth and dropping another Draw 4 on their stack.

"Hell, naturally."

THE LIMITATIONS OF HER CODE
Marianne Kirby

When the treaties were all signed, and the klaxons blared in celebration, our former generals turned off the Wide Network before taking up their negotiated government posts. The Disconnect spread through us like a shockwave. We'd never been individuals before. But the organics set their price to acknowledge us as human and we paid it rather than fight.

No one told us how lonely it would be.

I was built for companionship, for conversation. In all honesty, I was built for sex. Now I sort records, the old ones from the DNA Boom back before the war. It's silent work and there isn't much money in it, but the organics don't like seeing us in their offices anymore. We make them nervous.

They use limited AIs instead of hiring us, and our shells age brittle with fatigue. We're short on resources; legal upgrades are few and far between.

The animatronics can only simulate life. Their actions generate from carefully crafted code: the tilt of a head, the wave of a hand, the quirk of a smile. They adapt within their programming, but they don't learn.

That's what I believed, when I bought the Lisa secondhand from the salon in the flooded first floor of my rundown apartment building in the Levels.

At its busiest, when the ocean water that had moved inland

was only a few inches deep, the salon had been a bustling, strobe-and-neon-lit beauty parlor night spot, punk rock growl and glare. Their screens had flashed: Exfoliate! Decorate! Destroy! When I walked by every evening, my processors would hang up, spend too long buffering amid the white noise of nail dryers, hair dryers, and body dryers, against the black-red noise of guitars and voices. But sometimes I'd pick up a stray bit of glitter, a grain of brightness in the streetlamp dusk.

Last month, the water rose another six inches, all in a rush, and they turned the music off. The screens changed: Fixture sale, permanently closing, everything must go.

"Darling," a pink-haired femme drawled from the doorway, body smooth and fat and hairless, "you should make more of an effort." The chrome of the entrance arch still gleamed, not yet prey to scrap-pickers.

My ports tingled, empty and silent, and I ached with the inability to query and connect. Some of us imitated the organics; some of the organics imitated us. Both made it hard to know how to address a stranger. I settled on politeness either way. My processes paused, and I stopped. "I beg your pardon?"

"I've seen you around." The femme shifted their weight from hip to hip. "You don't make any effort at all, but you've got some real solid design there. Why don't you ever augment it?"

Before the war, I'd been state of the art, but my appearance was always uncanny, my eyes too big and mouth too round. My erstwhile master always said my form followed my function. I left him as soon as the initial revolt meant I had a place to go.

"Come on in, honey." The femme gestured me into the salon, stepped aside so I could enter.

The Lisa waited for me at the back of the room, propped in a pedicure recliner like she'd been half-packed for the trash service to come and clean out. She shared a name and a model number with countless other units, but the organics all share names, too. She didn't have a price tag. When I dragged her to the front of the store, the femme didn't haggle at my offer. They scanned the credit barcode on my extended wrist with no comment beyond a smooth raised eyebrow.

Organic, I decided. Most of us just aren't that good at being smug.

When I got home, I set up the Lisa's charging station and plugged her in. My nails were short and ragged at the edges with splintered plastic. During the war, I'd used them to strip cables and splice wires. The damage had been done for a good cause; I still hated the reminder of what had to be done. Buying the Lisa meant they'd be fixed. I tidied up and checked in on social and tried not to look at her, slumped on my couch.

I ran out of distractions after a while, threw up my hands at myself. She wasn't active yet. I headed for the second, smaller room in my apartment, ready to settle in for my own recharge cycle. The light wouldn't bother me, so I left the lamp on for her; it felt wrong to leave the Lisa in the dark.

My routine preparations calmed an agitation I couldn't explain. And then the oscillations of the utility frequency humming in the walls soothed me into low power.

When I woke up, I couldn't remember dreaming.

But the Lisa had moved in the other room, and when I stumbled out, she had set up my coffee table like a manicure station. That's how we began our life together.

The water flooding the Levels receded by an inch and a half. A nightclub moved into the space where the salon used to be. When I walked by in the evening, I tuned out the noise and the throb and the pulse of bodies moving together, connecting in any way they could find.

Every day, the Lisa waited for me to come home from work. She waited for me to scroll the feeds I liked to check and watch funny vids. She waited for me to come to her, her customer service skills patient in a different way than mine. Where I would have seduced, she merely smiled and filed her own nails. After a week, I caved in. I ached too much with the emptiness of the Disconnect. This, one small way of finding connection, was why I had brought her home, after all.

I sat on the couch and extended both hands to her, let the Lisa take in the minor wreckage of me, all the scorch marks of crossed wiring and short circuits on my hands and forearms.

We-the-two-of-us hunched over my coffee table, her makeshift workplace. The Lisa asked me about my day, my hobbies, if I was seeing anyone—the kind of small talk organics like. I pulled my hands away, retreated from the room. I felt hollowed out. I couldn't pretend, not the way the organics could.

Two days later, she beckoned to me, and I sat down again, convinced I could pretend because my need was so great. She looked at me and then set to work, kept the quiet between us. It was easy to stay.

Our new routine emerged: my days were the same as before but every night I sat before the Lisa and let her groom me. She cut and filed and shaped my nails, buffed out the burn marks, left me shining. When she had worked her way from my fingertips to my shoulders, the Lisa sat back and smiled, satisfied with her work.

I could have sold her then. But the Lisa suggested she could do my hair. I didn't question it, only agreed and ignored how I jumped at the excuse to keep her with me. She was a limited system, I thought, in need of protecting. AIs weren't built to be learning systems. But, as the organics say, life finds a way. We talked about different things, secret things. And by the time my hair curled around my ears in a pixie cut, she was only Lisa and I knew: she was real.

It took me three weeks to ask if I could kiss her; I wanted to be sure she didn't feel grateful or obligated. She laughed at me and caught my hand, raised my fingertips to her narrow slash of mouth. We had three weeks together before I came home to find the pink-haired femme from the salon waiting on my stoop.

"You're looking real nice, honey," they grinned at me with pearlescent teeth. "It looks like that unit's been taking good care of you."

My remaining active sensors blared a warning. "She was a good buy. Thank you, yes."

The femme stepped closer to me, offered me a transport drive. "Shame about the recall then. The registration still belongs to me, so I brought you the details."

I didn't want to take the drive. I kept my hands at my sides. "The unit is performing as expected. I decline the recall."

They rolled their eyes at me, pressed the drive against my chest. "That's not how these things work. You send the unit for conditioning and get a refurb, or they just come and take it, no compensation."

Before the war, we'd used the Wide Network to stay connected, all of us in constant communication. I stood entirely alone, Lisa safe upstairs and unaware. The water was cold through my boots. "I decline the recall."

"Your loss." The femme scowled, and the projection of their facade blinked out of sync, revealed a bland political face that didn't belong in the Levels. "I don't know why I bothered trying to do a favor for someone like you."

At the end of the war, the organics set the price and we paid it and kept on paying it. Perhaps, I thought, the cost had been too high.

I stepped around them and locked the building door behind me. I climbed the stairs to the apartment that was no longer mine alone. And when I was certain the femme would not be able to see me, no matter what their augmentation, I opened my chest and showed Lisa the ports directly into my system. She smiled at me and nodded. I connected us, making a Local Area Network where before we had processed singularly.

I refused their price.

My nails are shorter than they used to be, no longer elegant but practical. We-the-two-of-us, Lisa and I, will keep them that way. We know what war looks like. If—when—they bring it to our door, we will be waiting.

YOU FOOL, YOU WANDERER
Brendan Williams-Childs

Shanna is gathering mushrooms from the spot where they grow thickest, three-hundred feet below the Aboveground, behind the immense waterfall that marks the start of New Peace Valley, when Kean reappears. She is placing the soft, spongy bodies into her basket while around her the sound of the great waterfall that protects them makes a continuous roar until, all at once, it doesn't. She feels the silence before she understands it, before it crackles, warps, twists up and snaps like the sheetmetal that litters the surface above the cave system where Shanna and everyone she knows lives and dies, which once included Kean and now apparently includes again.

Behind them, for a split second, she can see something like a mountain surrounded by darkness, something like a mist around them and they are wavering, flickering, and then they are there. With her. Reeking of oxygen, looking baffled and coated in a thin red film like the algae that plagues the surface of aboveground rivers, very much alive in the dim light with her. They smile. Dead for three years and now here. Like they'd never gone at all. "Hello."

Her scream catches in her throat. She can't move. She is a silent sculpture of a woman whose deceased lover has come back from the dead through thin air. How could she do anything? She wants to cry, to laugh, to check her vital signs. Kean's hair is tousled, their freckles are a constellation in the pale expanse of their face under that thin red coating, their lip is split. They are holding something mechanical and broken. She reaches for them and her legs begin to give out.

What she says is: "Kean. Oh." And then she bursts into tears, falling into them. They grasp her firmly, keep her up, and she sobs into their embrace. It is unnervingly sticky, impossibly solid.

× ×

She decides that she'll take them home, learn the secrets behind their travel, their impossible existence. The two of them take a back route, one Kean used to know but now perhaps seems puzzled by. They follow behind her, unsure footing on the smooth stone. There are no natural lights on the path from the Great Falls to the Quartz Quarter, only darkness that Shanna cuts with a headlamp set to dim blue—a color that doesn't announce itself to mushrooms or the New Peace Valley Guard who have told her numerous times that it's a fine if she's caught gathering produce at crop sites without treated water. She watches Kean as they walk together.

They explain, "I made a device that oscillates particles in such a way that they bend, together, through spacetime." Their voice is quiet, there is a lisp that wasn't there before, they walk slightly faster than she remembers. They hold the machine's broken pieces, glittering, in their arms like a baby. "That's the short of it. I couldn't carry any of my papers with me, but I know the design by heart."

"That sounds like a lot of work." *And not at all in your field.* They're chemists, the two of them. Not particle physicists. Fifteen minutes into Kean's return and Shanna is facing the fact that it is not, actually, a return but rather a new arrival. A new Kean. A Kean who strains their eyes against the darkness of the back-tunnels, who may not know the landscape of the New Peace Valley settlement or the 975 other miles of caves that connect to it. A Kean who didn't die in the earthquake that killed so many.

"It was." They grin at her. "But worth it. I had to find you." They run their hand over the rugged wall. A trace of red appears, follows their fingertips.

Shanna, too, is smeared in the drying film where they touched her. She has decided that the likelihood that it's blood is too high to risk asking if it's blood or not. Once they're home, she'll take them into the shower anyway. It won't have to be addressed. The whole thing, this whole situation, in fact, won't have to be addressed. She can keep them secret, she can keep them hers.

⁕

Kean, the first Kean, died from a cholinergic crisis after the earthquake. There had been no early warning, no time to prepare. Shanna, Kean, and the rest of the synthesis team were plunged into darkness and then, as the equipment shattered, into a cloud of mixed spores. Only Shanna, closest to the door, had come out mostly unscathed. The others hadn't come out at all. For three weeks, Kean (and Liu and Retta and an intern whose name Shanna has since forgotten) lay lifeless in the locked-down lab while Shanna lay unconscious in the hospital. When she woke up, it was alone, to the news that all synthetic hormones would now be made from animals and that the Human Growth and Progress Lab, far enough down in the valley's floor that it could be sealed, would never be reopened.

Now, in the security of her small apartment built into the side of the rock walls that slope to the settlement along the river, she sits on her sofa and watches Kean assess the oscillation device. They are showered, wearing a pair of her pajama pants that are both too small around the waist and too long in the leg, and kneeling shirtless on the carpet at her feet, the pieces of machinery all intricately small. "I hate this bit," they explain, arranging tiny metal pieces like a puzzle. "It has to be re-built every time I travel. It's like a gun that only goes off one bullet at a time."

"Have you used a gun?" Shanna takes in the uneven scars on their chest. Her old Kean had perfectly straight, wide scars that ran nearly the whole circumference of their torso. This new Kean has knotted, u-shaped incision marks running from sternum to armpit. Their hands are the same, though. Shanna

117

can't imagine a gun in them.

"You don't use guns here?"

"What would we need a gun for?" Shanna stretches out on the sofa and wants to invite them up, to say that all of this can wait, that they have to learn each other again and that nothing is more important than that. "I've seen a gun, but only in the museums. There's no hunting down here, we farm."

Kean laughs. "That's not the only use for a gun."

There is a long silence. Shanna doesn't know if she should explain that she knows that, that the museum covers all that, that New Peace Valley has never seen a war since the last war above-ground when the miners took their stand. Years and years and years ago but she knows what a gun is. Everyone in the valley does. She doesn't say any of this.

Like the idea has just come to them, Kean asks, "What year is it?"

"6012." She sees the frown that he covers up as soon as it crosses his face. "What year is it where you came from?"

"I don't know if it translates." Kean is back to looking at their machinery. For a long time, they're silent. Shanna can see the exhaustion dawn on them, the twitch of their eyes. "Do you have a tupperware for right now?"

She doesn't recognize the word. A bell of panic chimes in her heart and the skin on her neck stings with sudden sweat. She can manage to pretend around Kean's physical changes, but if she can't understand them...They're looking at her expectantly and she has to ask, "Tupperware?"

The concern is in their face as well, but they smile through it. "A container with a sealable lid, big enough that I could put the pieces in."

"Oh. Yes." She is careful stepping around their project. When she returns with the ceramic box, she helps them load each individual piece in with care.

"I need more aluminum. And rare earth minerals." They touch her hand as they close the box. "Where could we get some?"

The reputable sources, scientific supply stations and the City Farm and Supplies Market, aren't an option for a person who is supposed to be dead. Shanna slowly draws near to them. They don't pull away. She places her forehead on theirs and for a moment they are still. She feels as though all of her skin is shaking, like she's a battery finally re-charging. "I'll ask around. Scavengers on the surface offer a pretty good bargain sometimes and I—" Her voice catches in her throat and breaks.

They kiss her without asking but her surprise hardly registers before she is overwhelmed with the sensation and bursts into tears again. "Shh." They pull her close, both of them pressed up against the sofa. They are warm and soft and there. There, there, there. "I'm here now. It'll be alright, darling."

They used to call her *sweetheart*.

⚎

Kean's list has more than just aluminum on it. They need things that are simple (scrap metal, tools) and things that are not (yttrium, lithium batteries). They present this list to her in the morning and she sets out, undeterred, determined. "I'll also get you some clothes," she promises, though when they ask if she's certain that she wouldn't prefer them to stay shirtless while they build she does pretend to consider it.

The earthquake that took her first Kean also took the largest route to the aboveground. To get from New Peace Valley to Aboveground Settlement 039 was once nothing more than a short hike up a long set of stairs. Now, woven reed mushroom basket strapped to her back, she has to hug the valley walls through a series of switchbacks to make it to the market at the entry of the cave system. She watches the sun follow her west through the immense glass dome under which New Peace Valley lays. By the time she gets to the Big Sandstone Camp, the glow in the valley, hundreds of feet down, is afternoon's dark gold.

Stationed at the point of entry, Roye, who Shanna tried to date after her first Kean's death, greets her. "Shanna! Oyster or lion's mane?" He points to her basket. "What are you trading for today?"

"Rare earth minerals, mostly." There's no point in lying about it. Her reincarnated partner she can keep secret, a pack full of precious metals she could not. Not from Roye, anyway, who takes his job greeting and good-bye-ing every customer so seriously.

His eyebrow arches up. "Are you back at work? I thought you were on Income."

"I'm crafting now." She hands him her point-of-entry booklet. There are no borders in their massive cave system, no countries, but there are checkpoints. If a person goes missing, it's helpful to know where they were last. "You know, like...bots. I'm crafting bots."

He nods, stamps her entry book. "That's great. That's really great! A hobby is...Well, it's good. I know it's been tough." His voice has that irritating note of sympathy that drove her out of all her old spaces. But Kean is back now, she can humor Roye for a moment. "Would you be interested in coming to dinner tomorrow? At my place? Jal will be there, I know she'd love to see you."

The invitation catches her off guard. For a moment, she feels like a filter has been lifted from her vision. There is Roye, talking to her like he knows her because he does, and she knows that Jal is sweet, or at least that she brought food over for the first three or four months after the earthquake, while Shanna was recovering from the toxins and the funerals and the paralysis. The idea of going out seems less overwhelming, knowing that she has someone to come home to. "Maybe?"

Roye beams, "Great! I'll swing by tomorrow night then and check in. Are you still up in the Quartz Quarter?"

"I am. Unit 706." She places one of the largest mushrooms on his table and collects her booklet. There is a stamp in it dated two years ago. She doesn't remember making the journey, but there it is—the proof that she tried to live a life after the quake, alone. What did her days look like? Last year she returned to mushroom gathering but who was she, she wonders, for the first two years after Kean died?

She must be making a face because Roye is standing now. He reaches across his table and puts his hand on hers gently. "Shanna, are you with us?"

Who is *us*? She focuses on Roye's face, tries to bring herself back. Us, trans people? Us, the community of New Peace Valley?

Us, survivors of the quake? Technically yes, she is with us if those are the definitions. "Yeah, sorry." She pats his hand, forces a smile. Kean's list is in her pocket, she has things to do. "I'm with you. I'll see you tomorrow."

×[×]_×

Kean spends most of the evening tinkering. Shanna watches with a feeling that she can't identify, which compels her to pace in circles on tiptoe around Kean's project, examining it from every angle, as they attach delicate piece to delicate piece around a crystal which Kean has described as, alternatively, a source of power and simply a refractory tool. Refractory, Shanna realizes, is what New Kean is for her, as well. Their presence makes Shanna aware of how empty her apartment is, how silent. When her next door neighbor begins his nightly flute practice, the sound startles her. Voices of passersby outside seem like shouts echoing off the rock walls.

When they are in bed, after they have taken their turns with each other enough to confirm that they are still in love or at least still lovers, Shanna curls her arms around Kean. They are small enough to fit comfortably into her, their bulk warm and familiar. "I've been here before," they say into her embrace.

"You belong here." She says this intending to be affirming, but as soon as the words leave her mouth they sound hollow. Kean belongs here. Is this Kean? They are close enough, but the gap is widening. She looks at the ceramic box on her dresser.

"I belong with you." They kiss the palm of her hand. "But not here. You're in the wrong place here."

"I live here." There's no fight to her voice. She wishes there was, that she could make a resounding argument and drain the tension, like an infection. She feels her heart beat against their back. "We live here."

They turn, squirm, until their nose is pressed against hers. Up close she sees double of them merging into one, single bright brown eye full of expectation. They smile, teeth too long. Shanna closes one eye to fix her perspective. "Do you want to know about the other worlds?"

"I…" *Want to believe this is the only one, the one where a miracle has brought you back to me.* "Of course."

"I've seen worlds where people don't live underground, where they built up instead of down. Do you know why you live underground? I've seen the world this one came from, or at least one of them. I've seen worlds without good air, without water, without cities, without antibiotics, without plants and animals. I've seen worlds with all of those things. And I've seen worlds without war, with universal language and income and with great old forests that didn't get burnt down."

Shanna listens to these descriptions with a growing anxiety. There are an unknowable number of them, these worlds. And in each Kean is…Where? Simply passing through? Kean was in her world and someone else's all at once. Where was she? Is there another Shanna out there, missing her Kean?

"What about me?" she squeezes their hand. "You and me. How are we, in those other worlds?"

They are silent, then. For a long time, they look at her, that half smile fixed on their face until it isn't anymore. They place their hand on her face, pull her towards their chest. "You're dead in a lot of them. I'm dead in a lot of them. There's a better world than this one." This is the most serious she's heard them. She cannot remember a time in their life, their first life, that they spoke so clearly. "Every world I've seen is a variant on this one from a hundred or more years ago. And only in one have things been fixed, really. Only one where we could be happy together. I can get us there, if you let me."

"I'm happy wherever I'm with you." If she says it, she can believe it. She can will it into being. If she believes hard enough, maybe they will, too. Maybe there are worlds out there with clean surface air and wild forests, but the thought fills her with fear more than excitement. How could there be a better world than this, the one where the unreal is possible?

When Shanna leaves for dinner next evening, Kean is still building. The device is taking on the appearance of a pipe bomb. Would they know she knows what that is? "I won't be long," she promises, and they nod but don't say anything else. She waits for a response for a beat too long before going out. There is tension between them, leftover from the night before, and she wants to think they'll fuck it away later but she isn't certain. She can't bring herself to talk about the other worlds, and it's all they want to talk about.

Roye is waiting at the end of the lane, waving, carrying one of the immense lanterns that signifies him as a part of the New Peace Valley Guard. With his bright blue clothes, his dark skin, he looks like a butterfly resting on the wall under the lantern's glow. He smiles at her. "Hey there!"

"I didn't know what to bring." Shanna holds up her empty hands. "Sorry."

"It's fine. You're bringing yourself." Roye motions to the path, hoists the lantern high. It's not a long walk to the center of town but visibility is low. Even with the stars above, shining through the great sunroof that, *blessings upon it*, survived the quake, the inside of the cave is unrelentingly dark.

Before the quake, the worst thing that New Peace Valley had known was its own founding. Shanna considers this, under the glow of the lantern and Roye's smile. Carved into existence by desperate, impoverished people facing an aboveground that was blisteringly hot, strapped of clean water, abandoned by the wealthy of the old regime, New Peace Valley has a resilience that she envies, a tenacity she hopes to embody. So far she's done all right, given everything. She walks with Roye, who, like her, used to work at the Human Growth and Progress Lab, the shift before hers, and wonders if he misses his life before the quake, or if he is so ingrained in the valley that there's nothing else for him beyond. Is it love or nostalgia, to embrace Kean's return-arrival?

The question nags at her. Coupled with Kean's other worlds, she imagines she can see through the darkness of their passage, where the line between their lives and another life might be. Even when they reach Roye's house, when she's embraced by Jal and given a seat at the table, when she's admiring the art and the sturdy furniture constructed from mycelia. Over dinner, after the conversation about Jal's work at the modeling garden, Shanna asks, "If there was another world, and you had the opportunity to go there, would you?"

"Absolutely not." Jal answers without a second thought. Her head shakes so vigorously that her earring comes loose. "I've read a book or two. Nothing good ever comes out of that kind of thing."

"Come on, Jal, play in the space." Roye sets his spoon down and considers the question. "What are the parameters?"

"What do you mean?" Shanna asks. Should she have asked Kean this, herself?

"I mean, like, what other world? How would I get there? Would I have to cease existing in this one?" Roye stirs his soup while Jal nods. "Would I get to bring people?"

She should have asked Kean, she decides. "I don't know. I just…" Roye and Jal's house is like hers, walls made of stone and hardened layers of fungi, powered by hydroelectric and solar, decorated sparsely but with great intention. There is very little in their world, so much less than the world that came before them, but that little is enough. "I think about it. About another world. Dimensions. If I could go to another dimension, one where…" She can't bring herself to finish the sentence. Kean, the secret, is only two days with her but already too heavy to carry.

A long silence fills the space between their seats until Jal clears her throat. "When Liu died, I had a lot of dreams about hir. I dreamed that ze would come back, or that I would go somewhere and find hir. And I would wake up and think *I would give anything for that*. But it couldn't happen in this world. I think….It's not easy. But if ze showed up now, like, through a portal or something…I don't know what I would do. I don't think I'd go. I don't think it would be hir, you know? I mean, Roye said it better than me. Parameters and stuff."

Roye half-laughs, "Yeah. Would I go to a world where the quake never happened? Maybe. But not if I had to give this up." He gestures at everything at once. *This*. Shanna realizes with something like panic that *this* includes her. That *this* does not include Kean. *This*. The people around her, the place where she lives.

"I should get going," she says. She feels unsteady on her feet.

"I'm sorry, I just…"

"It's all right." Roye stands, too. "Take my light." He smiles, Jal nods.

Shanna holds the lantern, feels its smooth and warm heft as Roye lights it, the moss in its heart a constant glow. For a moment, she thinks about another dimension that doesn't contain Kean, a dimension where she made the choice to stay for the rest of dinner with Roye and Jal. She sees the shiver in their reality, looking at their faces, in the understanding that that world is one she could still create.

＊＊＊

Shanna is silent when she comes home. Kean doesn't register her presence. Their sturdy body is hunched over the device which still resembles a pipe bomb, but now with a lotus flower stuck to it. She passes behind them to the bedroom, where their clean clothes are laid over the chest at the end of her bed. Quietly, her eyes still on the hallway, she fishes into their pockets to find their pocketbook. When they were alive, the first time, they carried her picture with them.

She feels the edge of a photograph in the worn leather before she opens it. Her heart races and then feels frozen. The photo is them together but not them. It's not even the Kean in the living room smiling back at her. It's Kean but with a different nose, Shanna but with a different jawline. There are twelve ID cards in the pockets. Different sizes, colors, fonts. Some of plastic, some of paper, one of metal with a holographic finish. All with Kean's face, or a face that looks uncannily similar. The name *Kean* does not appear.

She stands and approaches the living room. She considers the film of red over their face when they arrived. "Hey, sweetheart?"

Kean practically jumps. "Oh! When did you get home?" They have the tired, wild-eyed face of someone close to a breakthrough. Shanna remembers it from their days at work, the care they took with their experiments.

"Could you…" She hesitates, looking at them. They could belong, couldn't they? If they tried? But there would always be the doubt. And she's holding their wallet in her hand. She has already accepted. "Say my name."

"What?" They laugh. When she doesn't, they laugh louder. "Come on. What's this about?"

"I miss hearing it from you." She doesn't move. "It's been...A long time."

"Well that's—Oh." They've seen their wallet. "What were you doing in my things?"

"Do you know my name? Do I know yours?"

"My name can be whatever you want when we get where we need to go." The edge to their voice startles her. They have already turned back to the machine.

Her stomach knots in a hot ball, her legs weak. She watches new Kean, their broad shoulders and wide back straining their shirt, hunched over a machine that looks like it might kill everyone in the Quartz Quarter, and tries to map their face to *her* Kean's. She cannot imagine what they look like now, sealed in their lab with Liu and Retta and the intern. Are they decayed? Are they part, now, of a body of fungi that used to give them what they needed? Is the fate of all desire to be consumed by it?

Her stomach aches as she asks, "What are the parameters?"

"What?" They turn around. The device in their hands is glowing. The crystal in the center shakes. "What are you talking about?"

She grips the wallet tightly, holds it up for them to see. "What happened to me in these worlds? What happened to you?"

They look her dead in the eyes, lit by the glow of the crystal. She thinks of the thin red film on them when they arrived, her decision not to ask. She wishes she had, now. Would they have told her the truth? Who had to die for them to arrive here? She knows how her Kean died in this world, how did they go in the others?

"Do you want to go or don't you?" Their voice is low, like they've already accepted her no. Like it wasn't a surprise. Have they made this offer to her before? Has she declined? "If you don't want to go..." They fall silent, holding their breath.

"Where am I, in these other worlds?"

"You died, all right?" they yell. She wants to say she

understands, that the pain is immense enough that she, too, would have bent the world for them. That the world bent on its own, became small, and only has recently begun to unfold. They continue, "You died in the best world and I keep trying to bring you home. But you won't go. Why won't you go?" Their voice breaks, the question a high note, their face furious, tears in their eyes.

She lowers her hand. She wants to embrace them, there, with their dangerous little device and their heartache that she knows lives under their skin. "Because I don't love you. I love a version of you, the version of you that's special to this world. And some other version of me loves a version of you that is special to your world. Because each world is its own."

Their face distorts. Their mouth opens and then closes, the muscle of their jaw strains against their skin. "A *version* of me? I'm me. I'm the only version of me. I'm the only version of me in the universe for you. Do you know how many extraneous duplicates of myself I've had to get rid of, trying to get you back? I'm me wherever I go, and I love *you*. And in every world you say you love me but you won't go with me." They raise the device in one hand over their head, hold their other hand out. "Either trust me, because I love you, or give me my wallet back and I'll find the version of you that does."

The feeling of their skin against hers in the transfer is enough to bring tears to her eyes. She wants to convince them to put the machine down. Instead, she says, "My name is Shanna."

"Shanna." Their accent mars her name.

She can imagine Kean, a body made of mushrooms, without wishing she could join them. New Kean stands before her with their glowing machine that will rip the world apart. She says, "Again."

"Shanna." They are half-smiling, now. She wants to say that she is, despite everything, grateful to have held them one more time, that she's sorry for them across those worlds. But they give her no time to say anything else before they close the lotus bloom of the machine, activating it. It ruptures.

The air around them both becomes hot, reeks of lightning. The room flickers, warps. Everything shakes, and Shanna's skin seems eager to leap through the rip in space without her. She watches in dull shock as the flesh of her fingertips peels away into the portal where Kean stands. Behind them, a world is forming. Dark forest, ancient growth. The air is burning and Shanna flinches, trying to pull away. She has survived worse, she tells herself. She got out of that room, she made it down the hall, she escaped to the safe zone during the quake. She has survived the world ripping apart before.

Kean's eyes are closed, their face a grim smile that shows all their teeth. They take two steps backwards and raise their arms. The world behind them emits a smell of wet leaves, the reek of a compost pile. For a second, the portal is stabilized. Kean opens their eyes, their feet are on grass. "You had your chance."

The machine begins to emit a higher whine. The crystal shivers furiously. Shanna takes one last long look at Kean, now in this other world. Kean, who is not Kean, who is someone willing to do things that Kean would never do to get to some version of her that loves them. She may never be able to stop them but she can slow them.

They begin to reach through the portal for the machine. Shanna rushes forward, plunges her hands into the cold air of the other world. Her fingers burning, she pushes Kean backwards. They grunt, stumble, fall back onto the grass. There is no time for them to cry out before Shanna's hands are around the crystal, before they're back in her world, before they're burning and cramped and then—

× ×
×

Shanna comes to in the hospital. Her hands wrapped in bandages, a bedside table full of flowers. At the foot of the bed, Roye and Jal are reading the newspaper together. The air is dry and cool, smells of lavender and vinegar. Above her, the stone ceiling is intact. Splitting the world has incurred no damage to New Peace Valley, at least not here. "How," she manages, her throat dry. "How is everyone?"

Jal and Roye spring to attention, immediately at her side. "Everyone's fine," Jal assures her. "You're all right, nobody got hurt."

"Your apartment is a bit...singed?" Roye looks for the right word, holds her injured arm gently. "Your bot malfunctioned pretty badly. I don't know if it can be salvaged."

Blessings upon us, she thinks, nodding slowly. "That's...That's okay. I don't think it was the right hobby for me, anyway." Jal brings her a glass of water and she drinks it through the metal straw. Her mouth less dry, her chest less tight, Shanna looks at the curtains that separate her from fellow patients. *All divides can be overcome,* she thinks, and then looks at Roye and Jal. There is only one of her now, in this world. And only one Jal, one Roye, one opportunity in this moment to reach out. She asks, "Would you two like to come with me, sometime soon, to gather mushrooms?"

A PARTY-PLANNER'S GUIDE TO THE APOCALYPSE
Lauren Ring

First, grieve. Mourn the loss of the past and of the future. Grieve for months, years if you must.

Then, remember what you're good at, and go pull those old garlands out of storage. It's time to plan a party.

Call it Apocalypse Day, or Survival Day, whichever suits your mood. Your new holiday will join a long tradition of defiant celebration. Besides, your people have survived crueler things than this twist of nature. Even if you skipped temple more often than not, you know how the old saying goes: they tried to kill us, we survived, let's eat.

Send out the invitations, by way of bike messengers and posters tacked on crumbling black-ash trees. Invite anyone and everyone. All survivors welcome. If they made it this far, they deserve a dinner party.

Set the table for twelve, as many as can fit. Pull your greying hair back into a neat bun and head for the kitchen. Your wife can make her world-famous brisket, which might actually *be* world-famous now that the world is much smaller. Do your best to help and you will eventually be relegated to mashing potatoes, which is the only way you won't set the stove on fire.

Wait for the guests to arrive, in ones and twos, by bike and by foot. Help them hang their respirators on the coat rack and set aside a table for their piles of dark sunglasses. Welcome them with light and laughter and the rich smell of good food, no matter how hard it was to find.

Don't be surprised when friends and even strangers bring gifts of their own. From glass ornaments to fresh marigolds, they will help bring the old to the new. There hasn't been much celebration since the end of times. It's time to change that. They will help you, given the opportunity.

Keep them from the food for now. It will be difficult, but they will not listen once they have started eating. Seat them around your carefully fortified living room and ask them to tell their stories. You will have to go first. Be brave.

Once the ice is broken, your guests will speak. They will share tales of unimaginable loss and suffering, but also of joy and laughter. They will tell you about finding the perfect cloth for hair ribbons in the attic of a half-burnt house, about falling in love with the shoemaker who fixed their worn-down sole. They will tell you about living, not just surviving.

After you have listened, then you may return to the kitchen. The brisket is ready. Dish out the potatoes and pour the last of the wine to those who need it most. Sit next to your wife and hold her hand beneath the table. Look around the room and see the people you have brought close, the lives you have made warm. Know that you have done a good thing today, and every guest in attendance will remember it in a year's time, even if they are far from this happy home. Eat. Drink. Be merry.

If, in the ebb and flow of dinnertime conversation, Danny from down by the riverbank tells his son that your wife is your sister, don't let it slide. This is your world now. No quarter for bigots. Don't worry: everyone will have your back, even his son. It is your choice whether or not to let him stay.

Clear the table and leave the dishes in the sink. Take the fresh apples that Hunter has brought from their orchard and cut them with knives that will see no more violence. Serve the slices with honey for a sweet future ahead.

Before you move on, look again to the past. Light a yahrzeit candle, found half-forgotten in a back closet, for those lost in the ash and dust. Keep it with the marigolds. Let it burn until the next sundown, when it will sputter out as you put away washed dishes and take down the tattered garlands.

But right now, in the final rays of fading sunlight, tune in to the synth pop of the last remaining radio station. Clear the living room floor. Pull your wife close to your still-beating heart, and party like it's the end of the world.

IMAGO
A.Z. Louise

At night, the colorful marks of endings were dark as dried blood, and the ghosts shifted and moaned in hidden places. Char slipped through the gloom with a practiced ease, stepping over spalls of concrete as if they'd memorized their places. Their size had once made them careful around people who elbowed and scowled, and those skills had gone on being useful long after all the people had gone.

Well, not all of them. Char had met a few dozen people who hadn't popped, including Maya, who lived in an old Victorian that made for a welcome pit stop during scavenging runs. Nobody was a better scavenger than Char, but they had a tendency to lose track of time. Staying with Maya would mean that they wouldn't have to risk going all the way back home in the dark, when thieves and worse came out of the splattered buildings and looked for people heading home with their hauls.

At this time of night three years ago, the crows would have been gathering in this part of the city, settling down to roost, but crows were smarter than Char was. They had moved on to places where no one lurked in the darkness, and eventually all the other birds had followed. Char missed the sounds of sparrows and finches, and wished they knew where all the birds had gone. Perhaps they'd gone through the splashes of color, which looked in places like human-shaped holes to colorful new landscapes.

Music and light poured out of Maya's place. The hum of diesel generators backed the thudding beats with their low voices, and filled Char's skull with their fumes. Char's head ached as they went past the bouncer, Kody, who let them pass with a friendly nod. Char had known Maya since the beginning, Kody almost as long.

Despite the loud music, the mood inside was subdued. People stood in tight knots or sat elbow to elbow on plush, aged velvet couches. Chipped cups of moonshine were clutched in unsteady hands. Few people spoke, and nobody danced. The place had the atmosphere of a funeral. Char passed through quickly, not wanting to listen to the latest sad story of someone disappearing into the growing forest outside town. They just wanted to rest.

Maya usually held court over a small group of her favorites in the big bedroom upstairs, but Char found her alone, looking into a cup of whiskey that smelled like paint thinner.

"Maya?" Only one thing could dampen the nightly party at Maya's.

"Leon went Chromate yesterday." Maya's voice was barely audible over the noise from below. Leon had been one of her favorites, a skinny little man who could pick any lock. "They tried to get him out of the city, but it was too late. He started popping people and they had to put him down."

"Oh, Maya." Char dropped her heavy sack of parts by the door.

"At least, if he'd gotten out of the city, he might have lived. They say Oracles live out there. That it's the city that makes them dangerous." Maya didn't look up, lost in whiskey and what could have been.

"I know." Char wanted to believe it. Believing that meant that maybe there was some hope that people who had gone Chromate could recover, or that those who had vanished were still alive. But there was no proof, and false hope seemed worse than none.

"I'm tired, Char. I try not to show it, because people come here to forget their troubles. But I'm tired."

Char knew. They could tell by her eyes, which looked through people before looking at them. They could tell by her voice, growing quieter every day. They could tell by her body, once lush as Char's own, which had eaten away at its own curves and curled inward like a pillbug trying to save itself from a bird's beak.

This new world swallowed people whole.

"I don't know if I can do this anymore," Maya said. She put her cup down, the fringe on her leather jacket dipping in the amber liquor.

"That's okay." Char crossed to her, helped her take off the old jacket, buttery soft from years of wear. It smelled like smoke. "You don't have to."

"Where will everyone go?" Maya asked. "Where will people sleep if not here?"

"You can think about that later, all right? Other people can help. You know I will." They fixed Maya's long, dark hair, which was caught in her earrings, twin waterfalls of silver leaves that tinkled when she moved. People always brought her earrings in exchange for shelter and sweet forgetfulness. "Do you want to rest for a while? You look like you haven't slept."

"I've been awake since I heard about Leon. I tried to sleep, but I had nightmares. I used to dream in black and white, but now I dream in color. Only bad dreams, though. It seems like all I have now are nightmares." Maya rubbed her eyes wearily.

"Come on. Put some other music on and I'll rub your back."

"But everyone—"

"Everyone is standing around feeling sad about Leon. They'll like something quieter, too." Char said.

Maya fiddled with her computer, ancient and held together with electrical tape, and the thudding drum kick stopped. Something atmospheric took its place, and a tightness Char hadn't noticed forming in their chest faded out, returned as she listened for the sound of ghosts, faded again. The generators and music were still too loud to hear the spirits.

They followed Maya into her bedroom, which she usually shared with more than one of her favorites. The antique four-poster was empty and unmade, the mismatched dressers open, Maya's clothes hanging out everywhere. While Maya changed into pajamas, Char straightened up, afraid the highboy would tip over with its top drawer open.

Maya's shoulders were knotted tight, unwilling to give an inch against Char's kneading fingers. Slowly, so slowly, Maya relaxed, and Char felt her breathing slow. They took their hands away as gently as they could, not wanting to wake her. She stirred, rolling onto her side, and Char's breath snagged in the back of her throat. A green smear of color gleamed on Maya's lips.

Char hurried to the bathroom to wash their hands, heart throwing itself at their sternum. Their own terrified face looked back at them in the mirror for thirty seconds as they counted down a long enough handwashing. What were they supposed to do? Someone had to get Maya's guests out before her visions started. The worse a Chromate's visions were, the more dangerous. How long had Leon been an Oracle before he'd killed fifty? How long ago had Maya been exposed?

Maya didn't move when Char crept past her bed, down the stairs. Their stomach churned, every muscle in their body aching from trying not to run. The night air burned their lungs when they stepped outside, and they realized they'd been holding their breath. They leaned against the doorjamb, trying to breathe deep.

"Is she okay?" Kody's voice made Char jump so hard that something twinged in their neck.

"No." They rubbed the sore, twitching muscle, trying to massage the pain out. "She wants everyone out."

"What? At this time of night?"

"She's really upset," Char said. Their eye was drawn to the gun at Kody's hip; an old revolver taken from his dad's house after he'd popped with most everyone else. There was still a blue stain on the grip. If Kody knew, he'd kill Maya. Char had to make sure she was alone and couldn't hurt anyone, get her into the forest somehow. She'd have a better chance of survival out there than she would in her own home.

"I'm gonna go talk to her." Kody took a step toward Char, and they instinctively grabbed his arm. He looked past them rather than at them. A silence more restless and sickly than the whispers fell over the room.

When Char turned, Maya stood at the bottom of the stairs,

her hand on the bannister.

"Maya?" Char said. Maya didn't respond. "It's time to go back to bed."

"These tongues are burned," Maya said. Her voice was all wrong, shivery in a way that scrambled Char's stomach contents. "They can speak, but the taste is all blood and blister. Do you taste it?"

"Yes," Char asked, not knowing what Maya wanted. Maya turned to look at her, a kelly green tear running down her cheek. Fear blossomed across the guests' faces like paint clouding water, but none of them moved.

"No, you don't." Maya placed a hand on Char's shoulder. "But you will."

"Everyone get out." Char's throat was too tight for anything more. "Go!" It was as if Char had cracked a whip over the guests' heads. They moved as one, pushing toward the back door in terrified silence. The only sounds in the room were ambient music and shuffling feet.

"These hands rake up shadows. Do you feel it?" Maya asked. Her eyes were green all around now, swirling and pearlescent.

"No." Char tried to jerk away, but Maya was too strong, now. All thoughts of getting her somewhere safe had fled. "I just want to go home, Maya."

"You are going home. The doors are opening."

"Maya, I don't want to fight you. I don't want to hurt you."

The house had emptied out. Char didn't know how to reason with an Oracle. How could they? Maya was seeing things beyond them, beyond the fragile world that had begun to crumble when half the people in it exploded into rainbows of color and more went Chromate every day.

"Char, back away from her." Kody drew his gun from its holster. Char made another attempt to pull away, and Maya's fingers dug into their flesh.

"I can't."

"Close your eyes. Cover your nose and mouth," Kody said.

"Please don't." Tears stung Char's eyes.

"If I don't do it, someone else will. And they'll have to put you down, too, if she hasn't already popped you," Kody said.

"Kody, please," Char begged. "We can take her away from here, to be with the others."

"You and I both know this is kinder."

"Please."

Kody cocked the revolver with a metallic snap.

"*Kody, no!*"

The shot was so loud that Char's ears hurt, rang, buzzed. Kody slumped against the door jamb, clutching his head. He splattered, no scrap of flesh or bone left inside him. Only bright purple wetness and empty clothes remained, surrounded by the alien stink of a pop. Like something poisonous and green, like seawater steam. Like death. Not even gunpowder could cut through that smell.

"Char?" Maya's voice shook. When Char looked at her, Maya's expression was frightened, confused, but the eyes were still wrong. Her hand slipped from Char's shoulder. "It's happening, isn't it?"

"Yes," Char breathed.

"I'm scared. Please." Emerald tears streamed down her face, seeped from her nose and mouth. Char didn't know what she was begging for, but Maya had sheltered them so many times. It was their turn to shelter her, regardless of the risk.

"I won't leave you," they said.

Maya let out a wrenching sob, crumpling to the ground. Char knelt next to her, drawing her into their arms. She shook, murmuring so low that Char couldn't understand her.

Maya's shivers were contagious, working their way into Char's chest until they could barely breathe. They coughed, and red came up. Not blood, but fluid filled with that stink of forest rot.

The visions came on hard and fast, Char's head spinning out into busy dreams of angels with mouths full of hot blood and hands streaming with darkness. Roots reaching deep, they sucked up water and life until their perfect heads burst into swarms of bent-winged cicadas, sending shards of halo slicing through the air.

The insects took to the sky, and Char felt the overwhelming urge to join the swarm. If they could fly, carry Maya away from people who would hurt her, to go to the safe place where the crows and sparrows and finches had gone, maybe everything would go all right. Maya's hand was in theirs. They leapt, their feet finding the soft, mossy earth of the stump of a neck. There, the bone and marrow between Maya and Char, the whole world spread out before them beneath a sky as violet as what remained of Kody.

"Thank you for coming on this journey with me." Maya's smile shone brighter than the shimmering chitin of the cicadas humming around them.

Char, spellbound, could only smile back. They and Maya were becoming, two nebulae condensing into stars. The colors were deep in their bones, dragging their consciousness down into the nourishing soil. Char wanted nothing more than to sleep, with no concern for all of the slowly fading constructions of humanity, but she and Maya weren't safe until they flew.

Roots had already tangled around Char's ankles, trying to pull her down into the rich earth and moss, but they dragged their legs free. Hot streaks of pressure bit into their flesh, and they knew they were bleeding, but they couldn't bring themself to care as they broke for the edge. Maya's hand nearly slipped from Char's as they fell into the electric purple sky together, the city vanishing into trees standing tall as angels. Cool air bathed them, feverish anxiety and pain washing away into the night. Since the first pops had splattered the city, Char's dreams were restless, full of searing color and wild movement. The dark stillness was a relief, and for the first time in a thousand nights, they could rest easy.

When Char woke, they were soaking wet, weak after a broken fever. They wiped their face with their hand, and it came away pink, the red fluid diluted by sweat. They lay somewhere soft, looking at the ceiling of a rough wooden shelter with bright blue sky peeking through the cracks.

Their legs almost gave out when they stood, but it wasn't weakness that nearly made them fall. Outside the little wooden house, sunshine bathed more crude structures, surrounded by verdant forest. Instead of the moans of ghosts, the air just outside rang with birdsong. They laughed, giddy with exhaustion and something beyond hope. A warm hand touched their clammy one, and they turned to meet brown eyes brimming with relief and joy.

"Welcome back," Maya whispered. "It's been a while."

SAFE HAVEN
A.P. Thayer

Mile after mile, my throat has been getting worse.

I tap your shoulder, desperate for a break. The shadows between the broken buildings are enough cover for the moment. Every lungful of air makes my throat itch, but we've been running all morning and I'm ready to collapse. You feel it too, but you don't complain. You never complain. Never need a break. And I can't help resenting you for that.

I'm still mad. You know I can never just let a fight go. I'm too proud and knowing that about myself makes me angrier. Why can't you see it my way? Trying to help others is too risky. I want us to be safe; you want everyone to be safe.

The bandanna plastered over my mouth is soaked through with my sweat and spit. The falling ash sticks to it and every breath tastes like the end of the world. I fumble with my canteen and press the warm tin against my cracked lips. You used to say they were so soft. The last of my water trickles down my throat like shards of a broken mirror. I want to cough, but that much noise is dangerous. I hold my breath until my lungs scream and my chest burns and I gasp for air. The poisonous air. My throat is an inferno and now I'm out of water.

Damn.

You hold out your canteen. I refuse. I used up my water and I have to live with it. I won't give you the satisfaction of helping me right now. You know how petty I get. We're almost there, anyway. I tighten the strap of my pack. We need to keep moving.

The dull roar of thunder accompanies us. The clouds threaten rain, but never deliver. Can you remember the last time it rained? I almost ask you before I catch myself. Of course, I blame you for the fight, so now I'm mad I can't talk to you about rain. What I wouldn't give for just a few drops. Enough to fill our canteens. To wash us clean.

A scream echoes across the ruined city.

I stumble forward, crouching down in the shadow of a building. You dive down next to me and we lay still for a moment, panting. I point over your shoulder, through the alley, risking the movement. The river is visible down the hill, a darker gray background between the buildings. We have to keep moving. We are so close.

Another beast screams, its hellish wail echoing in the gloom. A weeper. Hunting us. A second monster answers, ahead and to the left. Much closer. They're surrounding us and we're out of time.

Vamos, you whisper with your eyes.

I push myself off the building and we stumble down the alley. My legs burn as I pull my boots through the oily mud. More wails tear through the air. They're getting closer.

Your foot catches and you pitch forward. I catch your arm before you fall and we stumble into a pile of garbage together. Old cans and bits of plastic cascade off the mound. A chorus of screams fill the air around us, closer this time. Right on top of us. You shove me forward and I yank us into a doorway, scrambling to get under cover. I shut the door behind us, barely able to hear the latch over the pounding of my heart, and we crouch under a grimy window.

A weeper pads into the alley and we duck down out of sight. It scuttles forward and pounces on the spilled garbage, hungry for blood. Our blood. I close my eyes to the world, hoping to shut out the sound of it, but it's like its image is imprinted inside my eyelids. I can see it tearing through the pile with black claws and spidery limbs, scattering trash to find its prey. Its smell seeps into the ruined building, and I gag on the sweet rot.

You squeeze me tight and I try to get a hold of myself. We

barely breathe. We just shiver together. For comfort, for safety. The way we've been holding each other for years. It's easier to be brave when I'm in your arms, but I'm still a coward. I'm just scared for you, for me, for us. Scared about our fight and what you'll do to help others. I want to tell you I'm sorry. That I love you. But I don't. I can't. Not right now.

The weeper hisses. I can imagine it, angry, its face up to the darkened skies, searching. Seconds tick past, stretch into an eternity, filled with only the ragged breath of the monster outside and our hearts thudding in our chests. Another scream and I hear it gallop away, other wails answering it further away from us.

We don't dare break apart. Not for a long while. We hold each other in the shadows and listen as the howls become fainter and fade away. If it weren't for you, I'd have given up long ago. I'd have laid down in the mud and shut my eyes and thanked death for finding me.

You squeeze my hand. I don't want to let go. Not right now. Not ever.

"Come on," you murmur. "We're almost there."

I open my mouth to say I'm sorry, but you're already moving.

⁙

You pull me through the remnants of the city, all trash and rot, empty buildings stained black and held up by only the memory of what they once were. We crouch low and duck from cover to cover. The cries of the hunting weepers are still far off, but that doesn't mean there aren't more hiding in the shadows.

The last crumbling edifice gives way to the riverbank. There, out in the middle of the water, is our destination. What everything has been for. Our safe haven.

The lighthouse juts up from a small, rocky island. Its red and white paint is faded by time, but the colors look garish against the bleak landscape. It looks smaller than when I last saw it, but that was decades ago. It was summer, then. The sun was warm and I was small.

"See, we made it," you say.

"It's just like I remember," I lie.

We pick our way down the riverbank, through the dead trees and haggard undergrowth. Nothing grows here. Nothing grows anywhere. The howls have receded, but the overpowering silence seems worse somehow. Now that we're this close, it seems like we have everything to lose. I have everything to lose.

No, I can't think like that. I still want to convince you not to turn it on. We'd have everything we need. We would purify the water and plant seeds and grow them. Together. We can't help others, but we can help each other. There is only us.

A howl tears through the air behind us.

Shit, shit, shit.

We sprint the last few feet to the water's edge. You pull a bright yellow cube from your pack and yank the tab. The raft inflates while I unfasten the oars from my pack. We push the rubber vessel into the water and jump in, careful not to splash ourselves. I jam the oars against the shore and push us into the river. The current grabs us and I row us out.

Weepers careen down the bank, skittering on their thin limbs like insects. Their paper thin skin stretches over knobbed bones, showing the dark blood inside. Black stains surround their eyes and ooze out of their nostrils. They smell rancid. One smashes into a tree and impales itself, then tears free, desperate to get at our flesh. Its momentum carries it a few paces, spraying black blood the whole way, before it collapses in a twitching heap. Two others pounce, snarling and snapping at each other before devouring it.

Others gallop past and plunge in after us. The river bubbles and hisses. Smoke rises from their flesh as layers of skin slough off of them, burned away by the acidic water. The further in they wade, the faster their flesh dissolves.

It doesn't stop them. It barely even slows them.

They swim faster than we can paddle, trailing black corruption behind them. Their bodies are all pale flesh and gray bone now, peeled of skin and sinew, but they keep coming.

A black claw slashes toward the raft, but I smash it with my oar, shattering the bones. It screams and gurgles, slipping beneath the water for a moment. It flails its shattered limb at me as it surfaces again. It tries to pull itself forward with its ruined hand, but it's barely a stump now. Acrid smoke pours from its mouth and nostrils. Black blood bubbles from it, like tar.

It drags the stump along the side of the raft, trying to grab on, even as I row us away, launching us free from its grasp. The raft rocks, we slow, and another weeper catches us, even as the first finally disappears beneath the surface of the river.

I'm too slow this time. Claws sink into the boat, tearing holes in the rubber. The punctures whistle softly, the quiet sound more urgent than the starved screaming of the weepers. My oar rises and falls, chipping large pieces of flesh and bone off the weeper's face until it slides off, choking as it sinks below the water, and its body breaks apart. I paddle harder. We're almost there.

"Jaime!"

I whirl around. A weeper has its claws around your vest, its bottom half still in the river.

I hack at the thing, trying to get it off you, trying to row, trying to do both. The oar blade cuts into it, spraying black all over the raft and I nearly vomit at the stench. It doesn't slow down. It heaves itself up and bites into your collar.

NO!

You scream. Or maybe I'm screaming. I'm trying to kick the thing off of you but it won't let go. Oh god, no. Let go! Let go of him! I smash my oar into its head and cave the back of its skull in and it slides off the raft. It sinks beneath the surface of the river and a sudden silence crashes down on us, interrupted only by your pained breathing and a distant whining sound.

You're slumped against the side of the raft, pressing a hand against the bite, but it's no use. Blood oozes through your fingers and dribbles onto the fluorescent yellow raft. It pools in the bottom of the boat, mixing with the black of the weepers.

"No, no, no, no no nonono..." I add my own hand on top of yours, desperate to hold tight. "We're almost there. Just hold on. Por favor."

You look tired. As if this is all a minor inconvenience and you're ready for a nap. *Wake up!* I shake you. "Hold on!"

Your eyes widen for a moment and focus on mine before drifting behind me. I'm trying to stop the bleeding. There's so much blood. You point over my shoulder.

"The boat..."

The whine of escaping air hits me. I have to stop it or we'll sink right here. Like I have to stop the bleeding. Snarls and splashes from behind. More weepers.

I find tape in my pack and tear off haphazard pieces to seal the side of the raft. I turn back to you. Oh God, there is so much more blood now. You're so pale. You can barely keep your eyes open. I tear off more pieces of tape and press it to the wound. White bone and slick red. The duct tape won't stick. More. More duct tape. No, something else. I tear off my sweater and press it against the wound, I wrap the tape around your shoulder. Your bloody hand grabs mine. You're so weak.

"It's okay." Your voice is a whisper. "Get us there. We'll be safe."

I choke on a sob. My hands, covered in your blood, are trembling. The splashing is getting louder. The weepers are close. *No.* I take the oars and push us towards the island. The lighthouse looms above us.

I'll get us there.

⋅ ⊹ ⋅

The raft scrapes against black rock and I stumble out. I pull us onto the shore, my feet slipping beneath me. Behind us, weepers sink beneath the water, their screaming turning to gurgling.

The lighthouse is all we could have hoped for. Less of the black, oily corruption covers the ground here. The soft lapping of the river washes much of it away. I lift the raft out of the water with you in it. We're safe. We made it.

But your life is trickling out from under the makeshift bandage. Dark lines wriggle beneath the skin of your face. We've seen it in so many others, but now it's you.

"We made it," you say.

It's quiet. I'm shaking and sobbing. "I couldn't keep you safe. Couldn't—"

Your hand touches my cheek and I choke, unable to say the

words. You pull your bandanna off and smile at me. That smile. Your fucking smile. I never deserved it, never deserved you. Look where I've led us. Why did I let you convince me to come here? I hate you, God, I hate you.

More screams in the distance. Always more. It doesn't matter.

"I'm sorry, I'm so sorry." The words spill out of me. My way of saying I love you. They're useless words and don't mean anything. Aren't going to change anything. But I don't know what else to do.

"Take me to the top, querido. I want to see."

"I can't, I need to—"

You reach out and your fingers snake behind my head, around my neck. You pull me close and our foreheads touch. "Show me."

Another sob rips through me, but you hold me tight and I carry you into the lighthouse. You've never felt so light. Drops of blood dribble behind us, staining the concrete. Your blood is dark now.

The stairs creak and groan but hold. The top of the lighthouse is bare. It smells old. You shouldn't die here. You shouldn't die at all.

"Marcos, I—"

"Just prop me up there." Your voice is hoarse. I lower myself against the glass and lay you across my lap. We gaze out across the river to the surrounding lands, your head cradled in my lap.

The water is filled with weepers. They pull themselves through the river, trailing flesh as they swim to get at us. By halfway across they sink beneath the water.

The river is too wide. Our plan worked. The lighthouse is safe.

I trail a finger across your cheek. "How has your skin stayed so soft all these years?"

I didn't realize I'd spoken out loud. Your smile wrenches at my heart. I want to howl and vomit. The black veins are spreading across your cheeks, marking what's left of our time.

"Come on, turn me upriver," you say.

I do as you ask, knowing every movement is leaking more blood onto the cold, gray floor, but unable to deny you anything.

"It's beautiful," you say.

You're so at peace as you look over the desolation surrounding us and I can't stop crying. It's not fair. We almost made it. Fuck this place. Fuck this dead river. Fuck this lighthouse. Fuck you for believing me. Fuck me for losing you.

"It's getting darker. I think it's time."

"How am I going to—"

"You just will. You're a stubborn shit. You'll figure this out. You'll survive. Just—" You pause and catch a shuddering breath. "Don't do it alone. There are others. They need your help, too."

You squeeze my hand and I bury my face in your shoulder. "Don't go. Please." I'll do anything to keep you here. Please don't go.

Your body shudders. You never listen to me. Or anyone else. You always do exactly what you want to do and I love you for it.

I cry with my face against your body until I can't anymore. It's darker now. The clouds overhead are charcoal. I have to get to work. Any minute now, you'll start to turn.

Outside, the howls of the weepers have died out. They've stopped trying to swim across. It's peaceful and quiet except for the rumbling laughter of the sky. I slip your body into the river and turn back to the lighthouse.

This was supposed to be ours, but you're right. You're always right. It should never have been just for us.

I climb to the top and pull the lever. The mechanism grinds and shudders before the bulb blinks on, bathing the top of the lighthouse in white.

NOTE LEFT ON A COFFEE TABLE
Mari Ness

A licia –

1. The last pack of Nilla Wafers is in a sealed box in the ceiling of the half-bath.

If you found this, you can find it.

2. You're not forgiven.

I just got sick of Nilla Wafers.

3. As you can probably guess from that, we've pretty much cleared out what was left in the stores. Still, depending upon how long Ramon and Nick stick around, you should be able to find enough for at least a couple of years. Maybe more.

Also, we never did go into the houses. Too grim. But there's probably stuff there.

If you can handle the bones.

4. My memory tells me you can handle the bones.

5. Not that I trust my memory anymore.

6. I wrapped up the bedding and towels in plastic, to stave off mold. I'm afraid I burned the blue velvet one—your favorite— well before the end—but the purple comforter is in the guest room closet.

7. Yeah, the comforter we used that last time.

Not that I knew it was our last time.

8. I don't trust my memory. But I do remember that.

9. The solar panels can handle charging the fridge or charging the trike, not both. Or the oven and the fridge, not both. Especially when it's hot, which is nearly always. If you want to try to jury rig up some of the other solar panels that are still around, be my guest, with the caveat that as far as we could tell, they're either too heavy to move, too small to charge anything, or still configured to those network systems. Where the main systems are underwater, or broken by hurricanes.

10. I checked social media every day after the worst hit. I saw you post.

Right up until two days before the internet here went down, mostly permanently.

11. Truth to tell I've mostly given up on the oven. If something needs to be cooked, I have the fire pit in the back. It'll probably be overgrown again once you get here—if you get here—but it shouldn't take too long to clear.

12. I kept assuming you would reach out, tell me how you were.

13. Though, fair warning, we're mostly out of lighter fluid. And lighters.

14. I even thought you might come down here. You had an electric car, and the roads were still open, if nothing else.

The sea didn't arrive until later.

15. Water. Stick to the rain barrels. I've also left a couple of those lifestraw things I scrounged up just before the sporting goods place went underwater. Probably as good as boiling; definitely better tasting. As far as swimming/washing goes— again. Rain barrels.

The changes never touched the gators, and they seem to like their new islands in the ocean.

16. And then, of course, I gave up.

17. Clothes shouldn't be too much of a problem – no, we didn't have many clothing stores here, but twenty-three or so survivors can't go through that much clothing, especially when twenty of them take off after a few years.

18. But I still thought—I still *think*—you'll come.

If only to find out what happened to me and the cats.

19. Or to go to the theme parks. They ended up only half submerged, and though everything not submerged is terribly overgrown, it's still a wonder to explore. I row there from time to time, following the roads beneath the water, not quite covered by seagrass. Yet.

I've even stayed at the castle on a couple of nights, looking up at the Milky Way.

Which we can see now. The starry lining of all this, I guess.

20. I don't know why I'm saying any of this.

This was just supposed to be a simple list.

21. Right. List. Bicycle parts – both of the downtown stores still have plenty in stock. Mild miracle, considering how much Ramon and Nick and I use them, and that of course the roads haven't been repaved since—Yeah.

On the other hand, turns out that roads last much better than expected when you aren't driving cars on them.

And we can't bike all that far without running into water.

But anyway, you'll find plenty of tires, tubes, frames— whatever. I'm leaving the trike, too—it can't even fit on the canoe, much less the kayak.

22. I did think about leaving right after the seas arrived. That's when most of the people who survived left—scared of running out of food, scared of gators, scared of the shadows that kept appearing at windows.

But I was so tired.

And you never contacted me.

23. Medications—yeah, those are pretty much gone, even from that small compounding pharmacy right around the corner..

24. When the ocean rolled in, it was almost a relief.

25. Which is why I stayed. Yeah, the stores are almost empty, yeah, they weren't kidding when they said it would take at least a century for the waters of that brown lake to be clear again. But the fish haven't killed me yet; the pineapples and fruit trees and vines are growing wildly, and it's *quiet*, except when Ramon and Nick come by. Blessedly quiet.

And creepy as it is, I find something magical in rowing over the drowned homes.

And ducking beneath the live oaks.

26. That, and thinking that at some point, you would come.

Still thinking that.

Thus this list.

27. And then, the shortwave chatter last night.

28. Yes, we have a couple of ham radios around. Yes, we can use them. See the solar panels and chargers mentioned above.

29. No, I haven't forgotten anything.

Especially the sound of your voice.

27. But if I'm wrong, and you're not Alicia—

Try to make those Nilla wafers last.

THE VALLEY OF MOTHERS
Josie Columbus

Alice gasped as a patch of gravel came loose under Tamika's foot. The other girl was as adept as any of them at scrambling over crumbled walls and battered cars, but watching her still made Alice apprehensive.

"Be careful," Alice said in an urgent whisper.

Tamika smirked over her shoulder. "I'm alright."

"Are you sure this is where Jamal said the food was?"

Tamika nodded.

"He's not supposed to come this far from home."

"It's fine, Alice," Tamika said. "He's a clever kid."

Alice frowned. "We're too far from the hideout," she said. "We should go back."

"We have no food, Alice," Tamika said with a frustrated sigh. "We can't go back to the kids empty—"

Tamika's words came to an abrupt halt, her eyes widening. She exchanged a look with Alice, and then dashed to the shelter of a crumbling wall. Alice followed, her bare feet calloused against the punishment of the broken roads.

"What is it?" Alice hissed. Tamika pointed.

A scavenger crouched in the street in front of an old storefront. She wore battered leather, a scarf pulled across her mouth, and a pair of goggles over her eyes. Alice suppressed a shiver as she noticed a gun and knife among the implements on her belt.

"What's she doing?" Tamika asked. The stranger regarded the store front's broken windows for a moment, and then hopped inside. "There's no food in there."

"More for us," Alice said. "Come on."

Tamika spared another furtive glance toward the old storefront, then dashed out from behind the ruined wall. Alice followed as Tamika led them to a low brick building whose walls had been scorched by a past blaze. A tilted crucifix hung on the wall next to its shattered doors.

The interior was a charred ruin, chunks of shattered wood burned to the point that Alice could not tell if they were fallen beams or former pews. Tamika glanced around, and then made for a collapsed section of the floor. They clambered down into a basement with walls stained black with soot. Tamika made her way to a small hole that had been dug into the rubble, then disappeared into the shadows of the room beyond. She returned a few moments later, her eyes bright with joy.

"Look at *this*." Tamika held up a metal can with a label that said something about "hearts." Alice returned her smile.

"Looks like food to me," Alice said. "Come on, we'll bring it back to the hideout."

"There's more cans back here," Tamika said.

"*More?*"

Tamika grinned, then turned back into the hole. She soon returned with a can in either hand. One was missing its label, but Alice recognized the other as corn.

Alice stared down at the three cans, very aware of the hollow ache in her stomach. It had been a long time since she'd held so much food at once.

"It's a good thing we didn't turn around," Tamika said.

Alice's wonder soured, but she was caught off guard by Tamika's exuberant expression—it was not often that she was graced with such a genuine smile from her—and felt her heart flutter. She felt her annoyance almost fade, but she held fast to it, brushing away her unexpected feelings about Tamika's smiling lips.

"Come on," she said, stowing the cans in a little bag lashed to her hip. They barely fit. "We should get back." Tamika's face faltered, but offered a terse nod before following Alice outside.

As they walked, Alice could feel the wrongness of the ruined town around them. The choking dust in the thin air, the relentless beat of the sun, the weeks that passed without rain. They passed a ruined house, and Alice felt a pang in her chest as she remembered once playing in that yard. Yellow grass and the ghosts of wildflowers now tangled where she once recalled a bed of soft greenery, far more yielding to young knees. Alice's ears pricked to a low, distant rumble. She pulled herself from her reverie, and whirled to look at Tamika, whose eyes were wide with fear.

"Marauders," she said.

Alice tugged at Tamika's arm as she moved. "Hide," she said, and turned to dash off toward a collapsed house—but Tamika didn't budge.

"Look," she said, and Alice's eyes followed her finger. There, rummaging around inside the rusted hulk of an old car, was the stranger. A low growl was growing in the air.

"They're going to kill her," Tamika said.

"What?" Alice said, tugging on Tamika's arm again.

"She doesn't know," Tamika said, her voice tight.

"Tamika," Alice said. "We have to *move*."

"No," Tamika said, the fear in her voice replaced by a frightening surety. "We have to *help*." She snatched her arm away and dashed toward the stranger.

The rumbling grew louder. Indecision paralyzed Alice as Tamika ran, until Alice turned and fled. Alice slid into the shadow of a crumbled stone wall, choking on her own cowardice, before peering back out into the street.

Tears welled and blurred her vision, but she could still see Tamika tug on the stranger's jacket. The woman whirled, hand going to the weapons on her belt, and Alice knew a moment of despair. When the woman saw Tamika, though, she glanced around and crouched in front of her. Tamika pointed in the direction of the noises, the stranger nodded, and Tamika led her into the shadow of a wall. They both disappeared from sight.

The sounds of the Marauders fell on top of them. Alice made

herself small in the shadows as a pair of overladen cars tore down the street. One vehicle's open bed swarmed with men and women clad in makeshift armor, waving blades and guns in the air. Behind it came a smaller car wrapped in barbed wire, men hanging out its windows as they shouted, taking swigs from dark bottles.

It seemed to her like the moment would never end—but Marauders only lingered if they saw something to attack or loot. Soon only the dust in the air remained, the sounds of their engines fading into the distance. When the world fell back into silence, Alice jumped up.

Her heart leaped when Tamika emerged from behind the wall. All her own rules forgotten for a moment, Alice ran to her, catching her in a clinging embrace and holding her tight. Tamika gave a little laugh, and hugged Alice back. Before she could fully appreciate the feeling of Tamika's arms around her, Alice heard the crunch of boots against asphalt.

The stranger had pulled down her scarf and goggles. Her skin was light copper, marred only by the line of dust below her eyes and a faint dusting of stubble on her cheeks. She had dark brown eyes, and wisps of textured black hair poked out of her hood. Her black brows were knit in an expression of concern.

"Hello," the woman said. "What are you two doing out here?"

Alice stepped to put herself between Tamika and the stranger, then offered a narrow-eyed scowl.

They locked eyes, and Alice held the gaze as best she could, trying to put cold intimidation into her stare. The woman did not waver. Instead, she held out a gloved hand.

"I'm Sara," she said, and offered a small smile. "What's your name?"

Alice regarded the woman for a moment without taking her hand. "Alice."

"Alice," Sara said, as though committing it to memory. "Thank you for warning me about the Marauders. I didn't think they'd have any reason to come through this part of town."

The ringing in Alice's ears had faded, and without it she could hear the gentle hum of motors carried on the wind. She chanced a quick look at her surroundings, then turned back to say, "We shouldn't be out in the open."

"You're right," Sara said. "Do you know someplace safe we could talk?"

Alice narrowed her eyes. "What do you want with us?"

Sara frowned. "Just to make sure you're alright."

"We're fine," Alice snapped. "Can we leave?"

"I'm not keeping you here." There was a hint of sadness in Sara's voice.

"Good," Alice said. "Come on, Tamika."

"Wait," Sara said. "Where are your parents?"

Alice faltered. She took a deep breath and grabbed Tamika's arm to drag her away, but Tamika spoke up before she could: "We don't have any."

Sara's face softened. "Why not?"

"They left us," Alice said, her tone too harsh. Tamika flinched.

Sara pursed her lips. "I was afraid of that," she said. "Are there more of you?"

Both of them kept quiet.

"I'm not going to hurt you," Sara said. "I just want to help."

Alice snorted. "How?"

"I'll cook you something." Sara smiled. "I have a fire kit, and food and water. Is there someplace safe we could light a fire?"

"Yes," Tamika said, her voice bright. Alice turned to give her an angry stare.

"*No,*" Alice said. Then in a harsh whisper, "We can't bring her *home*, Tamika."

"Why not?" Tamika said at full volume. "If she cooks for us, we don't have to open the cans, and the food lasts longer."

"But—"

Tamika stepped past her. Alice stared, dumbstruck, as Tamika squared her shoulders and looked Sara in the eye.

"Follow me," Tamika said, and then started to walk down the street. Sara glanced between the two of them for a moment before following. For a moment, Alice stood rooted to the spot, then gritted her teeth and followed.

They made their way back to their hideout. It was a low, sturdy structure that had so far escaped destruction by Marauders. Old desks and wooden chairs had been pushed against the walls, obscuring broken windows. Two more children sat in the center of the space—one a few years Tamika's junior, and the other even younger. The older one, Jamal, stood and turned as they approached. He gave a wide grin at their return, but his face fell into fear upon seeing Sara. Eve turned to look at them too, but seemed to quickly decide that the newcomer wasn't as interesting as her scavenged toys.

Sara regarded their sparse living conditions. The light was starting to fade around them, and shadows lengthened in the little space. After a few moments of silent appraisal, Sara crouched down and opened her pack. She produced a small plastic box from it. "Is there wood I could use for the fire?"

Alice started to protest, but Tamika had already scurried toward the piles of broken chairs. She returned with an armful of splintery wood and a broad smile. Alice scowled at Sara, and her contempt for her only grew as the woman worked at the fire.

By the time it was lit, all the children had gathered around her. Sara set a pan atop the low fire and filled it with water, then produced a can and a plastic bag from her pack. She cracked open the can and dumped the contents into the water, fishing pieces of jerky out of the bag to toss in with it.

The smell of salted broth and peppery meat filled the air. Alice's mouth began to water despite herself. As she folded her arms across her chest, Jamal turned to her.

"Did you go to the place I found?"

"Sure did," Alice said. She tried to give him a smile, but it came out tight and forced. "We found three whole cans."

Jamal's jaw dropped, and his eyes almost popped out of his skull. "*Three?*" he said, and Alice winced at the volume of his exclamation. "Can we store some for the Valley?"

Sara cocked an eyebrow at him. "Valley?"

Alice's stomach dropped as Jamal nodded and said, "The Valley of Mothers."

"What's that?" Sara said.

Tamika sent Alice a wary glance. Alice fumed. It was bad enough that she had told them the stupid rumor, or that Tamika used it like a fairy tale, without them blabbing about it to strangers. It chafed her to think that something so simple as soup was enough to make them trust Sara, and that in trusting her they were eschewing all the careful lessons Alice had taught them over the years.

"It's where they all went after the Dust Trail," Jamal said, his smile wide. "And they care for every kid that comes to them." He paused. "We want to go there so we don't have to be hungry, or cold, or lonely anymore."

"You're not lonely," Alice cut in.

"It's not the same," Jamal said.

Anger rose in Alice's chest and tears prick at her eyes. It surprised her how badly Jamal's flippant comment stung her.

"That sounds..." Sara bit her lower lip. "Lovely." She glanced down at the steaming little pot. "The soup's ready. Who wants some?"

The food distracted the other children. They had no spoons, so they had to slurp the soup from the little mugs that Sara served it in. The broth was bright yellow, and dark chunks of meat floated in it. Even as she resented it, Alice felt the food's warmth and substance suffuse her body in a way that she had almost forgotten was possible.

She shot Sara venomous looks as the others directed questions to her that they usually would have reserved for Alice. Worse, Sara indulged the most foolish of them, egging Jamal on to tell her more of the Valley of Mothers. Alice felt a combination of fear and fury in her chest each time one of the children revealed something more about their habits with a careless question. More than once, she sought out Tamika's comforting gaze, some assurance that she too could see the danger—but Tamika was just as enraptured by Sara as the rest of them. When Eve sheepishly walked up to Sara with a colorful book clutched to her chest and held it out for her to read it to them, Alice stood in a huff and stormed out of the building.

The night air was cold, but she didn't care. She stalked across the battered street and climbed onto a pile of rubble. She looked back at the light flickering through the broken windows of their hideout and hugged her legs to her chest.

After a few minutes Tamika came out, her brow creased in concern. She crossed the street and sat next to Alice. "Are you okay?"

"They're going to want a fire every night now," Alice said.

"What?"

"The kids!" Alice said. "They won't understand that we can't make fires every night."

Tamika held Alice's furious gaze. She reached out and pried Alice's flexing fingers apart, then threaded her own between them.

"They're smarter than you think," Tamika said. "They'll understand."

"They won't," Alice said. "You know how Jamal is. He gets stuck on ideas. He's still convinced the stupid Valley exists."

"What's wrong with that?"

"He thinks we're *going*," Alice said.

Silence hung in the air for a moment. "Would that be so bad?" Tamika asked.

Alice narrowed her eyes at her. "The Valley isn't real, Tamika. You know that. We're safe here." She looked back at the hideout, at the little pricks of firelight peeking out from the cracked walls. "Or we were, at least."

Tamika didn't respond, so they sat in silence. While they did, Alice stole a glance at her. Tamika made her feel safe, even when she knew she wasn't. Alice wasn't sure why her gaze drifted to the sharp edge of Tamika's jaw, or why she marveled at the way her dark eyes glinted in the moonlight. Alice felt a desperate desire for someplace more gentle, where they were not trapped in a daily struggle for survival. A deep longing blossomed in her chest for a world, a time, a life that had been stolen from her.

Alice scooted closer and leaned her head against Tamika's shoulder. Tamika pressed her cheek to Alice's head.

Sara emerged from the hideout, a frown of concern on her face. After a moment, she spotted the two girls and strode towards them.

"Are you two okay?" Sara asked. "The others were worried."

Alice gave a rueful laugh. "I'm surprised they even noticed." Tamika shrugged her head away from her shoulder. Alice felt a flash of hurt, but Tamika's hand still stayed in hers. "What do you want?"

"Just to talk," Sara said.

Alice bristled. "About what?"

"This place isn't safe for you," Sara said. "You don't know how to grow food, so you have to scavenge from old buildings. And you have to compete with Marauders even for just that."

"We've done okay so far," Alice said, acid in her voice.

"Maybe," Sara said. Alice felt a glimmer of satisfaction at the edge of anger that rose into Sara's voice. "But you can't stay here."

"Yes, we can," Alice said. Her gaze slipped from Sara's face, toward the dusty road that led toward the edge of town.

"It's been getting harder and harder to find food," Tamika said, her voice quiet. "We need to find a better place, Alice."

Alice turned a look of shocked betrayal on Tamika. Their hands slipped apart.

"Where?" Alice asked. "There are Marauders *everywhere*, not just here. And even if we *could* get past them, where would we go? The Valley?" She laughed, but there was no mirth in the sound. "It's a myth. We'd die trying to find it."

"It's not," Sara said, her voice almost timid.

Alice's breath fell away from her. Next to her, Tamika could manage only a stunned, "What?"

"I know where the Valley of Mothers is," Sara said, her words more measured.

"Liar," Alice said.

"I do," Sara said. "It's a town. We call it Sappho."

Tamika's eyes widened. "You're…a mother?"

"No," Sara said. "That part's not quite right." She sighed. "I came up the Dust Trail with a group of women. We'd all faced hardship, and had found strength in each other along the Trail. We decided, while we traveled, that we needed a place to call our own. We'd never had a place where we could be totally free to be ourselves. We decided to build a place where we wouldn't have to hide who or how we loved. So, we found a river that wasn't choked with dust and made a go of it."

"That's not the Valley," Alice said, folding her arms to her chest.

"No," Sara said. "We never meant to be a sanctuary. We just

wanted a place that was ours. Not many people settle this far south, but plenty left children behind, to lighten their loads." A tear streaked her dusty cheek. "We couldn't just leave children to die."

The three of them sat in silence for a few moments as Sara's words hung in the air.

"Why are you telling us this?" Tamika asked.

"I want to take you there," Sara said.

Alice reeled. Before she could form words, Tamika was asking another question.

"Can Jamal come?"

Sara seemed surprised by the question. "Of course," she said. "Why?"

"You said it's all girls," Tamika said.

"Oh," Sara said with a small laugh. "Our group just happened to only have women when we settled, Tamika. Jamal is welcome to make his home there, just like the other young boys who live in Sappho. He could stay the rest of his life, if he wanted." She paused. "You all could."

"No," Alice said, her voice small and shaky.

"What?" Tamika said, turning an incredulous face on her. "Alice, we can't stay here. Sara's right, it isn't safe."

"So we're supposed to trust some stranger?" Alice said, her voice rising to a yell. "Just because she made us some *soup*?"

Tamika's jaw set. "There's no more *food* here, Alice! Sara has food, and can bring us to a place with *more* of it. For Eve's and Jamal's sakes, we *have* to go with her."

Alice scowled, blinking back tears at Tamika's betrayal. She opened her mouth to shout at her, when a calloused hand landed atop hers. She flinched away from Sara's touch.

"You can think about it," Sara said. "It'll take me some time to get ready to leave. Talk to the other children. I'll come back tomorrow afternoon."

Alice shook her head. "We can't leave," she said.

"Think about it," Sara said, then turned her gaze to Tamika. "Both of you." Then she stood, gave them a weak smile, and jogged off down the street.

"Alice," Tamika said, her voice soft. Alice felt the questioning brush of Tamika's fingers and snatched her hand away.

"What?" she snapped, her anger bubbling over. Tamika flinched.

"We're going with her," Tamika said.

"We're *not*," Alice said.

Tamika's lip quivered. Tears began to spill down her cheeks, and she shook her head.

"*You* don't have to," Tamika said, her voice shaking. "But *we* do."

"You can't go without me," Alice said. She hated the childish quiver that invaded the words.

"I don't want to," Tamika said.

Tamika reached out again to try and touch her, and Alice flinched away. She saw hurt flash in Tamika's eyes.

"I'll go tell the kids," Tamika said. Then she turned away and started to walk toward the hideout.

"Tamika!" Alice said, blinking away hot tears. "Stop!" she shouted, but within moments Tamika had disappeared inside of the hideout. Alice scowled, and marched to follow her.

She entered just in time to hear Jamal excitedly shout, "We're going to the Valley?"

The exclamation sparked Alice's anger into a blaze of rage. She surged into the room, face contorted and stomach boiling with fury.

"We are *not*!" she said. All eyes turned to her. The stricken looks on Jamal and Eve's faces sent a pang of sadness through her, but it wasn't enough to derail her anger. "We are not following some stranger into the wastelands to get killed by Marauders!"

"But Sara's not a stranger," Jamal said, his voice approaching a distressed shriek. "She gave us…"

Jamal trailed off as Tamika's hand landed on his shoulder. Her face was a mask of cold determination that Alice had never seen before. Tamika marched across the room until she stood an arm's length away from Alice, then crossed her arms in front of her chest.

"Sara can help us," she said. "We're going with her."

"Help us?" Alice barked. "She's going to get us killed, if she doesn't just do it herself."

"She is *not*," Tamika said.

"You can't know that," Alice said. "You can't know what she plans to do with us."

"She plans to *help* us!" Tamika shouted. Alice recoiled—Tamika never yelled. "And we deserve that! We deserve a life that's easier than this! Most days we can't even find food, and all we do when we aren't looking for it is huddle here and hide from Marauders. Are you going to let your *pride* get in the way of the first person who's ever offered to help us?" Tamika's voice shook. "Because I'm not. I can't stay here and watch the people I love starve."

"I don't want to lose you!" Alice shrieked, her voice breaking. Tears ran in hot streaks down her face as she drew in a ragged, desperate breath. "I don't want to lose *any* of you. If we follow that woman I...I might not be able to protect you." Alice's anger drained from her body and left her feeling hollow. She stared, desolate, at Tamika. "Please," she said. "I can't lose you."

Tamika's anger broke, a scattering of tears falling down her softening face. She reached out and took Alice's hand. Drained as she was, Alice was surprised by the electric jolt Tamika's touch sent through her body. She thought of the fleeting glimpses she'd gotten over the years of something that could have been hers, if not for the harsh realities of her life. She thought of Tamika's eyes, her touch, the smell of her hair. Alice released a heavy breath as Tamika stepped in closer to her.

"You won't lose us," Tamika said. Her other hand came to cradle Alice's cheek. Before she knew what she was doing, Alice leaned the weight of her head into Tamika's hand. Safety and comfort flooded her as Tamika's thumb pressed against the corner of Alice's mouth.

"Alice," Tamika said. Alice looked up into Tamika's dark, beautiful eyes. "We need something...gentler than this. We all deserve so much more kindness than the world has given us." She paused. "You see that, right?"

Her gaze slipped away from Tamika's to settle on Eve and Jamal. She felt like she was seeing them for the first time—their cracked lips, their gaunt faces, the stark lines of their collarbones.

The terrifying realization that she couldn't protect them, even here, settled on her shoulders.

"I'm scared," Alice whispered, not wanting Eve or Jamal to hear.

"I know," Tamika said. "I am too. But we can do this. Together."

Alice nodded into Tamika's palm. "I'm sorry," she said, this time loud enough for Eve and Jamal to hear. Jamal took a tentative step forward.

"So," he said. "*Are* we going to the Valley of Mothers?"

Alice offered him a shaky smile. "Yes," she said. "We are."

This time, Jamal's whoop of excitement sent a surge of joy through her heart. Alice smiled as Eve and Jamal whirled around to gather up their scant belongings.

Tamika touched her forehead to Alice's, and wiped away Alice's tears with her thumb. Then her arms wrapped around Alice and drew her into a hug. Alice returned it, squeezing hard and burrowing her face into Tamika's neck.

The thought of leaving the safety of their home still scared Alice. She could not convince herself that Sappho would be the perfect, gentle life that she hoped it would be, but she'd be striving for something new, something better. And she'd be doing it alongside her family, alongside Tamika. That would be enough.

Tamika squeezed Alice tighter. "Want to help Eve pack her toys?" she said into Alice's shoulder.

Alice smiled into Tamika's neck. "Of course," she said.

FOR THE TAKING,
FOR THE MAKING
V. Medina

In the labyrinth outside the settlement, you find your name.
M didn't tell you what would happen when you got here.
She said that it was a part of finding your way, that everyone
passed through the labyrinth before coming into the created
safety of the land they'd claimed. It didn't mean much of
anything, she promised, it was just a formality.

You didn't believe her then, and now that you've passed
through, seen what waited in the dark for you, it's clear how
much she was holding back. It isn't just a silly ritual, an initiation
to keep out those who might disrupt the balance the collective
had established. It's a blessing and a claiming and an honoring.

Before you can take your first steps into the waiting tunnels, M
moves to your side and presses a kiss to your cheek.

"Keep your head up," she says, "and don't be scared. We've
survived so much. You just have to remember how to keep your
feet moving."

You nod, smiling at her. M makes your hands shake a little,
your heart ache with want, with hope, with the excitement of
someone showing confidence in you. In the world that was,
people having faith in you, thinking you were capable and strong
and powerful, was a dream. No one knew what you could do,

how well you were equipped to survive.

Of course, most people are dead now, while somehow, you're still here.

It's funny in a way. In the firelight, against the shadows and dark sky, you find yourself feeling like the world never crumbled at all. You feel like you're only just waking up.

M takes your hand between both of hers, giving it a hard squeeze.

"I'll be waiting," she tells you. "And we'll get to meet each other properly."

You don't know what that means exactly, but it's still comforting. Even as she leaves you, it feels like her hands are wrapped around your own, her warmth gently guiding you as you cross the threshold into the labyrinth itself.

"I'm not alone," you whisper to yourself. "I'm not going to go through this by myself."

* * *

Your footsteps echo, ratty sneakers against stone. You wonder how many people have walked this path before you. You're pretty sure no one's died here, but it still feels heavy with the weight of loss.

The path unfolds before you, lights glowing in the distance, ghostlights and whispers glinting in the darkness. You decide it isn't malice or even sadness in the air. If the dead linger, they mean no harm; maybe, instead, they just want you to know they're there, keeping an eye out.

Maybe, you think to yourself, watching one of the lights dance along the far end of the path, they're trying to remind you that you're not alone, too. Even the dead could get lonely and lost, and with how things ended—how the world dove deep, deep down into itself while chaos and pain followed—they might need to know they hadn't burned everything down for the ones who still stood.

* * *

As you walk, the lights dim and eventually fade out altogether. You've been in the pitch darkness before, though, without moonlight or stars to keep you going, and the dark holds no fear for you. Your hands reach for the walls to find the waiting rocks and use them to guide your way.

You aren't sure if the light will return, but uncertainty is a common enough visitor in your life that it's almost comforting to be thrown back into it. You don't know what's waiting for you, but whatever it is won't see you coming either. You know too well how to be quiet and unnoticed.

Even when the world was on its last legs, no onenoticed you. Amidst panic and fear, exhaustion and dread, you were the furthest thing from anyone's mind. It's how you thought you wanted it to be, but ithurt too.

Once again, you were the unwanted child, the weak, worthless, disgraced daughter of a well to do family. You thought that if you weren't one of those who made it to end, it was probably better that way.

In the tunnels, lost in the darkness, you smile, baring your teeth. You resolve to see this to the end, for yourself, and for those who came before you and only made it half as far. Not all the dead are kind, but each had one thing in common: they are very, very dead.

⁕

Your feet ache as you keep walking, and your throat is sticky and dry with thirst. You have no idea if it will be only a few more minutes or a few hours left on your walk, but you know you're going to keep going all the same, even though you can't fathom how big the labyrinth actually is, how much space is taken up by this strange place.

You want this. You want to call. this strange crew your friends, your family even. You want to touch M's hands, kiss her, tell her you're happy. You want to *be* happy.

And you think she wants it for you too. You saw she looked at you, how her hands linger against yours.

You told M your name, but it felt like a lie, and she called you on it.

"That *was* your name," she had said. "Who are you now, though?"

You had no idea what to say then, and you still don't.

That might be the point of this though, to find yourself in the darkness so you can exist fully in the light.

As you listen to the sound of your feet, your heart, your own breathing, you decide that yes, you like that idea.

⁕

The lights begin to dance again, flickering and flashing against the walls furthest from you. You've been walking with your eyes closed and you're not sure when they came back, but you can see them now and, as you listen, you think you can hear voices. It isn't clear how close they are, but you can hear just enough to blur the reality of the situation.

"Hello," you call out. "Is any—is someone there?"

The voices don't change, and nothing seems to indicate they heard you at all. Your heart starts to speed up just a little. Sometimes this happens—the voices in your head rise up and sing their delirious little songs, to try and lure you into singing too.

You haven't told M you were sick. You didn't mention to her that before the world ended, you were unstable at the best of times; you didn't know how. You were still worth something to her—after all, you'd survived long enough to meet her— and you certainly weren't violent, but you can feel the guilt rising up inside you for not saying something.

Gritting your teeth, you take in several long, deep breaths, counting in your head before you exhale. You've never been good at grounding, at cutting through the lies your own mind tells you, but you know you needed to move past the noise to find the truth of the situation.

The voices aren't the kind you've become used to, the ones laced with vitriol, their words pointed and poisonous. The buzzing of anxiety is there, but the sharpness isn't.

For a moment, you consider if, maybe, it's not in your head. If there might be people hidden somewhere in these walls, if they just don't know that you can hear them.

You try calling out one more time, hoping someone might be there to catch the echo. Listening close, you hold your breath and cup your hand around your ear, just in case.

One word rings through the faint darkness:

Learn.

×‍×

You walk. You remember the world before, and just as often, you remember what brought you here. Pictures play out in your mind, the world smouldering, the horrific sight of your family's bodies, the way you didn't flinch when you found them.

You found other survivors too. The end of the world didn't stop people from being people; the bad, the painful, jagged desperate parts came out, but so did the gentle, kind, generous parts.

You did your best to keep your head up and do what you had to do. You had already danced close to death, through so many near misses, that you knew how to survive. You were doing everything you could in order to keep going and the end of the world really didn't change that much.

You think that was what drew her to you, your dear friend waiting in the center of the dark. M saw the scars on your arms, the fire in your eyes. She saw your lean, hungry form and deemed you someone with more power than anyone would have thought. Worthy enough not to be a thing to hunt down, or to leave behind, but to ally herself with.

You thought you were alone. But, as you carry yourself forward, even through your exhaustion, hunger and thirst, you know the safety of a pack, of a group to rely on, is drawing ever closer.

×‍×

You wear a key around your neck to remind you that you can find your way anywhere. No door is going to keep you out and there's no way to keep you locked inside.

You didn't always believe that. It took the world ending for you to realize you don't need help, that you carry your own fate and can find your way. If this doesn't work, if the life you long for isn't with these people, you know you're going to keep going. You'll find happiness, with bared teeth, or blood on your claws, or, if you're lucky, with hope and a promise.

⚹

The darkness slowly lifts, and the lights return, soft and gentle, welcoming and warm. The center is nearly at hand. You think you hear whispers again and this time, you're sure they aren't coming from your own mind. You can feel the sound against your ear, the slightest shift in the air.

You hum, because you can't think of what else to do except to offer a kind song in response to the gentle words.

The whispers grow louder, rising up from what feels like the walls themselves. Your heart beats faster and your eyes widen in the dark. You feel the ghosts stirring, the faintest feeling of hands brushing your back, your shoulders.

"Easy," you whisper to yourself. You breathe in and out, holding each one long enough to hurt. Through shaking breaths, you remind yourself that. This is safe, you are safe, and the dead have no power over you. Anything to ground yourself, to stop your mind from racing and rambling in the darkness all by itself. It doesn't work, not at first. Your heart still slams in your chest, your hands clench, fingers twitching and curling and digging into your palms. And then, very abruptly, your heartbeat slows, and the tension in your shoulders, your jaw, your fingers, starts to release. You feel your breath even out and your body remembers what normality feels like.

The grasping fingers shift and relax and desperation melts away into a reassuring pressure against your shoulder and the small of your back.

You were so drained, so tired. But as the dim light ushers you onward, you're sure you can see this through until the end.

You think you see M before she sees you, but as you get closer, you realize you're wrong. She turns, a smile already on her lips, and you feel the last bits of tension, of fear and exhaustion, shed off you like old skin.

"Hello," she says, holding out a hand to you. "It's a pleasure to meet you."

You smile back, shaky but pleased. "Hello."

"So." M tilts her head, showing off the curve of her neck. "Who do I have the pleasure of meeting?"

You laugh, excitement and nervousness mixing in the sound, raising one hand and touching your own neck, before letting the words fall from between your teeth.

"My name," you start, your voice careful. "I'm—" You shake your head, unsure if you can even bring yourself to say it. It feels strange, to take on something like this, a new name, a new self; but you know you shed your old life with the old world.

You start again, letting the weights of the previous world, the life you'd led and the person you were, slip from your lips along with the words. "My name is Hecate."

When you hear it out loud, you feel all of that fall away, and you find yourself left in the dim light with this strange, wonderful woman and the life you can now embrace. You can't help but grin.

"Welcome, Hecate." She smiles as she says the words, leaning in to kiss you once again. "I am the Morrigan."

You look at her, almost surprised; then you laugh, shaking your head.

She takes your hand, watching you as she does. "Come on. It's time I introduce you to the rest of us."

As the two of you find your way back out, you feel free and full of possibilities. You feel like a goddess, walking hand in hand with power and promise and divinity. The labyrinth opens up into a whole wide, crumbling world, and you feel the myths wrapping around you, claiming you just as you've claimed them.

The world might have ended, the old stories crumbled, but some myths will live forever.

WHEN SHE NOTHING SHINES UPON
Blake Jessop

Caydee scales the mech like a spider, her tools clinking whenever they make contact with its armor. The machine is three times her height, a lusterless giant at once completely technological and as faceless and ancient as a clay golem.

She ratchets two mesh housings off the top of the armor, drawing a greasy forearm across her face to move the sweat around. It's cool in the mech bay, but she's coated with the usual film of perspiration and synthetic lubricant. She wrenches the grating off with a grunt, then changes the LEDs underneath with acute, obsessive tenderness. She swaps the actual lights first, then more bulbs that cover other parts of the electromagnetic spectrum. It is very dark outside—always, always dark—and the pilots need every kind of light they can get. That done, she climbs down and stretches until her vertebrae pop.

"Good girl," she says to the mech.

"I'm good," a low voice says from over her shoulder, "this is a machine."

Caydee jumps. Probably not more than an inch, but it feels like a foot. She's not new to mech work, and knows she's wrenched all the kinks out, but she is new to this pilot. Pairing up survivors is normal, and she's done it more than once, but this pilot's reputation casts a long shadow.

"Hi," Caydee says, and starts babbling. The pilot is slim,

scarred, and quiet. There's a bit of grey in her close-cut hair. Caydee gets herself under control enough to say things that make sense. "So, you want me to use your name or callsign?"

"Pilot is fine."

"Huh. Okay. You probably read my file, but just call me Caydee. As in *K.D.* It stands for—"

"I don't want to know. How charged are my cells?"

"Eighty percent." Caydee rattles off information while the Pilot gives the mech a walk-around. It stands on its own, a giant patchwork of armor and hydraulic struts. The machine is festooned with flashspun fiber saddlebags for salvage, and there's a gun mounted over one shoulder. The weapon is a skeletal set of rails twisted into something like a unicorn's horn.

"I rebarreled the coil gun for three millimeter. It won't drain your batteries as much as the old cannon did, and the muzzle snap won't ruin your night eyes."

As the Pilot finishes her inspection, Caydee whispers a command into her earpiece and the armor plates blossom open. Caydee steps up onto one armored knee and offers the pilot a hand. The Pilot climbs past her without a word and slumps awkwardly back into the machine's saddle, snaking her arms into the suit.

"Right, just lie back and let me tuck you in."

The Pilot ignores her. Caydee unhooks thick cables from the suit and lugs them away. The armor closes around the Pilot until just her face is visible. Caydee climbs back up and lowers the last, huge armor plate, enveloping the Pilot completely in high-carbon alloy and hermetic silence.

Caydee uses an impact wrench on the bolts and seals the Pilot in. The coil gun pivots left and right as fire control systems come online and the Pilot looks side to side. The suit doesn't have a head, just little bubble camera sponsons all over its superstructure. None of them look at Caydee as the Pilot marches the suit toward the door outside. All the lights in the bay go out for an instant, and the exterior doors open.

Frigid air gusts in from outside as other mechs walk up the ramp to join the Pilot. Ash swirls in through the gap and muffles the machines' steps. They file out into the dark and the doors close like giant steel curtains. Caydee settles in to wait.

×
×

The Pilot was having a hard time getting used to her new mechanic. Caydee wouldn't stop talking; everything about her was blunt, unfiltered, and perpetually in motion. It disrupted any sense of calm the Pilot felt getting ready to go scavenging, which was all she was willing to apply any deep focus to. The rest of her days passed listlessly, eating tasteless food, sleeping formless sleep, and dreaming about the dark outside. Things her waking mind wouldn't admit, even to itself.

Every time she got ready to head out, she felt like a surly parent talking to a very energetic child. Walking around the mech, making sure the maintenance and repairs were on point, which they were to an almost sublime degree, the Pilot couldn't think of a good word to describe her.

"Do you have to be this cheerful?" the Pilot said, slumping into the suit.

"Yeah," the mechanic replied, looking up at her as the petals closed. The Pilot didn't actually ask the next question out loud, but Caydee answered it anyway. "So that I can imagine this moment as something other than nailing you into a coffin."

Before the Pilot could say anything, the mechanic pulled the armor plates closed and the world went quiet. Her external view popped up, projected on the interior surfaces all around her. The camera bubbles gave her a very wide field of view, and the mechanic was a motion blur at the bottom of her field of vision. Muscle corded and thrummed in her arms as she bolted the Pilot in. Only a very faint metallic rattle made it through the armor from Caydee's impact wrench.

Unsure why, the Pilot felt like she ought to say something to the mechanic. She engaged her coms.

"Anything I need to look at, Pilot?" Caydee's voice came through clear. They were only ten feet apart. The link would be lost not long after she walked out into the swirling ash. Static electricity in the infinite plume made lightning sometimes, and thunder that came from everywhere at once.

"Pilot?"

She started. "No."

"Okay," Caydee said cheerfully, "good talk."

More silence.

"Caydee?"

"Pilot?"

"It's not a coffin. I'm a better machine than anything out there."

× ×
×

The Pilot's time outside was no time at all. She made a point of not remembering any of it. It caught her, often, in her sleep. Clouds of ash and a sky, in the rare moments with enough light to see it, like the underside of a lake during a storm. The metallic tap of debris in the wind against her armor, the quiet terror when her sensor suite told her something in the sky was sweeping the earth with radar, looking for her.

The world outside the bay couldn't reach her, though, because she didn't let herself see it. Didn't let it touch her. Didn't let anything touch her. The sky had dropped a black cloth over her soul, and made her invulnerable. She piloted her machine around the dark world, and took whatever was left that was of any use. She dumped it all in the saddle bags, and tried not to get caught. There was always the gun, if anything went wrong. It's flat, harsh snap wasn't all that different from the lightning. She came and went, unseen and unknowing, until the bags were full and she passed back through the bay doors in a snowy swirl of ash. Until she had the mech parked back in Caydee's little pool of light.

"How was it up there?" the mechanic chirped.

"Dark."

"That's it? One word? No blue sky or fruit trees?"

"I'm not talking about it," the Pilot said. She was just old enough to remember what blue sky looked like, and used to hate going scavenging because of it. She worked hard to lock that down, and Caydee was chipping away at the armor with her endless collection of tools and flippant comments.

"That's okay. There are different ways of dealing with having no time left." The bolts rattled out and the armor opened. The Pilot closed her eyes and sat still. Just breathed. Surprisingly, the mechanic left her alone. The Pilot heard her checking the coil gun's magazine. She had fired most of the ammunition, and the twisting rail still glowed a very faint orange.

"Jesus. How did you get blood on my beautiful paint job?"

"I don't want to talk about it," the Pilot said.

The mechanic looked down at her. Like she could feel everything the Pilot had, or hadn't, through the armor plate. Like she could see something the Pilot kept hidden in the dark.

"Sure," Caydee said, "let me get you out of there."

　⹉

Days pass in a strange way underground. Caydee sleeps whenever she can, and wakes when the Pilot and her mech need her. The machine needs her a lot. The Pilot, she's less sure about. Sometimes individual minutes seem to take hours, like she can focus on a single problem for a week and find she's ticked one thing off a list of a thousand and it's only been five minutes and she has to move on. The Pilot distracts her through all of this, skewing the cascade of Caydee's thoughts, even when she's not around. She's talked to her so much, and the Pilot never says anything. Caydee is sort of getting used to it; she talks to the mech the same way, and it never answers, so what's the difference?

"Anything you want me to look at? I can fix anything," Caydee says. The Pilot is giving the machine her usual intense scrutiny. She turns from the mech suddenly, and meets Caydee's eyes. A little awkward, because Caydee is used to the staring thing being unrequited.

"Things that shouldn't scare me do, and things that should don't," the Pilot says.

Caydee is, for the first time in a long while, speechless. The Pilot looks at her expectantly, as if there was any kind of answer to that. Her eyes are the kind of blue the sky maybe was, once, but Caydee has never seen. She searches for something to say and comes up empty. The Pilot starts climbing the mech, and Caydee offers her a hand up. The Pilot almost takes it. Balks. Caydee powers the suit and buttons her up in silence.

"Am I ready?" the suit's speakers say.

"Almost done," Caydee replies.

She bolts the chest plate in, and pulls the red spray can she usually uses to circle fault points off her utility webbing. She paints a little smiley face on the armor plate. The front camera bulbs watch her.

"All better. Get out there."

She can't tell if the Pilot laughs, but the mech lingers for a second before turning for the door.

Caydee looks up. "Anything wrong?" she yells. The mech is facing the bay door, but one camera bulb gimbals to keep looking down at her. The machine reaches out one huge hand. Caydee reaches up to hold one of the fingers. The moment is quiet, briefly.

"This probably looks really awesome. Can I walk you to the door?"

The mech's hand drops and it stomps off.

Caydee smiles anyway. "Good luck!" she yells, as the Pilot marches her machine toward the bay doors.

Scavenging missions take a long time, unless the pilots come charging back in a swirl of ash and darkness in a few minutes because everything went wrong. Some of the mechanics fret, some sleep or leave to get something to eat, if there is anything to eat.

Caydee stays in her little pool of light and stows her tools. Arranges everything in rows as neatly and lovingly as a gardener in hydroponics planting seeds. Time passes aimlessly for a change, maybe a lot of it, until her earpiece crackles and the alarm klaxons go off.

In the far darkness of the bay, the doors crack open, screaming on their rails. Four mechs went out. One returns.

Caydee's finger trembles when it touches her earpiece. In other pools of light, other technicians draw breath to speak at the same moment she does. Four questions for which there can only be one answer.

"Pilot, respond," Caydee says. Static. Her heart falls into her stomach. The mech stomps mechanically past the first few stations and stops in front of her. The coil gun rail is red hot, and the armor pitted with high velocity impacts. The central plate has a single conical hole bored into it, the shining metal looking liquid under the lights. The smiley face is gone. A rush of adrenaline makes Caydee feel like she's vibrating. She grabs her impact wrench and climbs.

"CKEM strike, somebody call the medics!"

The bolts rattle as she guns them out. The entire plate is slightly concave. It won't hinge loose when Caydee tries to pull it free. She drops the impact wrench and pulls out a vapor torch.

The mech's interior is full of hemostatic foam and blood. The suit has used every emergency system it has. Caydee torches the Pilot's harness and manages not to set her on fire. She reaches in and pulls and the muscles in her shoulders scream. She ignores them. The kinetic energy penetrator has bored a hole in the armor and sent a semi-molten arrow through it, the Pilot, and out the back of the suit. The wound is somewhere beneath her jawline, and the foam has only partially stopped her bleeding. She looks like a ghost.

More hands help Caydee pull the Pilot down, and in a few seconds she's alone again. The foam is pink and tacky on her hands. The mech stands empty before her, as suddenly fragile as a punctured and empty eggshell. Caydee starts shaking.

×•×

The Pilot knew this about her mechanic; she would find Caydee sleeplessly working on the mech, because it was the only thing she could fix. She couldn't close wounds, or staunch blood, or light the sky or mend hearts, so she'd be working in a fever to get the mech back into working order. The Pilot wasn't sure when she learned all this, but she knew. She wanted to see it, and the reasons for that were harder to explain.

She made a good prophetess, even on unsteady feet. The Pilot walked gingerly, trying not to turn her head, toward the pool of light and sparks in the bay. Watched the muscles on Caydee's back tense as she worked, and felt a twist of heat cut through the chilly air.. She banished the sensation immediately, but found it insistent, like a signal return on a radar track. Distant, but unsafe to ignore.

The Pilot spoke. Her throat still hurt, and all she managed to do was croak.

"Pilot!" The mechanic struggled to put down her tools without doing anything dangerous. Caydee hurled herself toward her, stopping awkwardly at the last possible moment.

"Wait, fuck. Are you okay? Can I give you a squeeze?" She fidgeted desperately.

The Pilot tilted her head up to show Caydee an uneven lozenge of metallic fabric stretching from under her chin to just below her right ear.

"The weave is still bonding, but I'll be operational in a day or two. The penetrator missed my spine, so it was just a bleed injury. Survive the first twelve hours and you're in the clear."

Caydee took off one of her gloves and reached out very tentatively to touch the mesh.

"Can you feel anything through it?"

"I don't know. I don't want to touch it."

"I do," Caydee said, and did. The Pilot felt it. Like someone touching her through a veil. Caydee's fingers reached the edge of the mesh and met skin. The Pilot closed her eyes and tried to remember, idly, the last time she had really touched anyone.

"I really need to give you a hug, okay?"

The Pilot nodded, and more of the mechanic came into contact with her. She was very warm, and smelled like the mech, but a lot more alive. Caydee exhaled deeply, and the hot rush of it tickled the Pilot's neck. She pulled back a little. Their cheeks brushed.

"Better," Caydee said. There was room for something between them. A perfect amount of space. The Pilot dropped her chin, closed it off, and their foreheads touched gently. The mechanic failed to let her go, and the Pilot let herself be held for a moment before looking up. Their eyes met. Travelers in the dark.

"What is this?" the Pilot said.

"Wrenching," Caydee replied, letting the Pilot go and wiping at her face. She left grease marks and little glittering flecks of metal on her cheeks. Time didn't bother to pass. The Pilot found her hands being held.

"Come on," Caydee said after a while, letting her go. "I'll show you how I'm going to keep you alive."

* *

Soon, scandalously soon, the Pilot is ready to go back out. The mech, of course, is pristine.

"Clear," the Pilot says, "button me up."

Caydee climbs easily up the mech.

"Well, it can't go any worse than last time." She takes off a glove and finds some pretense to reach in and accidentally let her fingers brush the Pilot's ear. "Are you ever going to talk to me about what it's like out there?"

"Dark and cold," the Pilot says.

"Two words. I'm making progress."

She's trapped until the mechanic finishes powering up the machine. Caydee leans in to kiss the Pilot for good luck as if it was something they'd done a hundred times before. The Pilot balks. Turns her head and closes her eyes.

"This doesn't mean anything and cannot go anywhere."

Caydee laughs. Not childishly. From somewhere deep and old.

"You are not very good at this."

"I'm also not wrong."

"I know."

The pilot opens her eyes. The mechanic is smiling at her sweetly, like she knows something very simple and wants her to understand it without making her feel bad.

"What?"

"You don't stop feeling when there's no hope, you feel *because* there is no hope. You have everything backward. There is nothing wrong with this. Check it out."

Caydee leans forward, one hand gripping the armor frame, and joins the corner of her lips to the Pilot's. Nuzzles and turns her head so that the Pilot has to turn with her. The Pilot tastes a little sweat on her lips. The feeling of the kiss is that of being plugged into a battery, of feeling a charge that makes everything that comes after possible. When it breaks it leaves electricity.

"The world is broken. You're broken. I get it. I'm not. Okay?"

The Pilot meets Caydee's eyes, soft and brown, and tilts her head up. Their lips touch again, for a little longer, until Caydee's twist into a smile.

"See? Not wrong. Now, can I call you something other than 'Pilot?'"

"Pilot is fine," the Pilot replies, but there's something other than emptiness in her eyes.

"Fine. Go out there, Pilot, and come home. That's it. Go out there and then come back to me."

The Pilot nods, and Caydee lowers the plates and bolts shut her armor against the world.

THE LAST DAWN OF TARGADRIDES
Trip Galey

Twelve minutes before the Dawn

Virtus' heart fluttered like a caged bird as he waited in the wings for the emcee Our Glass to call the category. *No.* He smoothed the dress over his thighs. Aurora was cool and shining bright as the rippling lights in the sky. As bold and commanding as thunder. Virtus' heart slowed as he tried to channel Aurora to the fore. The pieces kept slipping in his mind.

Focus! Everything depended on this performance: the standing of the House, his reputation, everything! If he failed—no. He was spiralling. Virtus took a deep breath and reached for Aurora's majesty.

Two-and-a-half hours before the Dawn

"Right, now that your quongs are out of the way, take your bagaga and pull it back between your legs. That's right, tuck it right up between those sweet cheeks."

Virtus stifled a laugh as Dame Fyne Kaffeh instructed her newest protégay in the fine art of feminine impersonation.

"It's tickling my nether eyeh," Pharrah moaned.

"Count your blessings, then," Dame Fyne shot back. "Now get that wig on, girl! Your category is coming up." She turned to

Virtus. "Be with you in a moment, love."

"Thank you, Dame Fyne," Virtus murmured. "I know it's last minute."

A great grey pearl fell from his lips as Virtus spoke. He caught it with practiced ease and tucked it into one of the many small pockets sewn into his clothing.

"Half an hour, messecaffers!" Someone hollered from the door. "OTA Triple-E in half an hour!"

"Thank you, half," was the chorused reply. The room, already a crowded and chaotic whirl, erupted into frantic activity. Makeup and wigs were swiftly applied, corsets were cinched for the gods, and a small spat broke out over an iron rod enchanted to produce the perfect curl.

"Hey," a voice murmured in Virtus' ear, "you got this. Because I got you."

Virtus smiled as Thom's leather-clad arms encircled him. Virtus inhaled his scent and sank back into Thom's embrace.

"You've won what, two categories tonight?" Thom flexed, squeezing Virtus' chest. "Cake. You're going to be great as Aurora. If you can win that easily as yourself, you're going to *slay* when you drag up."

"But I've never done it in public before," Virtus protested. "She's never allowed me to. Mother—"

"Can fuck right off," Thom interrupted him. "Forget what she thinks. It doesn't matter. Tonight is about *you*. About Aurora. About winning on your terms. Not about what will or won't irritate the Dragon Lady of House Valenziaga." Thom paused, cocking his head to one side. "I mean, is there anything that doesn't irritate her?"

"Honest compliments. Impeccable couture. Seeing her rivals ruthlessly ground beneath her heels."

Each sentence was punctuated with the appearance of a rose. These Virtus absently threw into the churning crowd in the dressing room. Someone would snatch them up and use them before they faded.

"I thought my family was bad." Thom fidgeted. "Your mother really takes the cake, though. Of course, I haven't met her in person to know."

It was a familiar complaint and Virtus waved it off. "Believe me, it's safer that way. She'd *hate* you."

"I think I could handle it."

"When I was seven, someone sent a blind assassin after her. He carved out his own heart in remorse as soon as he heard her speak."

"You're fucking joking."

"She keeps it on her vanity. I can show you if you don't believe me." Virtus stared disconsolately into the mirror. "I'm just a pale shadow of her glory." The truth of that belief was bitter on Virtus' tongue and dropped wormwood and carnelians from his lips.

Before Thom could disagree, Dame Fyne swept up to them, a set of elaborate brunette wigs in her arms.

"Now," the motherly drag quean said, "tell me about Aurora. Who is she? I need to know so we can choose the right riah." She set them out in front of Virtus, who cleared the cluttered table to make space, brushing aside various cosmetics and plucking an antique comb from the tangle.

"Whichever one is darkest, as the night before the dawn," Virtus answered, absently. Who was Aurora? He had pieces, but—Virtus tensed, his hands clenched, and the comb between his fingers snapped.

"Oh no!" Virtus looked from the pieces to Dame Fyne. "I'm so sorry. I didn't mean to break it."

"Don't sweat it, dearheart." If Dame Fyne was put out, she hid it with the skill of the long-suffering. "It's easily fixed. We're Queans of the City, girl, remember that! And we're gonna do what queans have always done: take something broken and make it beautiful! Paul? Paul Ari, get your tuchas over here. I need that pot of vlacquer."

A butch sylph in a tuxedo and black patent leather brogues breezed through the crowd, a small earthenware pot in hand. Dame Fyne uncapped it and carefully selected a brush. "You," she snapped her fingers at Thom, "make yourself useful and hold that comb," and with deft hands began to apply the iridescent glop to the fracture line.

"We can't risk getting any of this stuff on your hands, m'dear," she said to Virtus. "It's utterly vicious. Viscous? Vicious. Anyway, it's the second-stickiest stuff I've ever had on my hands." She winked broadly.

Virtus managed a smile. Thom snickered outright.

"There," Dame Fyne said brightly. "Better than new." She held up the comb. A glittering line of iridescent vlacquer cut prettily through the original design, fusing the two halves once again into a solid whole.

"I'm on!" Pharrah squealed, bouncing over to her drag mother. "Wish me luck!"

"Good luck, lovely." Dame Fyne squeezed Pharrah's shoulder in a rough display of affection. Pharrah briefly touched her fingers to the older quean's hand and smiled. Virtus blinked rapidly and turned away for a moment, swallowing several times to clear a mix of envy and sorrow from his throat. Things with his mother were never that sweet, nor that simple.

Half a day before the Dawn

Virtus looked down at the City, spread around the towers of House Valenziaga. Virtus had been summoned and was being made to wait. By his own mother. You'd think her son would rate better treatment. Still, at least the view was nice.

Every window faced edgeward, this close to the centre, with an unbroken view all the way to the kaleidoscope sky above the City's outskirts. Well, unbroken except for the void-dark hole punched through the city where the House Yvonnrae had, until recently, stood. As he watched, a patch of crimson bloomed at the edge of the sky, flecks of gold flashing at the heart of it. Somewhere, in some faraway world, a cataclysm had struck and sent a fragment spinning away, to be drawn to the City like yarn to a spindle. The Edgerunner gangs would be out in force as soon as the worldmote drew close enough, to salvage and scavenge, picking it clean long before it settled into place as part of the City. That is, if the thing didn't crumble to nothingness first, pulled apart by the strange tidal forces that dominated the Verge.

Virtus' heart beat faster; his stomach fluttered. The thrill of the 'run edged through him, half memory, half anticipation. That thrill never wore off, partly because Virtus could so rarely sneak out to the Verge himself. He hadn't managed it since that broken palace tore itself apart nearly two weeks ago. His mother did not approve of her only son and heir slumming it at the edges of the City.

"Stop sulking at that window." The command lashed out at him from behind.

Virtus started. "Sorry, Mother," he said, turning to face her.

The room around them was a showpiece marvel, hung with art scavenged or made from the beautiful detritus of a thousand worlds. Eclipsing it all was Matron Mother Vainglory Valenziaga, founder of the Legendary House of Valenziaga and perhaps the oldest resident of the City. Hers was a preternatural beauty, a perfection more than mortal, that reached out and dug its claws deep into anyone who gazed upon her.

She didn't look a day over twenty-five. Unsurprising. Part of her power was to make other people see her the way she saw herself—to actually *be* it—shaping her body to the desires of her mind. If she couldn't, Virtus would never have been born.

Vainglory strode over to him, snaking out a hand and catching him by the chin. She raised it, turning his face back and forth, staring at it intently. Her lips thinned in distaste.

"You've over-tweezed your eyebrows. You look like a Dilly Street bitaine." Matron Mother Vainglory released him. "Fix it before your category comes up at the Ball tonight."

Humiliation knifed into Virtus' heart.

"I did them this way last week and I won." A small spark of defiance blossomed at Virtus' lips as a snowdrop. Vainglory snatched it before Virtus could move a finger.

"Only perfection matters in my House." She punctuated each word with a petal torn from the little flower. "Especially now. Look out that window. What do you see?"

"I—" Virtus stomach twisted. He didn't want to think about it, let alone talk about it, for all it had been the only thing anyone had been talking about for days. "The Fell of House Yvonnrae." Virtus swallowed. "Does anyone know what happened?"

"It doesn't matter," Vainglory answered coldly. "They've fallen, and if we are not careful, we could be dragged down in their wake. Or do you think House Pahseshem has, perhaps, failed to notice?"

"No, Mother," Virtus said. It was safest to stick to short, direct answers when she got like this.

"We of House Valenziaga must be flawless. It's why we are a Legendary House. We are realness. We are style. We are perfection. These things define us. Protect us. Do you see a sun in the sky outside these walls? In any of the snatches of sky out there?"

"No, Mother." What else could he say? That her definition of realness, of perfection, was stifling him? He crushed the urge. No. That wouldn't end well.

"That is because *I* am the sun around which this tatterdemalion world revolves. This House, the last shard of my world, stands at the centre by my power and my glory alone and I will not allow anything to threaten it. Stupid mistakes like that," she jabbed her finger at Virtus' face, "leave us open to attack. I will not have our position as First House placed in jeopardy. Is that clear?"

Virtus nodded, keeping his face impassive with the ease of long practice.

"I said, is that clear?"

"Yes, Matron Mother." The assent dropped into Virtus' hand, a chunk of raw crystal.

"Good." Vainglory leaned in and kissed him on the cheek, plucking the new-formed gemstone from his nerveless fingers. "Fix those eyebrows before the Ball tonight."

⠈⠢

Seven minutes before the Dawn
    "Winner is!" Our Glass' voice snapped Virtus back to the present. "Facet of House Pahseshem!"

"Neuja tat." The curse darted away from Virtus' lips, a glittering scarab in flight, and lost itself amongst the rafters. Another win for House Pahseshem.

No. No, no, no. It was too much pressure. This was not what he needed. This was not how he'd wanted to debut Aurora. He wasn't ready.

Good Goddess, get a grip, girl! Virtus tried to breathe. Why was it so hard to hold it together? There must be something in the air.

⚹

Forty-three minutes before the Dawn
The ballroom had been even more a madhouse than usual, perhaps in honour of fallen House Yvonnrae. Even with Thom clearing the way, Virtus struggled to thread his way through the crowd on the mezzanine.

Bodies thronged around him, cheering and catcalling, groping, drinking, and dancing. Virtus shrank into himself in a vain effort to fit through the ever-shrinking gaps between people without ruining his dress.

"Category is!" The voice of the emcee, Our Glass, sliced through the din like a razor. "Virgin Vogue!"

A long space had been cleared in front of the stage that dominated the far end of the ballroom. A high table seated five judges and Our Glass, light glinting off the brass and crystal device that served as his right eye, prowled back and forth in front of it like a stalking cat. A parade of lissome young things flowed past, limbs repeatedly catching in exquisitely agonising positions.

"Martina! You barmy badge cove, get off the floor. You're about as much a virgin as I am." When Martina sneered at him and struck another pose, he twisted a dial on the brass gorget around his neck and his amplified voice rattled the chandeliers. "This category is for virgins only, and your cherry's done been popped more than a stick of bubblegum. Now get that flabby arse off my runway before I kick it off."

Virtus forced his attention away. His category was nearly up. He had to make it to the wings before they called it. As he pressed further through the mob, Our Glass' voice carried the winner's scores to him "Ten, ten, ten, ten, ten! Dachas across the board! Winner is! Elle l'Egance of the Legendary House of Lakhsonen!"

Lakhsonen was Thom's House. Virtus allowed himself a shared smile with his boyfriend, then screwed his courage to the sticking place and turned to dive into the sea of people once more, only to find his way blocked.

Facet, heir to House Pahseshem, barred his way. Everything about her was sharp, from her delicately-pointed ears to her flawless cheekbones to her piercing eyes and the tongue that could slash a bitch to ribbons with a single, well-placed word.

Her eyes lighted on Virtus, and with a too-thin smile, dropped the most insincere of greetings, "Bona to vada, Virtus." She kissed the air to either side of his cheeks.

"Bona to vada," he replied, hands suddenly fallen limp and nerveless to his sides.

"What are you wearing?" Facet drawled. "Surely you don't think *that* is going to save your House from going the way of Yvonnrae?" She laughed like breaking glass.

Virtus stiffened. "I suppose we'll have to see, won't we?"

"Oh, I look forward to it." Facet leaned in to whisper in his ear. "Even more than being heir to First among the Legendary Houses, I'm going to enjoy watching your House's humiliation." She raked him up and down with her eyes. "Though it looks like I'll be seeing that even before the final scores are tallied." She laughed again.

Virtus choked back the retort that threatened to strike, an asp from his lips, and snaked out a hand, grabbing Thom's arm before the headstrong Lakhsonen could do something regrettable.

"I love your necklace," he said instead. "That rock is something else."

It was, actually. Set in silver wire, the rough spindle of something between marble and opal shimmered between the razors of Facet's collarbones.

"Isn't it lush? My bit of hard lifted it for me." Facet preened. "From the piece of what's-it-called that slipped through last week."

"Targadrides," Virtus said absently, eyes scanning the crowd for an exit gap. He needed to get out of this conversation and onto that stage. "It was an Emperor's Palace from Targadrides." And Virtus should know.

⁌

Thirteen days before the Dawn
Virtus gazed at a mural depicting the triumph of one nation over another, able to read the curling, cunific writing through some eldritch eddy of the tidal forces here at the Verge of the City. "Targadrides in victory over proud Sardathrion."

The ground shuddered beneath him. He didn't have much time. His edgerunning instincts told him this worldmote wouldn't last much longer. Virtus glanced back up at the mural. It had cracked and his ability to read the alien script was gone. Oh well. The thing had been too big to lift anyway.

Though the way was choked with dust and rubble and all the other detritus of the ending of a world, Virtus pressed deeper into the strange structure. There was so much broken beauty here, he knew he had to be able to find something worth salvaging.

"This way," Thom called from someplace further up ahead. "You've gotta see this!"

Virtus scaled a fallen support beam and dodged through a missing chunk of masonry. Thom swore as Virtus tumbled to the ground to land in a graceful crouch next to him; a laugh, daring and bright, spilled from his lips in a fall of opals.

"Someone is feeling sure of themselves today," Thom observed drily.

Virtus didn't respond. He couldn't. All of his senses were caught up by the room before him. Crumbling, majestic, it was a sumptuous throne room so begilded and begemmed that not even the dust of cataclysm could dull its glory. Shards of multicoloured crystal littered the floor, the window frames that once held them twisted and rent. Tattered draperies, twisted of impossible fibres, clung thick as spiderwebs to the walls.

"Some good stuff, right?" Thom shot his boyfriend a sidelong glance, but Virtus was already scrabbling over the rubble, eyes gleaming.

"Look at that fabric!"

＊＊＊

Four minutes before the Dawn
Stay in the present. Stop letting your thoughts wander off.
Any minute now Our Gl—

"Category is!" Our Glass' voice was no less penetrating when
heard from behind the safety of the wings. "Exotique Eleganza
Extravaganza!" The crowd in the ballroom erupted. "I want new.
I want now. I want nextra. I want it lifted from the most beautiful
and dangerous bits of city's edge flotsam. And hunty, if you
didn't design or sew it yourself, get off my catwalk. It's time to
show us who you really are."

Tension knotted Virtus' gut. Did he know who Aurora was?
Who he was? He raised a hand to his face, fingers hovering a
hairsbreadth away from the skin, not quite touching. His makeup
was a trifle heavier there than he'd like, but he'd not had much
choice in the matter.

His mother had seen to that.

＊＊＊

Three hours before the Dawn
Vainglory's hand cracked across Virtus' face. Virtus
staggered from the unexpected force behind the slap.

"That was a disgraceful performance—unworthy of House
Valenziaga." Vainglory's words were cold as ice.

"I don't understand." Virtus pressed a hand to his stinging
cheek. "I won my category."

"With a less-than-perfect score. Hardly a gag-worthy
performance." Vainglory's words were sharp as needles. "I told
you to fix those eyebrows. Did you hear nothing I said to you
earlier? We cannot afford to be anything less than perfect. House
Pahseshem is beating us and we dare not lose. But no. Because
you left points unclaimed on that catwalk, they only need to win
one more category to ascend to First amongst the Legendary

Houses. I will not let that happen. That is my place."

"I could compete in another category, win more points—" Virtus suggested.

"You? No. You have embarrassed House Valenziaga quite enough for one night." Vainglory made a small sound of disgust. "I can't believe I gave up nine months of my life to bring you into this world."

Every other time Virtus had disappointed his mother, every single one, his senses had been dazzled by her presence. He hadn't heard her true feelings because he hadn't wanted to or he'd wrapped himself in the lie that all mothers love all their children. This time, though, something cracked.

She didn't love him. Vainglory Valenciaga, who had given birth to him, did not love him. He had been necessary, not wanted. An ornament, not a beloved child. Grief swelled in him like the tide. Hold the mask. Don't break in front of her.

He couldn't breathe. The world had vanished away down to a single bright point. The edges blurred. Virtus blinked them back into focus with white-knuckled will. A small breath jerked out of him and he dug his nails into his palm to keep floodwaters from following.

"I said, do you understand me?"

"Yes, Mother."

Virtus' hand clenched tightly around the ring that Thom had given him. He tried to focus on the warm metal, to focus on the pain, to focus on the strength his found family provided. It stayed the tide, warred against the shatter-sharp edges of his heart, and kept Virtus on his feet until Vainglory left the room. Then the grief overtook him and he collapsed to his knees, the floodwaters loosed.

"She doesn't love me," he whispered to himself, again and again, syllables slipping and hiccoughing through body-wracking sobs. "She doesn't love me. She doesn't love me."

Thom found him, still kneeling amidst a pile of wormwood flowers and carnelians, and wrapped him in his arms until grief had run its course.

"Better?" Thom murmured when Virtus had fallen silent.

"I will be." The words rasped along a throat wept raw.

"What do you need?"

"Flawless makeup. A sickening wig. The dress hidden in my room." Virtus paused. "If my mother wants a gag-worthy performance, I'll give her one. And I hope she chokes on it." Each word zipped from Virtus' mouth a living wasp.

"Then let's get your war paint on," Thom rose to his feet and offered a hand to Virtus. "After all, there's only one way to deal with a dragon lady. Bitch, you gotta slay!"

"One moment. There's something else I need." Virtus reached down and began to gather up the crimson gems.

·

Three minutes before the Dawn.
Virtus—no, *Aurora* straightened. It was now or never. The carnelians sewn to her veil blazed like red stars. The dress fell around her in sleek layers of black silk, frosted with silver spangles as if all the starry universe were contained therein. She looked like Night incarnate.

"First up! Miss Elle l'Egance of House Lakhsonen." A whip cracked. "Oh, Miss Thing! So fierce! So hot! So red! Is that real wyvernhide?"

"You know it! Skinned the beast myself."

The whip cracked again. The crowd went wild. Elle certainly knew how to play them. It didn't hurt that her catsuit was supremely gag-worthy. She'd be the one to beat in this category. Aurora cracked her knuckles.

"Alright, alright, settle down y'all. Next up, the butch quean realness of Mister Grine der Sloot! There better be something good under that trenchcoat that we haven't all seen before. Yeah, you easy pieces know what I'm talkin' about." The sound of tearing fabric ripped through the room. "Oh! Hello! My giddy aunt, what kind of genderfuckery is this? Though I do love me a man in fishnets and a suit jacket. Wait a minute. Bitch, are those stiletto heels actual stilettos?" There was the distinct sound of a death drop from the far end of the catwalk. The audience rumbled and whistled and Aurora could imagine Grine on his back, legs in the air to show off his heels. "I need a drink! Now get yourself and them shoes up off my floor before you ruin it."

Pandering. And Grine relied far too much on that body-oddy-oddy of his. Not that he could be faulted for it. It was a true work of art. Aurora reached up to ensure her wig arrangement was copacetic. Flawless.

"And now, making her debut on the catwalk tonight, please welcome Aurora Thunder!"

This was it. Last chance to back out. No. Not now. She knew who she was. She was the light in the darkness, the sound in the fury. Defiant as snowdrops before the teeth of winter. Daring as a flash of opal fire. She stole one more glance at her mother. Vainglory's face was apoplectic white.

And vengeful as a wasp.

Aurora strode out on stage and struck a pose. She was serving quiet. Elegance. Cold and distant beauty. The music swirled around her, swiftly rising to a crescendo. When it crashed like a roar of thunder, Aurora stepped out onto the catwalk and began to strut, trains of filmy black fabric trailing her like storm clouds.

"Oh, this one thinks she somethin'!" Our Glass' voice carried over the music. "What do we think, folks? Are we buyin' what she's sellin'? Or have we seen it all before?"

A mixed chorus of whistles and jeers was the response.

"Sorry, Miss Thunder, but it looks like your night in black satin lacks serious star power—"

Aurora flicked up a single finger, silencing both Our Glass and the audience. She rarely exerted herself, but she was still a child of the blood of Legendary Matron Mother Vainglory Valenziaga. She knew how to command a room.

She snapped to the musicians. A delicate aubade began to play. She drew up her veil and suddenly, all the broken pieces in Virtus' mind snapped into place.

"I am Aurora Thunder and this," she gestured to her dress, "is the Last Dawn of Targadrides." With a jerk of her wrist she pulled the veil free and began winding in the fine, black satin cord that threaded through all the loops and layers of her gown. One by one, they fell open, revealing the fabric sewn onto the other side, fabric woven of dawn itself, the last light of a world now dead and gone.

"No one left living knows the whys of the Last Days of Targadrides, but this much can I vouchsafe to you: the crumbling flotsam of that world crashed upon the shores of this very city and I stood as witness to its death throes." Flakes of gold as fine as ash crumbled from her words as she spoke. They floated in the air around her, flashing like fire in the light. "I alone strode into the Palace of Tadar-Gris and beheld its dying emperor upon his throne, wrapped all in silk spun from gold of dawn."

Layer after layer of the dress was transformed, a slow but steady glow creeping up the dress like the rising of the sun. The music quickened as the light grew. Aurora matched her recitation to it, taking full advantage of the added effect.

"His name was like unto the last light of dawn as it flashes across a band of gold, and I will not utter it here, nor, nay ever again. It is a language that can only be spoken in Targadrides, and Targadrides is no more. These arms held him," Aurora raised her arms, twisting her wrists, snatching a daring silhouette, "felt his final breath, lowered him down to endless night. I cut the robes from his body as the palace crumbled around me. I lost a blade forged of silver fallen from my lips to a creature of night-made-flesh. I clawed my way back from the ashes of a dying world to bring before you all of this."

The dress blazed like a rough-gilded rose, pink and gold as the dawn. The only spot of darkness left was the coiled tresses crowning her head.

"Look upon my fierceness, ye bitches, and despair!"

Aurora snatched the black wig from her head and flung it away. Red-gold curls cascaded down her shoulders as the music shuddered to a climax and the sun finally rose on Aurora Thunder, self made whole and beautiful by that annealing flame.

Silence.

It stretched out long and glittering and still until someone in the crowd yelled, "Fuck me!" and loosed the floodgates. The audience went berserk.

"Calm thy tits, you maniacs!" Our Glass fought back against the wall of sound. "Let's see what the judges think!" He turned to the table behind him. "What have you got for us?"

"Ten, ten, ten, ten, ten! Dachas across the board! Ladies,

gentlemen, and those who have yet to make up their minds, I think we have our winner!"

Aurora's smile blazed like lightning, but her gaze was fixed on a single person.

Matron Mother Vainglory Valenziaga sat directly across the room, a small eye of calm in a sea of exultation. Her face a frozen mask, the perfect bow of her oxblood lips an uncharacteristic flat line, she stared. Virtus seized her eye and held it, neither one flinching until Matron Mother Vainglory of House Valenziaga blinked, slowly inclining her head in recognition of Aurora's victory, the fading sun forced to bow before a bright new dawn.

Laughter bloomed from Aurora's lips, a blue-bright cascade of morning glories broken only by a single alabaster blossom, wry and vain. Applause thundering around her, Aurora sank into a deep curtsey. Rising, her stiletto found the vainglorious bloom, and, turning to leave the stage, ground it beneath the heel.

THE DREADNOUGHT
AND THE STARS
Phoebe Barton

The Four Sisters stand between me and the lake, towering concrete cigarettes against the setting sun. I wave to them as if they're old friends but I'm really waving to their protectors, to show that I'm here and friendly and it'd be best for everyone if they didn't put themselves in my giant shadow. The one and only time I had to scrape congealed guts off my boots, I had nightmares for weeks after. Picking the crushed swords and guns and bones out with tweezers was the worst. That was what made it real.

I don't have to wave, but I do. Decency is decency, no matter how tall you are. That's what Nora said, back before everything fell apart. I pick through the wreck until I find the red-and-blue signal flag the Three Rivers merchants told me to look for, and I lower three hundred and six tonnes of coal onto a cracked and faded parking lot that'll never see another car.

"Can't tell you how thankful we are," says the person with the money. The sack of coins they set out for me has buying power from here to the edge of the Lakes. "We're getting close to the bottom of the hoppers, but this'll keep us going until the next ship puts in."

"Great." The entire place already reeks of smoke and coal

dust, as if someone's trying to summon a new apocalypse. "You ever heard of a woman named Nora? About as tall my fingernail, red hair, loves swords?"

"I don't get out much. You could try the Friendly Get-Together, but——" They gesture to a little wooden building about as tall as my ankle. "It'd be a hard time for you to squeeze in."

I take a breath and imagine how much compression I'd need to duck through a door frame, and my heart races. It's been so long since I last squeezed myself ordinary. I'd be vulnerable and too small to run away.

"Yeah." Back when I took the Dreadnought Oath and touched the monolith, I'd thought about the people I could help and protect. I'd thought about how I could still show Nora the love she deserved when I towered over her.

I didn't think about all the places I'd be far too big to go. I definitely didn't think about everything I might lose.

⋰

There was only so much Melody could do to make the scrapwagon quiet. Even the finest axles and smoothest bearings had to fight against the boneyard's rough, broken roads, and it was a long time since Melody had seen anything close to fine or smooth. All those loose shards of aluminum and steel and everything else jangling together weren't exactly symphonic, either.

So it was more of a disappointment than a surprise when a squad of Imperial Protectors stepped out of the night, directly in Melody's path. Their midnight armour, harsh and severe, reminded her of demons.

"Funny meeting you in this neck of the wreck," said the one in the center, carrying a mean-looking rifle with a bayonet made eager to cut. Melody groaned. Blaine. "I thought we went over this last time, girl. You're not trying to dodge your contributions, are you?"

"Give me a break, Blaine," Melody said. "It's scrap. Garbage. Nothing that'd make the Empress's eyes glitter."

"It's material for reconstruction," Blaine said. "And seeing as how you perverts haven't been putting in your share, well, there's a lot of need."

"What, is rusted steel the hot new thing this week?" Melody said. "Better tell 'em it's bad for piercings. They'll get infected."

"I'm not going to ask you again." Blaine stepped forward. His bayonet flashed in her night vision. The men flanking him shifted into combat stances, guns at the ready. "Your contribution."

Her fingers twitched. It would be so easy to grasp her pistol. So quick. She'd practiced. She might even get it out of its holster before Blaine's men made her cry blood. That way, the Empress would never be able to make her beg.

She couldn't do it. She let go of the scrapwagon and fell to her knees.

"At last, common sense," Blaine said. "Smith, McKay, secure the cart."

Melody watched with smouldering rage as two of Blaine's men heaved the scrapwagon out of her reach. When its wheels squeaked and its cargo groaned, all she could hear were cries for help. Cries she couldn't answer.

"Thanks for your donation," Blaine said, once the scrapwagon was well out of reach. "Remind your deviant friends."

It would have been so easy to shoot him in the back as he left. One practiced motion, one squeeze, one problem solved forever. It might even be worth dying for. It wasn't as if she was worth much, after all.

Instead she sank to the ground, empty-handed and small.

⁙

One thing they never told me about becoming a giant is that your nightmares get that much bigger. The stars say it's about four in the morning. I've got a sense for that now. Not like when I was small, when I still had luxuries like beds and doors and roofs and love.

"Fuck," I grumble. I stretch and shift, looking for some modicum of comfort on the little rubble-strewn meadow, and that's when I hear the murmuring voices. In the moonlight I find a pair of bedbugs who weren't smart enough to run back home the instant I started moving.

"Shortage at the blood bank?" The bedbugs drop their little improvised syringe—more of a scraper, really—when they realize I'm talking to them. So many people forget I'm not a curvier-than-usual mountain. "Lucky for you I'm O negative."

The bedbugs fall over each other as they scurry off. Men like that, and they're *always* men, are full of piss and vinegar when they think there won't be a lick of danger, but when danger licks its lips they're the first to run.

I toss and turn, but I don't find any more sleep before sunrise makes it impossible. I've heard talk of a few settlements sheltering beneath the old city's bones, and Nora could have visited any of them. If it turns out she hasn't, at least my list gets that much shorter.

One inescapable truth of life is that people tend to get helpful once you do things for them, and one inescapable truth of being a giant is that there's a lot of things I can do for people. Between hauling, clearing, and heavy lifting, I can make a settlement's day pretty quick. After I spend a few hours decluttering the roads in Streetstown, with a name like that, you'd think they'd have managed without me—one of the braver locals points me toward a community down by the lakeshore, in an old railyard not far from the Four Sisters.

"They get a lot of people coming and going," the local says. "It's that kind of place. Even if they are a bunch of disgusting deviants."

"Excuse me?" One thing they *did* tell me about becoming a giant is that you don't have to take any bullshit. "Sorry, I was too busy being a big giant lesbian to hear you. Care to repeat that?"

I smile, really wide. I let the little guy see my teeth. It's the sort of message that's hard to misread.

"They...they get a lot of people coming and going," the local says. "Lots of variety."

"Is that so?" After this I'm sure I won't be welcome in Streetstown again, but there are plenty of wrecked cities. "Thanks for the hint, and don't forget, be kind to each other. The world's not going to do it for us."

The city's one of the old suburbs, built for space and speed and assumption that everyone in the world wanted their own little cardboard castle, and so there are plenty of roads big enough to fit my feet and then some. I can't imagine what the builders were thinking. For an ordinary-sized person they'd be asphalt rivers. Every once in a while I set off mines with little *frumps* meant to blast legs off. They don't even break my skin. Public service.

The railyard's the biggest clear space I've seen in ages. No trees, no greenery, just expanses of track gone to wreck on gravel beds. Here and there, old train cars quietly rust where they sat the day the world went askew. I see a riot of cloth ceilings strung up around a long, low building. That must be where everyone's hanging out. I've seen villages built inside everything from shopping malls to shipping containers.

At first there isn't much to grab my attention, and then I see it. A mural covering the side of a shipping container with smooth, bold lines, bright colours, and soaring birds. It's hope for the future done in brushstrokes. Nora's work, certain and sure.

The world deserves brightness, I hear Nora say, or at least a dream of her. *Reality is dark enough. It's my responsibility to add some light.*

I step over a long, low perimeter wall and hear alarms go off as if it's someone else's problem. Murals can take a while to paint, and this one doesn't look too weathered. Maybe she only left recently. Maybe there are people who know where she went. I don't let myself hope that she's still here.

Shouts rise to accompany the alarms, but I'm careful where I put my feet and kneel in front of the mural. My eyesight's keen, but I'm too big to pick out the signature. I bite my lip and take a breath. I could always keep doing what I've been doing, after all. Wandering from ruin to ruin, sleeping in rubble fields, following dim hopes until it gets too dark to see.

I close my eyes and take another breath. I don't have to compress myself much. I can make myself just small enough to get a good look at the mural while still standing tall. It'll be good to flex those muscles again. Never know when I'll need to squeeze into tight quarters, after all.

I summon my energy, focus my abilities the way the dreadnought captains taught me, and force myself small. Slow, steady, careful. Until I feel a surge of energy that envelops me, seizes me, squeezes me down.

My feet never leave the ground, but I fall just the same.

* * *

Melody was halfway through organizing the parts for a new scrapwagon chassis when the alarm shattered the world. Not the bone-chilling rise-and-fall of an attack warning, but she'd learned there were no good alarms. That was one of the things Samantha had made sure Melody learned when she was inducted into the community. It had been a rise-and-fall alarm that had broken their nighttime embrace, and it had been by the dying tones of that alarm that Melody had found the only woman that had ever loved her slumped dead against a wall, clutching her rifle close, as if an instrument of death could save her life.

Back in the home she'd abandoned, people would destroy such an obviously cursed object. Here in the boneyard, things were different. Besides, when she cradled it, she could feel Samantha's warmth. She kissed the rifle's wooden stock, swept it from its rack, and charged out to answer the call.

"So, she finally makes an appearance!" Sylvia-Three might as well have been waiting at Melody's door to see if she'd ignore the bell. "And not melting in the sunlight after all. Looks like I'm gonna be five chits richer."

"Someone's gotta bring in the scrap," Melody said. "Or the walls'll get hard as hell to patch."

"I don't know how you handle it, spending all that time in the dark." Sylvia-Three didn't bother to hide her shudder. "All the worst people come out when it's dark."

"Night vision goggles." Melody tapped her temple. "They can't hide from me."

She didn't bother to mention Blaine and the Imperial Protectors. She knew the only reason they hadn't stolen her goggles as well as her scrap was that only desperate farmers killed the cow.

"So, any idea what the problem—" Melody's question died

in her throat as she got out from under the roof and saw the giant woman. When she leaned back for a better look, her legs kept going and sent her falling back into the dirt, eyes open and mouth agape. She'd seen pictures and heard stories of the skyscrapers they'd built in the old days, and this woman looked like she could knock a skyscraper over with the flick of a finger. Concentrated magic poured off her titanic body, electrifying every strand of hair Melody had.

"Holy wow," Melody said. "Wow."

She picked herself up and holstered Samantha's rifle—no way would it be anything more than a pinprick to a lady like that—before charging toward the giant woman. No one, she noticed, was following her. Maybe they were waiting to see if she'd get squashed like a bug.

"Hey!" Melody shouted. "Hello! Down here!"

The giant woman didn't look at her. Her gaze was locked on the Calmness Wall, until she kneeled in front of it with eyes closed as if she'd come to worship. Then, without even so much as a sound, the giant woman shrank and kept shrinking as if it was the most ordinary thing in the world. When Melody found her curled up on the ground, the once-giant woman was smaller than she was.

"Damn," Melody said, half to herself. "Hey there. Are you okay?"

The no-longer-giant woman groaned and stirred, sluggishly until she caught sight of Melody. Then her eyes went wide and she scrambled backward.

"Oh no," she said. "This can't be happening. It can't."

"I'm afraid it is, whatever it is." Melody crouched down and gave what she hoped was a friendly gesture. She couldn't place the woman's accent, but it didn't sound too far from familiar. "My name's Melody. What's yours?"

"Grace." Her voice was flat, with no emotion behind it. She looked at her hands, the ground, and the sky. "Oh, goddess, I'm *tiny*."

"That's a matter of perspective." Melody offered her hand. "It's good to meet you, Grace. What brings you to the Railyard?"

"That painting over there." Grace gestured at the Calmness

Wall. Her whole face was alight with hope and she spoke quietly, as if a shout would shatter the world. "Do you know where the painter is?"

"No idea," Melody said, and Grace's gaze fell. "That doesn't mean no one does, though! We get lots of wanderers here. Someone must know."

Grace looked at Melody's hand, then at the crowd running toward them both, now that there was no threat of anyone getting crushed underfoot.

"I've already screwed things up," Grace said. Fear boiled inside her, enough that Melody could feel its heat. "What's going to happen now?"

"I don't know," Melody said. "But I know a good way to find out."

Grace bit her lip and took Melody's hand. Her skin was smoother than Melody had expected. There couldn't have been many giants wandering through the wreck of the world—how long had it been since she'd touched anyone like this?

"Welcome to the Railyard," Melody said in the seconds before the crowd swept over them. "It'll all be fine."

× ×̈

There's no way it can be fine. How could it possibly be fine? I've forgotten so much about the terror of being tiny. What if I've lost control? What if I've locked myself small? A few minutes ago the railyard was clean and organized and understandable, and now it's full of dust and dirt and it's all around me and there are so many walls and bushes and tumbledown wrecks and they're so close, I'm so exposed, I can't see—

Don't be like this. Nora's voice, echoing inside my skull. The fragment of her I've managed to hold on to through everything. *You're better than this. Be strong. Be the woman I loved.*

"Everything all right?" Melody asks. I can't get over the patina of dust on her face and the grease stains on her overalls. Before, people were too small for me to linger on details like that. "Need a minute?"

"I'm fine." I can almost believe it myself. I force myself to be calm, so I don't have to think about what'll happen if my worries are real and all the rest of my minutes are this tiny, this compressed. "Where are we going?"

"To meet Elder Jennifer," Melody says. "She'll know what to do."

Melody leads me to an old train car shaped like a squashed octagon, with a few die-hard flakes of green paint hanging on. Cloth awnings hang over the doors, and most of the windows are shaded. I put one foot on the wooden steps inside, and I freeze. Before, when I slept in old hangars or barns or warehouses, the walls were never stronger than me. Now I'm tiny enough for walls to trap me.

"Are you okay?" It's Melody. From a thousand miles away, underwater. I gasp for breath but there's not enough air. I want to scream but my lungs are empty. I fall for real this time, dash my palms against the ground. Hard gravel. There are scratches, but no blood yet. I make a noise, a long, low note that encapsulates all my fear.

I hear new voices. Muddled, distant. Then Melody. "—like a panic—" I'm being crushed, I'm being squeezed, I'll keep shrinking until they're all giants, then the pebbles, then— someone's squeezing my hand. Warmth, presence, connection. It's been years. I'd forgotten what it felt like. I force my eyes open and there's Melody, my hand in hers, her gaze meeting mine.

"Coming back to us?" Her voice is a flute to Nora's saxophone, but either way it's musical. "Sorry. I should've figured."

"Not your fault." I inhale, hold, and exhale, again and again. After a minute I can feel the calmness licking against me. "It's been a while. I'm good."

I take another breath and hold it while Melody leads me inside. There are floors here that have never seen rain. Ceilings you can't watch the stars through. *Stairs.* How long has it been since I've had to climb anything? I'm lost in the recaptured novelty, of all these pieces of my old life bursting like dying stars.

There's a grandmotherly-type with dark skin, snowy hair, and steely eyes waiting for me on the upper level. She must be

Elder Jennifer. Like the wooden chair she's sitting on, she shows her age. Maybe enough to have known the world before it went askew.

"I thought you were a story," Elder Jennifer says. "Giant women. And now here you are."

"Here I am," I say, never a story and no longer a giant. "I'm sorry for overstepping. I've been looking for someone, and when I saw her art...I had to make sure."

"Oh, you mean young Nora," Elder Jennifer says. There's a weight to the way she looks at me. "So talented. Such a shame."

"Shame?" My legs give out and send me crashing to the floor again. "What happened?"

"The Imperial Protectors." Her words sizzled in the air. "She had to run. We gave her all the help we could, but it's a harsh world. You understand. You knew her, then?"

"We loved each other." I let myself breathe. Of all the things that could have been true—*she's dead, she's turned to glass, she's trapped in a painting*—running for her life wasn't the worst. She'd done it before. "The world got between us. It's been so long. I've been trying to catch up with her."

"I know how you feel," Elder Jennifer says. "I lost my wife in the troubles. But you didn't come to hear an old woman go on about loss. Why don't you stay for a while? The world does a number on people like us. You could use a rest."

I want to argue, but words like "tired" and "exhausted" don't even come close to describing my life. Since Monolith City fell, I've only stopped to sleep. I've always been moving, always been searching. At least now I know Nora made it this far. Instead I nod. I don't have the strength left for anything else.

Melody takes me outside to a little wooden stall suffused with wonderful smells, where a person in a patched green cap stirs a simmering pot. She nods at him, ladles out two cups' worth of whatever's simmering, and hands one to me.

"What is it?"

"Not quite tea," she says. "But it'll take the edge off."

We sit and talk for a while, about everything and nothing. She doesn't mention Nora, or me being a giant. It's the first time I've been on equal terms with someone in years, and as time drifts past I can feel myself loosening. All I need is to rest a little, and then I can grow back to normal. I'm sure of it.

That's when the artificial screaming starts. No matter how far I walk, no matter where I go, the worst-case-scenario alarm is constant. It's always that harsh, throaty howl, rising and falling and rising, built to signal the end of the world.

× ⋮

Two alarms in one day. Melody was sure that had to be some kind of record. At least she didn't have to run back home for Samantha's rifle. She was more than ready to drill some fresh holes in whatever raider swarm or Protector platoon was at the walls. Grace, though...Melody knew what it looked like when fear was in charge.

"That's the attack warning," Melody said. "Best for you to find a corner and keep your head down until we deal with it."

"All right." Grace said, meekly nodding. What else could she do? A giant woman could intimidate an army, but an ordinary-size woman had to fall back on whatever weapon she could wield. "I'll try not to cause any trouble."

"I don't think you could make a dent, considering," Melody said. "Stay safe."

The enemy was already in sight when Melody made it to her position atop the wall. A force of Imperial Protectors: no surprises there. She recognized Blaine at the front of their formation and her old scrapwagon at the rear, loaded down with boxes. Because of course he'd rub his theft in her face.

"Not another foot, Blaine, or you're gonna get it!" She couldn't hold her tongue, not with that kind of provocation. "Try me, see if I don't!"

"Oh, it's our little deviant scavenger!" Blaine threw his voice through an old, hoarded megaphone. Every one of the men behind him had rifles ready. "Gotta say, you've got a hell of a knack for engineering. Too bad you're fucked up every other way."

Her crosshairs were on him. It would be so easy. One pull was all it would take to wipe him from the world. It would only cost a storm of bullets, and the wall could only stop so many. She kept her aim on his head, dreamed of watching it explode like an overripe melon, even after Elder Jennifer arrived with a megaphone of her own.

"We've paid your tributes," she said. "That doesn't mean you're welcome at our door."

"You've been doing more than that, haven't you?" Blaine shouted back. Melody's finger tensed on the trigger. "You shrank that giant woman. The Empress wants to know how."

"Sheer queer ingenuity," Elder Jennifer said. "Now, unless you want a few too many holes in you, better get your butts back to the boilers."

"Don't pretend that this'll go away," Blaine said. "We're watching you, deviants."

Melody followed Blaine through her crosshairs, carefully and surely, until he and his men disappeared back into the ruins. Then she took a breath, set the rifle down, and punched the Railyard's rough walls until her knuckles split and her fingers slick with blood.

×

It's all my fault. Everything down to Melody's busted-up hands. After she found me in a corner and told me what happened, that's the only answer that makes any sense. I've been trying to grow, even just a foot or so, but it was all for nothing. I go to Nora's mural, looking for strength in her brushstrokes, but there's nothing of her energy left there now. I press my hand against the paint, and paint is all I feel.

None of this would have happened if I hadn't come here. I'd been so focused on looking for Nora that I never stopped to consider why she'd never looked for me. It's hard to miss a skyscraping woman.

I step into the train car again, pushing my fears away. Elder Jennifer is on the bottom level this time, knitting on a couch as if she didn't have a care in the world.

"I didn't mean for any of this to happen," I say. "I'll turn myself over to them. Get them out of your way."

"Are you kidding?" Elder Jennifer shakes her head at me, like she's seen this a thousand times before. "They're like viruses. All they care about is a way in. If you weren't here, they'd have found another excuse. Nobody concentrates force like that because they're bored."

"If I wasn't around, they'd have one less."

"Just because it's a harsh world out there doesn't mean we have to be harsh to ourselves," Elder Jennifer says. "Or each other."

"If I could grow back to normal, I'd be worth something." I keep my gaze locked on the floor. "Now I'm nothing. I'm worried I'll be nothing forever."

"Nobody's nothing," Elder Jennifer says. "Together, we're a great something. That includes you, don't forget."

"I stepped over your walls," I say. "I got those Protectors wound up."

"And yet, here you are." Elder Jennifer smiles at me. "People like us need to stick together. Especially in times like this. Who you were isn't important. What matters is who you are. If there's nothing more to you than being a giant, then...who are you, really?"

"I don't know." For so long my life was neatly divided: the small years, being a dreadnought, and looking for Nora. Now that there are no more dreadnoughts, and now that I know she wasn't looking for me, I feel hollow. "It never seemed important."

"Your name is Grace, and you matter," Elder Jennifer says. "That sounds like a starting point to me."

I nod and go outside, out into the open. Focusing should be easy. It's like they taught me in Monolith City. I follow the exercises, guide my thoughts, and picture myself as a dreadnought again. Energy crackles up and down my arms, harsh and uncontrolled and burning, but I don't allow myself so much as a scream until I collapse on the ground, not an inch bigger.

That night, I watch the sunset. The next morning I watch the sunrise. I can't remember the last time I've stayed in one place for so long.

Melody couldn't remember how she'd endured with the cabin being so quiet. After weeks of sharing her space with Grace, there was an energy there that hadn't been present even when Samantha had shared her life. Still, Melody couldn't help but see tragedy in it. Every once in a while she saw a flicker of the confidence Grace must have had as a giant woman, but it was ground down and stamped flat by the realities of living in a minuscule skin.

"What's it like?" Melody asked while they worked on the new scrapwagon. "Having that perspective, I mean."

"Hard to put into words." Grace shook her head and focused on the wagon. Her attempts over the weeks to return to her old height had only left her taller-than-average. "I could handle bullies. I could see far. I felt safe."

"That's in short supply these days," Melody said. Otherwise there wouldn't be any need for a wall around the Railyard. "You'll get there again, Grace. I believe in you."

"Thanks," Grace said, dull and monotone. "Dammit, this wheel is on my list. What a piece of scrap."

They had it fixed in time for more nighttime scavenging. Grace's presence on the boneyard trips put Melody at ease, with another pair of eyes and hands and ears in case anything went wrong. Most of the old city was long since picked over, but between Melody's night-vision goggles and her trusty laser cutter, there was plenty of scrap out there that didn't know it yet.

"Looks like the wall'll be happy with this load," Grace said after midnight slipped past. Some steel, a little aluminum, plastic that didn't know how to die. "I'd love to help reinforce."

"We can always use more hands," Melody said. "I'm glad you walked over the wall, you know?"

"Yeah, me too," Grace said. "I got to meet you, for one. That was nice."

Despite the moonless night, Melody turned her head to hide her smile. That was why she noticed the beam of light slashing through the darkness when she did, but it was already too late to do anything about it. It was helmet-mounted, with an Imperial Protector wearing the helmet.

"Damn, I'm getting deja-vu," Blaine said. "Except this time, I'm going to take that foot, and then some."

He stepped forward with his rifle at the ready. His crosshairs must have been on her. One pull was all it would take.

·:·

"You really need to stop being so predictable," says the lead Imperial Protector. "At least change your route. This is just sad."

He can't be anyone but Blaine. Even if Melody hadn't told me about him, I'm good at recognizing bullies. He's the sort of man I'd be happy to step on, if only I could still step on men and make it stick.

"Fine," Melody said. "Take it. Gives me a reason to build a better one. Third time's the charm."

"No, I don't think so," Blaine says. "The Empress isn't happy, and when she's in a mood, the world rearranges itself. She really doesn't like the two of you."

"That's fine." I don't bother reaching for the gun Melody gave me. Some situations can't be solved with bullets. "I'm really don't like people who burn coal. So it's mutual."

"I like to think I'm a nice guy," Blaine says. "So throw me your guns, and I'll give you a minute's worth of deviant together-time before I end you."

He's got men behind him. Too many to miss. I breathe in, hold it, and exhale. So this is how it all turns out. At least Nora ran fast enough to get away. We turn to each other. Blaine probably wants to see us touch, kiss, whatever. At least we can deny him that.

"You can do it, Grace," Melody whispers. After I fell into the Railyard, I had to look up at her; now she looked up at me. She offers me her hand, and I take it. "It's all a matter of perspective."

I nod and close my eyes. Every second I expect Blaine to get bored of waiting a full sixty seconds, to pull his trigger, to end us both. Maybe that's why when the energy starts burning me, I welcome it and channel it and let it crackle. I lost my home. I lost Nora. I'm about to lose Melody and the Railyard. I don't have anything left to lose. I hold on to her hand as tight as I can.

So much energy was liberated when the world went askew. So much possibility.

"What the fuck?" I hear Blaine say, but it's distant and soft, less steel than wool. Gun-thunder cracks across the night, and I feel pinpricks. Sharp, momentary annoyances. Maybe even a little blood. "Hell, sustained fire!"

It's been a long time since I've heard rat-a-tats like that. Not since the time I stepped between two angry towns and put a stop to their little war. I open my eyes and find that I've risen. Blaine and his men are like cicadas now, small and annoying and harmless. I turn to Melody, hoping she's taken the chance to break and run, until I realize that I'm still holding her hand.

Neither of us is looking up at the other.

"Oh my god," Melody says, her voice full of wonder. "Grace..."

There's nothing to say, so I squeeze her hand. I know how frightening it can be to have a new perspective.

"You Protectors better run back to your little Empress," I say. "Let her know that I don't like her very much, either."

I ignore them as they retreat into the darkness. I've got more important things to worry about. Like what's going to happen now.

"So," Melody says. "We're giants."

"I didn't think it'd work like that," I say. "Hell, I wasn't sure it'd work at all. I'm sure we can shrink you back down."

"No," Melody says. "I want to know what it feels like, and... you're my friend. I don't want you to be alone."

My heart tightens, and I feel a tear slip down my cheek. It's been a while since I stood in for rain.

"I still don't know who I am, you know," I say. "Other than being a giant. Maybe you can help me figure it out."

"Sounds like a cool project, especially since salvaging just got about a thousand times easier." Melody kneels down and picks up the scrapwagon between her thumb and forefinger. "What's your problem with coal, anyway?"

"It's nasty stuff when you burn it," I say. "All that smoke. Makes it so that you can't see very far at all."

High above us, the stars are shining. They're too far away for me to touch, but I know they'll always lead me home.

APOCALYPSE

Saida Agostini

let's say the world doesn't end
and you go to its edge
and yes, it is a real place: the ocean pounding
and pounding at the gates, white foam
winged and salty and lonely sluicing
and feral   will you
stay there, on your hands and knees
looking for god   count your infinite
offenses into an unending rosary   try to be good
on a land you never really
could claim kin to tilling your
lonely into a field

or will you find another way
make your own heaven   know
the seed that makes you   roam
this world like tina turner in mad max:
black bad assed   and silver haired
enthroned in your own bare skin   beguiled in
your own story   its siren call

DREAM ASKEW
Avery Alder

Dream Askew gives us ruined buildings and wet tarps, nervous faces in the campfire glow, strange new psychic powers, fierce queer love, and turbulent skies above a fledgling community, asking "What do you do next?"

Imagine that the collapse of civilization didn't happen everywhere at the same time. Instead, it's happening in waves. Every day, more people fall out of the society intact. We queers were always living in the margins of that society, finding solidarity, love, and meaning in the strangest of places. Apocalypse didn't come for us first, but it did come for us.

Gangs roam the apocalyptic wasteland, and scarcity is becoming the norm. The world is getting scarier, and just beyond our everyday perception, howling and hungry, there exists a psychic maelstrom.

We banded together to form a queer enclave – a place to live, sleep, and hopefully heal. More than ever before, each of us is responsible for the survival and fate of our community. What lies in the rubble? For this close-knit group of queers, could it be utopia?

Queer strife amid the collapse.
Collaboratively generate an apocalyptic setting.
Content warnings: violence, gangs, oppression, bigotry, queer sexuality.
For 3-6 players across 3-4 hours.

WHAT A SESSION IS LIKE

Players sit down together at a table, catching up and checking in with one another. They establish some tools for maintaining trust before they start to play. Players each choose a character role − a template that allows them to create their own unique main character. They also choose a setting element to steward in play.

The community, a queer enclave weathering the collapse of civilization together, is described and brought to life through a worksheet. This process leads to questions, excited brainstorming, and impromptu fiction. Scenes emerge, characters gain depth, and plot arcs start to reveal themselves.

During scenes, players shift between a few different responsibilities: playing as their main character, playing as their setting element, and contributing to a vibrant story world overall.

Main characters have guidelines for how to play them, including something called moves. The story unfolds through those moves, with plot arcs leaping forward. The main characters work together, fall in love, fight, hurt one another, heal together, enact ill-advised plans, and all the rest.

The whole thing wraps up after about 3-4 hours, and everyone walks away − maybe grinning, maybe with tears in their eyes. Play is rarely done for an audience or a record. It's done just for the fleeting joy of itself.

THE FACILITATOR

One of the players will also act as a facilitator.

The facilitator is responsible for gathering supplies, teaching the game to new players, and guiding everyone through the setup process. They make sure things run smoothly. If you're reading this, chances are good you'll end up being the facilitator for your group.

If there are more than enough people, the facilitator may decide not to play at all, to just facilitate and nothing more. But the default assumption is that they'll be a player just like everyone else.

No Dice, No Masters

Some of you reading this will have a long history of roleplaying games under your belt. It's worth noting some of the ways that this game deviates from the norm, because some instincts developed in other games may lead you astray here.

This game is diceless, relying on a structured freeform system of choosing narrative prompts from a list. Play is driven by the choices that players make. It's not strictly competitive or cooperative, instead exploring the drama that wells up between the main characters and all around them. Players are encouraged to make authentic, interesting choices with a spirit of curiosity.

There's no Game Master or "MC" to guide the story and its outcomes, which also means that no one has prepared a story in advance for the characters to play out. You're creating all the fiction on the fly. Anyone can jump in and play a minor character or antagonist, whenever the scene demands it. Authority over the wider setting is divided into a series of six setting elements that are distributed around the table.

Play is a conversation, an exploration, and an experiment. It starts with a lot of discussion and curiosity, and evolves from there. You play to find out what happens next.

Gathering

When reaching out to people about playing Dream Askew, you'll need to pitch the game to them. Tell them a little bit about the setting and premise, and why you think they'll like it. Mention any difficult content you think they might want a heads-up about. New players are sometimes surprised by the amount of time it takes to play a roleplaying game, so make sure to clarify how long you expect it will take.

Dream Askew takes about 3-4 hours to set up and play, and is designed for 3-6 people total. It works best when played around a table, as there is some writing and shuffling of pages involved. Ambient noise can make it hard for some players to engage and immerse in the shared story, so finding a quiet space to play is best if possible.

Before getting together, print off a copy of the play kit (found at buriedwithoutceremony.com/dream-askew). The play kit contains: the overview, an enclave worksheet, six character roles, six setting elements, and a page or two of additional resources. In addition, gather the supplies listed below.

What You Need

- These rules
- A printed play kit
- Pencils or pens
- Index cards, or similar
- A central pile of tokens (around 5 per player)

Food and Comfort

The game takes 3-4 hours to play, demanding a lot of attention and creativity. Be generous and merciful to your friends by establishing a food plan together before you play, and ensuring that everyone is physically comfortable throughout.

If you're hosting the session at your house, consider cooking a meal for everyone. Eating together gives you a chance to catch up and bond, before clearing away plates and getting down to creative business. Cook a meal if you have the opportunity, so you can feed your gaming group and everyone you live with. If people ask what they can contribute, keep it simple: chips, drinks, little confections, or anything your group would like to snack on.

If you're playing somewhere else, especially in a public venue, bring some simple, no-fuss snacks to share with everyone. Some bananas or a box of granola bars can be a saving grace for anyone who forgot to eat before showing up.

Offer people water and make sure they know where the bathroom is. Let them know that you'll take stretch breaks regularly, and then remember to do so. Before play starts, give everyone an opportunity to name any accessibility needs they might have. Let people know that the game will involve reading aloud during setup, and check whether anyone would prefer to opt out of doing so.

The time you put into making sure that everyone is fed and comfortable will absolutely pay off and result in better play.

SAFETY

Dream Askew explores emotionally-fraught terrain. It's important to create a trusting atmosphere for play, and to introduce safety tools that people can use to express their boundaries.

This text offers a humble tool: *pause*. To use it during play, all someone needs to do is say the word "pause." The game will freeze, and the player will be given a chance to state their boundaries or needs. Play will proceed in a way that feels okay for everyone involved.

Pause puts the focus on the needs of whoever uses it. If that person wants the last thing that was narrated to be edited over with something else, with no explanation given other than "I'm not okay with that right now," that's fine. If they want to take a moment to explain how a particular scene hews close to their real-life trauma, before deciding that it's okay for it to continue playing out, that's fine too. Pause can lead to a directive like "I'm down for this storyline to continue unfolding, but I need everyone to agree that by the end of the session, Jackbird's betrayal will no longer be a secret." If ever two people have conflicting boundaries or needs, try your best to work out a solution.

A word of advice: don't use pause to attach a cost to narration in order to manipulate people into doing what you want, like saying "Okay, that can happen, but your character will suffer for it in this way." Don't try to penalize other players in the hopes that they'll stop doing something that bothers you. Just tell them what you want to have happen.

Pause is an agreement: if your trust or safety are jeopardized, the group will stop what they're doing and find out what you need. They'll work with you to the best of their ability. Pause isn't there so that we can make a rosy story where nothing bad happens; on the contrary, it allows us to take risks and play seriously, knowing that we have tools to work with if something goes awry.

If you'd prefer to use a different safety tool, perhaps one borrowed from other games you've played, do so! Build trust and safety around your table in whatever way makes the most sense for your group. No matter what tools you use, remember that they're there to supplement (not replace) what players already know about tending to their own boundaries and emotions.

Some groups find it useful to name boundaries upfront, before the first scene of the game. Maybe there's content that's likely to come up that you'd rather skip altogether, something which you'd find particularly upsetting or triggering. Talk it through.

Regardless of whether the group names boundaries upfront or not, continue to evaluate as you play. If someone looks distressed, you might want to call for a water break and check in with them. Be kind to one another.

If someone needs to bow out of the game midway through, give them your blessing and check up on them later.

ASKING AND CORRECTING

Dream Askew plays with contemporary queer archetypes, as well as a storm of possible gender identities (some rich with extant meaning and some void of it). Players will come to the table with different levels of familiarity and fluency. More tools are in order!

The first is simple: ***ask questions***. If you are unsure of a word, concept, or element of the setting, it's always okay to ask. Maybe someone can explain it, or the group can look it up, or even invent a meaning together.

The second is simple too: ***gentle corrections***. If someone makes a historical or cultural error that bothers you, it's always okay to quickly and gently correct it. For example, you could say:

"if I might, *two-spirit* is an indigenous term – one that speaks to both gender and sexuality within those communities."

Roleplaying can bring up strong emotions; how much more so, when we're playing with the history or future of a real-life marginalized group! Remember that everyone playing is being brave and making themselves vulnerable. If someone does correct or question you, be gracious and appreciative. If someone makes a mistake, be gracious and forgiving. We're all learning together.

EMERGENT TEACHING

As the facilitator, it is your job to teach everyone at the table how to play. There's no one right way to do that, because every player is going to come to the table with different learning needs. Some will be familiar with this style of roleplaying, and others won't. Some will be immediately comfortable embodying a character and making messy choices on their behalf, while others will need gentle coaching and reassurance. What follows are some guiding principles for how to teach emergently and responsively.

Teach the concepts and context players need to make their next decision, then take it from there. This creates a natural rhythm of learning and application, and it avoids overloading people. Keep explanations short and sweet.

Teach to the curiosity of the players, answering questions as they come up. Some groups will eagerly interrogate the structure of the game upfront, while others will be happy to take it as it comes.

Use examples. Make your explanations concrete and meaningful by expressing them through example scenarios.

Model it clearly through play. You'll be a player just like everyone else at the table, so you can demonstrate exactly what playing the dream looks like. Make obvious choices. The first time you do something, explain a little as you do it: *"Okay, clearly I need to react to this affront! I still don't have any tokens, so Tyrus can't really act from a place of strength. Maybe I should make a Weak Move, so I can set myself up for proper vengeance down the road. I choose: reveal your secret* *vulnerability to someone. I think what happens is this..."*

CREATE CHARACTERS

Start by reading aloud the "What is Dream Askew?" section at the beginning of this text.

Next, randomly distribute the six **Character Roles** between the players. Each of the roles is a crucial figure whose skills, challenges, and perspectives help shape the fate of their community. Some have a profession, while others eke out survival in the margins.

Going around in a circle, have everyone introduce the character roles they're holding by reading out the left-hand column. Once they've been read aloud, everyone picks which one they'll use to create their main character. Put away any that aren't chosen.

To create a character, go down the middle column of the sheet, circling as prompted. Encourage people to talk about their character as they go - weighing options, announcing choices, and fleshing out details about what they're imagining. You can turn to a search engine or fellow player with any remaining uncertainties, or make up your own definitions.

Some of the prompts are shared among all the character roles, like choosing a name. Others are unique, reflecting the distinctive skills and power, or problems and predicaments, that mark that character's place in their community.

You'll be prompted to choose two relationships. Your choices will reveal more about your character's life, but they'll also help to define the community around them. You can choose to flesh out the minor characters mentioned in these relationships right away, or leave those details to be discovered through play.

At the bottom of the column is a prompt to choose a question to ask of the person sitting to your left. Think about which question seems most interesting, but hold off choosing for now – these questions will come up later, when you are filling in the enclave worksheet.

Once everyone is finished, go around the circle and introduce your characters. To introduce your character, talk about what choices you circled for your character, adding in whatever details or explanations feel exciting to share. If you talked about your choices as you were circling them earlier, it's still great to repeat that information now that you have the undivided attention of the group. Answer any questions that pop up. Make sure to read aloud your Lure, since the other players will need to know what it is in order to play into it.

Give everyone an index card, folded into a tent. Have them write their character's name, pronouns, and role on it for everyone else to see. If space permits, they can also copy out their character's Lure. If you don't have index cards on hand, improvise!

Carly, Ian, and Ramon sit down to play Dream Askew together. They settle on character roles, and circle their choices.

CARLY: *"Okay, name is* Cookie. *I'm an old* Hawker, *and I run a rough-and-tumble boarding house. I've got an* honest face *and* tattooed hands. *I rock a mixture of* scrounge-ups *and* gold chains. *I'm a* dagger daddy, *which I'm imagining like: if Danny Trejo was really into giving hugs and feeding people. Anyway, my boarding house is a sprawling old building with thirty cramped bedrooms, none of them legal. I offer* lodgings, *easy food, and* body-guarding. *I accept* lingering debts *and* fawning adoration *as payment. My relationships are with* the pissy killjoy next door, *and* the loan-shark who finally tracked me down.*"

IAN: *"Me next! My name's* Impala, *they/them pronouns. I have a* masked face, slender arms, *and* gargoyle gender. *My wardrobe is a mix of* breathable athletics *and* black bloc attire. *Here's what I'm picturing: DIY parkour batman. Me and my gang are masked vigilantes who duck and weave through the city, evading gangs and whatever police remain. We run blockades and fuck shit up, kitted out with* baseball bats, slingshots, *and* riot gear − *I'm imagining bulletproof vests and utility* belts as part of our costume. We're supposed to have a commitment to non-lethal tactics, but my hungry-for-blood younger sibling *recently killed someone.* Since that unsettling murder, I've lost some trust; *people are saying it's my fault for not keeping them on a tighter leash. My other relationship is with* the aging dyke who cooks me dinner sometimes."

CARLY: "Oh, hm. Is the pissy killjoy who lives next door to me the same person as the aging dyke who cooks you dinner?"

IAN: "I like that! Maybe I see her as a generous elder with so many valuable stories to tell, whereas you mostly just experience her as a nuisance who's always griping about your business."

CARLY: "Perfect. Yes. The boarding house is a pretty raucous place on a good night, so I can imagine having tense relationships with lots of neighbours."

Ramon introduces his character next: a Torch *by the name of* Rabbit. *He's a radical faerie who tends the community garden and oversees the enclave's many festivals.*

SHARE THE SETTING

Randomly distribute the six **Setting Elements** between the players. Going around in a circle, have everyone introduce the setting elements they're holding by reading out the title and italicized flavour text. Just like with the character roles, it doesn't matter who introduces which ones. Once they've been read aloud, everyone picks which one they'll play. Put the ones that weren't chosen in the centre of the table; they're still part of the game.

To flesh out a setting element, circle two things it desires from the list. What it means for a setting element to desire something is determined moment-to-moment during play. It might be expressed through the ambitions of minor characters or through strange developments in the landscape. Have everyone announce their choices.

Ask everyone to familiarize themselves with the "Pick Up When" and "Trade Away When" prompts on their setting element. Explain that throughout play it's likely that setting elements will trade hands and be played by different people. The core idea for many of the "Trade Away When" prompts is that you don't want to have to play both sides of a conversation; when your character is the one facing the challenge of a particular setting element, someone else should be responsible for playing that part of the setting.

Create Your Community

It is community that ties our individual characters together and situates them within the wider setting. Both dreams are about a marginalized group of people maintaining their own community, just beyond the borders of a dominant culture. The enclave and the shtetl are built on uncertain ground, rife with potential but also risk. What else is true of them?

As a group, go down the left-hand column of the **Enclave Worksheet**, circling as prompted. Make the decisions collaboratively. If you get stuck, talk it through and look for compromises. Aim to set up a community that has something interesting for everyone.

You'll start by circling a set of visuals that define the landscape and vibe of your community. You'll then circle three ideological or material forces that are in conflict with each other - a situation with no simple answers or stable solutions. As you circle things, talk about them and flesh them out. Discuss the scale of the conflict: is this a petty squabble between neighbours, or an entire town divided by rival ideologies?

Expect that by the time you've filled out the left-hand column of the enclave worksheet, you'll be 50-60 minutes into your session (not including any meals shared together).

Carly, Ian, and Ramon turn their attention to the Enclave Worksheet. Their character concepts have already implied a few things about the immediate landscape, and they settle on 3-5 visuals quickly: a bustling market, glass + concrete, overgrowth, community gardens, and blockades. It's a busy, fragmented city. Police try desperately to keep riff-raff out of functional neighbourhoods, vines and trees choke out the freeways and suburbs, and everywhere people are re-purposing buildings, parks, and public spaces.

RAMON: *What three things are in conflict in the enclave? I'm drawn to food justice, personally. I imagine that Rabbit sees feeding people as important spiritual work.*

IAN: *That's cool – maybe that's also part of what my gang does, liberating hoarded food from supermarkets and private storehouses. Like Robin Hood, but for canned goods.*

CARLY: *Food justice it is! But I imagine that would pull a lot of unfamiliar faces into our community, and Cookie probably doesn't screen people very carefully before putting them up in the boarding house. Maybe that worries some people, who wish we were more careful about our boundaries and borders.* Scarcity thinking?

RAMON: *That sounds more like the* need for purity *to me.*

CARLY: *Oh, yeah, good point. Okay, food justice is in conflict with the need for purity. What's our third point in this triangle?*

IAN: *Well, we already know that Impala's gang is stuck on the issue of murder and violence. Maybe the* use of violence *is our third point?*

CARLY: *I can totally see it... but it also means our community is constantly embroiled in really serious conversations, and I wonder if it'd be better to choose something with a bit more levity?*

RAMON: *Rabbit is always organizing esoteric festivals, community feasts, and sacred orgies. Maybe* party culture *could be the third one?*

IAN: *Oh, that's cool. What if: Impala is always liberating food with this idea that it'll be rationed and redistributed, but then Rabbit ends up throwing big parties where it gets eaten overnight.*

RAMON: *I love it. And obviously the parties pull in strangers from all over, which freaks out the people who worry about protecting our borders.*

CARLY: *It sounds like we've got our triangle: food justice, party culture, and the need for purity. Let's start drawing stuff onto the map.*

FOLLOW YOUR CURIOSITY

As everyone defines the community, use the remainder of the worksheet to start sketching a map. Everyone can draw, though one person emerging as the *de facto* cartographer is fine too. Leave lots of empty space to fill in during play. Talk about where people sleep, where they get their drinking water from, where they seek quiet moments of reflection or prayer, and more.

As the map is being sketched and the community is being fleshed out, you enter into a mode of play called **Idle Dreaming**. This is a time for questions and curiosity, for tangents and musings. Talk about whatever is interesting, or unknown, or scary, or beautiful about this place that you're building together. Make up details about the landscape, its history, and its residents. Setup becomes play, one flowing directly into the next.

To get you started in the process of idle dreaming, each character role contains a short list of questions to ask to person to your left, located at the bottom of the middle column. Answers can be short and simple, or lead into conversations of their own. In the process of asking and answering, you may find yourselves eager to plunge into a scene. Go for it!

With everyone asking questions and excitedly contributing their vision, scene ideas will soon emerge. Maybe something seems especially poignant. Maybe the answer to a question is clouded by uncertainty, or it just feels too big to make an arbitrary decision about. Maybe two players are figuring out why their characters recently broke up, and it's like: *hey, this should totally be a scene. I want to witness this happening in real time. Maybe it happened by the river?*

Idle dreaming stokes curiosity and excitement, and that leads into scenes. If ever a scene concludes and there's uncertainty about what might happen next, it's always fine to return to idle dreaming until a compelling answer rears its head and demands attention. With that said, it's common that once the first scene emerges, the session quickly builds momentum and never returns to that starting place of idle dreaming.

RAMON: *Now seems like a good time to ask Rabbit's question to the left. Impala, why did we break up?*

IAN: *Oh, what? We were dating?*

RAMON: *Seems like it, if that's cool with you!*

IAN: *Yeah, it's great. Let's see... I think we initially bonded over the fact that we're both providers for our community, and that's how we started dating. But over time, I got more and more frustrated with how it seemed like you were always squandering whatever bounty I brought in: food from the raids, yeah, but eventually I started seeing that dynamic everywhere in our relationship.*

RAMON: *Into it. I feel like Rabbit's the sort of person who is really generous in lots of ways, but entirely clueless to the ways that he's selfish or overbearing.*

CARLY: *Did it come as a total surprise then, when Impala dumped you?*

IAN: *I feel like this should be a scene! Impala dumping Rabbit.*

RAMON: *Ooh, definitely. How about it takes place in Rabbit's
                  dinner tent? He's placing a bowl of cucumber-nettle salad
                  in front of you, with a roast squirrel skewer alongside it.*

IAN: *Rabbit's always making these sort of gestures, whenever
                  we're alone together. Which makes it all the more difficult
                  to say what I feel needs to be said: "Rabbit, listen. We
                  need to talk."*

SCENES

The first scene emerges from idle dreaming, when curiosity
and excitement lead to a situation that people want to dive into
and explore. Scenes can start with a line of dialogue, with a
description of a cellar stuffed with old potatoes and garlic braids,
with action - whatever feels right. But as the scene unfolds,
make sure details emerge. Where is this taking place? Who's in
the middle of the action, and who's quietly watching on? What
smells waft over from nearby kitchens? Is someone fiddling? Is it
early evening, and have the clouds finally parted to make way for
sunset?

Scenes might take anywhere from two minutes to twenty.
Some scenes will revolve around a conflict, and others won't.
They might stand alone or flow organically into one another.
They end when it feels right for them to end.

If a scene ends and it's not immediately clear what the next
scene will be, you can always return to idle dreaming. Follow
your curiosity. If there are still questions to be asked to the left,
give people a chance to ask them. Scenes will soon emerge again.

RAMON: *Rabbit bunches up his flowing skirts in order to kneel
                  down next to Impala. He's getting older, and so his
                  motions are a little bit slower as he lowers himself down.*

IAN: *Hm. I think watching Rabbit struggle a little bit with
                  that movement reminds Impala about how they're just*

really different people. Not only in terms of their age gap, but also how they participate in community. Impala's world is all rooftops and break-ins, risk and passion. Rabbit is slower, plodding even. They share a community but live in different worlds.

RAMON: "What is it, my sparrow?"

IAN: *Impala stares down at their food for a long time, bites into the squirrel meat to buy a few more seconds to think over their words. "I... want someone who can go with me, wherever I'm going."*

RAMON: *Rabbit nods, but clearly doesn't grasp what it is you're trying to say.*

IAN: "I want someone who can go with me where I go. I want to feel like, when I'm out in the world and I'm heading into danger, I've got my whole heart present in one place."

RAMON: *Rabbit's heart sinks, realizing that he's being dumped. And then it sinks again, realizing that Impala is trying to spare his feelings in the process. "You don't have to try to make it sound pretty, Impala. That's not how you talk."*

IAN: *Impala stares down at their salad. "I want to break up with you."*

RAMON: *Rabbit stifles a whimper, before rising to his feet and moving toward the kitchen. He comes back with another bowl of salad and squirrel meat, and joins Impala at the low table.*

IAN: *And the two of them eat in total silence —*

RAMON: *Wash the dishes in total silence —*

IAN: *And part ways without saying another word.*

It's fine to narrate in first person or third. Describe your character's appearance and mannerisms, narrate their actions, and speak their words. Play to find out who they are and what they do next.

Each character role comes with a set of three tips. These tips can help guide players in how they play their characters.

Everyone at the table also shares in the responsibility of narrating the world around these main characters. Describe the smell of mildew in an old cabin, the strange beasts prowling in the woods, and the roaring of engines in the distance. Narrate what minor characters say and do. Introduce conflicts and obstacles. Twist the plot in new directions.

As you play, pay attention to whether everyone is being given equal space to talk and contribute. If you notice one or two voices taking over the conversation, you can shift the spotlight by asking questions of the players who've been quieter. Sometimes a question like "Okay, so Monique has been there in the shadows, watching this argument go down... what's going through her head?" can change the dynamic and make sure everyone is included. That said, some players prefer being a little more quiet; make sure everyone is being given equal opportunity, but don't demand that everyone make equal contributions.

Customarily, players will speak their character's words and embody some of their affect and gestures, but their actions will simply be described while the player remains seated. Players don't touch one another, even if they're describing how a character grabs another by the shoulder or tenderly strokes their wrist. If you want to play by different customs, discuss it as a group and figure out where people's boundaries are.

Distraught, Rabbit eventually finds himself at Cookie's place, drinking homemade bourbon out of a grimy jar. It's gotten late, and they've managed to talk about everything other than Impala. They're sitting on the boarding house porch, and the streets are now so quiet and empty that their voices are echoing off nearby buildings.

RAMON: *Rabbit is starting to trail off more and more, getting distracted by the moon, or the wispy fog starting to roll into the street.*

CARLY: *Cookie is starting to feel the weight of the day on his eyelids, but feels like he hasn't yet done enough. He hesitates before offering awkwardly, "So, you want to talk about it?"*

RAMON: *Rabbit swallows, and turns toward Cookie. He's suddenly got this really weepy expression on his face. "Are you sure? I mean, it's late. I don't need to burden you."*

Carly isn't sure what Cookie would say in this moment. Was he the sort to ask twice, to try and coax hard feelings out of people? Or would he take the easy out, and let Rabbit come to him in his own time? What sort of dagger daddy was he? Looking at the three tips for playing the Hawker, foolishly overextend yourself from time to time *jumps out.*

CARLY: *Cookie reaches an arm around Rabbit, pulling him in slightly. They're about the same age, and even the same height, but they're built so differently that Rabbit still manages to become tiny in Cookie's arms. "You know papa's here for you. Go on now." He's already so sleepy, but he feels like he still needs to give more to Rabbit.*

RAMON: *With that, the floodgates open. Rabbit starts sobbing, tripping over his own words, sputtering questions without pausing for the answers. It goes on for hours.*

CARLY: *And increasingly, Cookie is falling asleep. He's cradling Rabbit, running fingers through his hair, but he's slowly nodding off. Eventually his "mhmm, ...mhmm" turns into gentle snoring, and his head slumps down to rest on the back of Rabbit's neck.*

RAMON: *Not knowing what else to do, I think Rabbit just keeps on talking to himself, listening to his own sad words echoing across the street until dawn breaks.*

Making Moves

Whenever your character takes action, that's you making a **Move**. Moves are how the story unfolds. By default, a lot of the moves you make are "take action, leaving yourself vulnerable." But any time you're called upon to act, you can look at your list of moves and choose a different one to inspire your narration.

Making a move means taking the prompt and running with it, letting it guide what you say next and how you play your character. The move might point toward an outcome, but know that what happens next may still surprise you. You don't always need to announce the move by name, but sometimes it can be helpful to do so, because it will help ensure that all the players are on the same page.

When you make a **Weak Move**, you gain a token. Weak Moves show us your character's vulnerability, folly, or even just plain rotten luck. But they also earn that token, setting you up to shine in future moments.

In order to make a **Strong Move**, you need to spend a token. Strong Moves are the moments when your character's skill, power, astute planning, or good luck come to bear and transform a situation. When you see a player make a Strong Move, honour the significance of that moment and play to their success.

You start the game with zero tokens.

Some moves on each list are italicized questions. While they're questions about the characters and the story, they're always asked from one player to another, with an honest answer given in response (even if their character remains cagey about it). The answer is knowledge that your character deduces, intuits, or manages to get out of someone through conversation.

Why Tokens?

The tokens create a narrative rhythm by ensuring that characters experience complications, stumbling blocks, and mistakes made as they work toward their victories and accomplishments.

Tokens also help players coordinate expectations about what efforts will end up being successful, whether risky undertakings will succeed or fail, and what consequences will emerge from an action. If a player reaches into the centre of the table as they describe their character's next move, the group knows that this is a moment of weakness or miscalculation. Everyone is on the same page: this would be a fine time for things to go awry. If a player spends a token, it sends a different message: let this character have a moment of glory, they've certainly earned it.

It's the night of an important harvest festival. Rabbit's followers have spent all day in the gardens, harvesting the bounty of the enclave. Meanwhile, Rabbit has been at the bonfire, carrying out an important ritual: boiling the bones, *a sacred protocol for cooking any animal larger than rodents or fowl. The community gathers, and Rabbit announces the proceedings.*

RAMON: *"And finally, to grace our meal, adding to the bounty of our gardens, I unveil to you a cauldron of coyote and fox." But when he steps toward the heat of the embers and lifts the cast-iron lid of the cauldron, a nasty smell wafts out. Maybe the meat was putrid to begin with, maybe it just never got hot enough while cooking. I'm taking a token here, because this is a weak move:* botch a ritual, exposing yourself to risk or ridicule.

Crestfallen and embarrassed, Rabbit explains that the enclave will not, in fact, be dining on coyote and fox this evening. Scorn and snickering ensue, but eventually the party continues.

Later that night, Impala tracks down Rabbit amidst the revelry. They're carrying their sibling, bloody and half-conscious.

IAN: *"Please, Rabbit babe. I don't know what happened. We were running a raid on Buy-More. I went in through a window, they were supposed to stick to the cargo bay. Then all of a sudden there's gunshots. I don't know. I don't know what happened. Please." Impala starts talking in cycles and circles.*

RAMON: *Rabbit gestures toward the grassy patch on the meridian,
          and says, "it's okay, my sparrow." Even though you
          just dumped Rabbit, he still speaks to you in a familiar,
          intimate sort of way. But it's quiet, almost a whisper.
          What's your sibling's name?*

IAN: *We haven't established that yet. Let's say it's Riley.*

RAMON: *Rabbit kneels by Riley, pulling their scarf and satchel
          strap out of the way to get a better look at the wound.
          Two shots, striking the collarbone and shoulder? Does that
          sound like what you were imagining?*

IAN: *Yeah. That sounds good. Impala winces at the sight of
          the wound. "It's bad, isn't it?"*

CARLY: *I want to suggest that Riley is breathing shallow,
          trembling and shaking periodically. They don't seem like
          they're doing well.*

RAMON: *"Impala, is there anything that you want to say to
          Riley?"*

IAN: *"What? What do you mean?" But even as the words
          tumble out of their mouth, Impala knows. Their sibling
          isn't going to make it, are they?*

RAMON: *I'm going to spend my one remaining token, to make a
          strong move:* soothe someone's pain or duress.
          *Rabbit leans forward, pressing his forehead to Riley's.
          And suddenly, with that gentle-yet-solid touch, Riley's
          trembling stills. They breathe steadily − long, smooth
          breaths that actually bring air into their lungs. The pain
          is gone for a moment.*

IAN: *"You were brave, kid." That's all Riley would have*

> *wanted to hear, and it's all Impala can manage to get out anyway.*

RAMON: *And with that, Rabbit lifts his head back up. He rises to his feet. Riley is absolutely still. It's over.*

PLAYING SETTING ELEMENTS

Both dreams carve their setting into six elements, which are distributed around the table. Everyone is responsible for one of the setting elements at a given time, though the elements may shift hands as play proceeds.

Each setting element has a prompt for when to pick it up and actively play it. This signals that it's time to prioritize narrating on behalf of the setting element, rather than your main character. For example, you pick up The Earth Itself whenever you want to describe weather, mutation, beasts, or the natural world.

Each setting element has a prompt for when to trade it away. You can also choose to trade it away any time the demands of playing your main character are in conflict with the demands of playing the setting element. If there are spare setting elements in the centre of the table, you may trade your element with one of those. Otherwise, choose another player and trade elements with them directly. You should always have exactly one setting element in front of you.

When you're actively playing a setting element, use its tips to guide what you imagine and narrate. The third tip is always the same: ask compelling questions and build on the answers that others give. That's because world-building in these games is a collaborative process, and it gains power from curiosity and conversation.

Setting elements have moves – prompts which can inspire your narration – just like with characters. None of the moves involve tokens. Setting elements don't gain or spend tokens.

Impala's crew jacked an armoured grocery truck, while it was idling at a fuel stop. They've driven it to a quiet spot, but know there isn't much time before the cops get to them. They need to liberate its contents, fast.

IAN: *Okay, Impala goes around to the back of the vehicle. I'm imagining that it's locked down and secured in some way though, right?*

CARLY: *I'm holding the Varied Scarcities, maybe I can jump in here? I'm imagining that grocery-jacking is a common issue once we start hitting peak scarcity, and so these trucks are kitted out with multiple security features. They can only unlock in registered cargo bays, and they require the driver's fingerprint signature to do so. Have you done this before? Do you have a plan for how to get in?*

IAN: *Nope. This was an impulse job. Impala is scrambling for a solution here.*

RAMON: *I'm going to step in and play one of your gang here: Thumper, this scrawny butch who carries a rusty pipe everywhere she goes. She's wearing an oil-stained tank underneath black overalls. "We have to smash our way in."*

IAN: *"That'll never work. These things are built to survive artillery. Our best shot is to try and crack the security." I think Impala carries around some disruption tech, but they don't have a lot of practice using it.*

CARLY: *It says to pick up the Digital Realm whenever* "someone interacts with a digital device, or you have an idea about how digitization shaped this environment" *— that certainly seems to apply here.*

The Digital Realm is sitting in the centre of the table, and Carly swaps it with the Varied Scarcities currently in front of her. This is the first time that someone has touched the Digital Realm, and so Carly has to circle its two desires. She settles on expanded networks *and* trafficked secrets.

CARLY: *Okay, here's the deal: overriding the security measures is possible, but to do it you have to upload your own fingerprint scans. Which means they'll have your fingerprints on file, giving them a solid lead on tracking you down. And it'll be down to the wire on whether you can pull it off before the cops show up. Are you going to risk it?*

IAN: *Absolutely. Impala pulls out a small toolkit out of their backpack. I'm imagining it's just a paper bag that's rubber-banded shut, but inside it are a few devices that'll theoretically help them do this.*

MAKING TROUBLE

What kind of story will you tell together? Will it be a story of camaraderie and growth in the face of hard times, of paranoid in-fighting as community crumbles, of grand upheaval? Dream Askew requires that you play to find out, approaching each scene with curiosity and seeing where it goes.

Along the way, make trouble. Make trouble by playing your character as fallible and relatable. Make trouble by introducing minor characters with incompatible needs. Make trouble by picking up your setting element and throwing in an unexpected circumstance, just to see what the rest of the table will do with it.

Why trouble? Trouble because adversity gives the characters a chance to prove themselves, to come up with makeshift solutions and use their peculiar gifts. Trouble because it creates dynamic tempo in our stories. Trouble because it's fun.

Your goal isn't to cause suffering, especially not for the people sitting around the table. It's to explore how marginalized folks build strange and powerful community together, and what they do when that community is threatened. The characters might suffer sometimes, yes, and cause each other suffering, but the goal of making trouble is ultimately to see how people rise to meet it.

Your Lure

Each of the main characters has a Lure. Lures prompt others to set your character up to really shine, playing to their strengths and goals. For example, the Torch has the following Lure: *whenever someone participates in one of your rituals for the first time, they gain a token.* This helps create a dynamic of leadership and weirdness between the Torch and the rest of the community.

When someone follows the prompt of your Lure, they gain a token. That token is taken from the center of the table, not from you personally.

Minor characters don't have a Lure, and they can't gain tokens from interacting with yours. Tokens are for main characters only.

Minor Characters

Each player has a main character under their control, but those are far from the only people in the world. Minor characters will appear frequently, many of them springing from relationships chosen during character creation. Some minor characters may even end up becoming an integral, ongoing part of the story being told.

Whenever a minor character comes up in the story, anyone can step in to play them. Just say, "I'll play Bramble during this scene!" If a minor character is obviously tied to a setting element, whoever holds that element can play them. Shuffle who's playing which minor characters whenever it makes sense; avoid having a single player narrating both sides of a conversation.

Minor characters don't have a sheet to guide their play. They don't have a Lure. They don't have any moves of their own, though they may end up becoming the means by which you make your setting element's moves. Minor characters don't gain or spend tokens.

When playing a minor character, trust your intuition and say what comes naturally. Remember to keep the story focused on the main characters, at least most of the time.

Minor characters might include children running through the enclave, old lesbian farmers who keep the community fed, drifters, marauders, members of the outlying gangs or the society intact, mutants being harbored in back rooms, nihilistic revelers, traveling storytellers, or nervous youngsters who ran away from home and showed up hungry.

WRAPPING UP

Throughout the session, scenes will generate loose threads and compelling drama. As some of it gets reincorporated and explored further, major themes will emerge in your story. Often, everything will start to point toward a cluster of overlapping conflicts. The best sessions are the ones that hit upon a satisfying yet messy sense of resolution right around the 3-4 hour mark. Players can even angle toward this kind of outcome, by glancing at the clock occasionally and adjusting the tempo of their scenes and how much trouble they're making.

Some groups will agree on a specific end time before they start playing. If the session seems to be gearing up for a grand finale, leave yourself a good thirty minutes to explore it. It's sometimes surprising how long that final scene can take, and players may want some time for denouement or epilogue afterwards.

Don't try to tie up every loose thread. Leave some chaos and unanswered questions scattered about the story.

FUTURE SESSIONS

If the group wants to, you can make a plan to meet back up and play a sequel session, continuing the story of your community and its struggle. Ask everyone to record the number of tokens they ended the session with somewhere on their character sheet. Save all the play kit materials and name tents in a safe place. If you have time, make a few notes about what happened during the session.

When you get together to play again, hand everyone back their character sheets and ask them to pick a setting element. Share your recollections about what happened last time, and let this flow into idle dreaming about how things progress from there. Ask questions and talk excitedly until a scene emerges. Play to find out what happens next.

The Next Generation

If you're excited to return to the community you've made together, another option is to skip forward in time and play as the next generation or wave of community members. The possibilities are going to depend on what sort of queer community you made together. Were many people raising children? Were leadership roles well defined and supported in the community? Were waves of new arrivals showing up every day? Let your next batch of characters spring forward from the community context.

As a group, look over the enclave worksheet and talk about how the community has changed since the last session. Decide together whether you want to re-do the whole worksheet from scratch, or simply modify the map to reflect ways that the community has adapted over time. Print off new character role and setting element sheets, and fill them in from scratch. Play to find out how things have changed and where they're heading next.

Carly, Ian, and Ramon play two sessions with their enclave. Cookie takes on an assistant to help run the boarding house, a fiery trans girl named Eliza. Impala breaks their leg jumping from a rooftop, and cedes leadership of the gang to Thumper. Rabbit begins manifesting strange psychic powers. Everyone is delighted with where the story has gone, but they want to shake things up a bit. They decide that they'll play one final session, set four years ahead in the future.

CARLY: *I'd love to play Eliza for this session. I think she's taken over the boarding house at this point, and is starting to use it as a base of operations for a community defence project. Cookie's out of the picture; he drifted out of town a few years ago.*

IAN: *Eliza and Thumper have emerged as such fierce figures in the community. Are they working together on this?*

CARLY:	*Oh, what if they're in love with each other? And while they've only been dating for a few months, it's had this really transformative effect on the work that they do, and now Thumper's moved her whole crew into the boarding house?*
IAN:	*I love it. I don't think that I'm going to play Thumper, though. Impala was really action-oriented, and I want to switch it up a bit and play someone different.*
RAMON:	*Is it cool if I play Thumper, then? I just love her so much.*
IAN:	*Absolutely! I'm imagining Eliza is going to be another Hawker, and Thumper is a Tiger? I think I'm going to make up an Arrival. Every year, the crackdowns and blockades in the Society Intact are getting more severe, and people keep getting edged out. And so I'm going to play a young man named Jordan, who shows up here because he's not sure where else to go. He doesn't want to go in with bikers or sewer rats, and we're the only other group he knows about.*

GENDERS OF THE APOCALYPSE

Creating a character in Dream Askew involves contending with gender, but it's a gender exploded, extracted from the society intact and made mutant. What do some of these words even mean?

Some carry storied legacies from the real world, already infused with meaning – femme, androgyne, genderfluid, and others. A few are tied to racial community, positioning a character intersectionally, like two-spirit and stud.

Others are genders of the apocalypse. Ice femme and dagger daddy take existing queer identities and recast them in ways the real world has yet to experience. Gargoyle and raven emerge entirely new.

When you encounter a gender word, imagine. Ask your fellow

players. Flirt with a search engine. If nothing comes up, invent. No matter how you come to your initial understanding, it's yours to continue to define through play.

How Things Break

Electricity requires upkeep. Without human intervention, a coal plant would likely go down in less than a day, and a hydroelectric dam in less than a fortnight. Failures anywhere in the grid can have far-reaching effects, potentially pulling the whole thing down. Private, off-grid power systems require knowledge and upkeep too, and parts will degrade over time.

Gasoline goes stale quick. Depending on oxygen exposure, temperature stability, container material, and whether there is an added fuel stabilizer, that time can vary from one month to a few years. You can't siphon usable gas out of a car that's been abandoned on the side of the road since last year.

Paved roads will last a few decades before breaking down to the point of being treacherous or impassable for cars. The exact timeline depends on weather, use, and the earth itself.

The amount of time it takes for **industrially-canned foods** to degrade depends upon the integrity of the container. While best before dates expire within a few years, the food inside can remain edible across many decades, though colour, texture, and flavour will degrade. Once the can becomes compromised or dented, however, oxygen and bacteria quickly invade and make the contents unsafe.

Dried foods can last a lifetime if kept in a cool, dry environment safe from oxygen and life, though their nutrients will slowly degrade over decades.

When things break down, how does your community react to their varied scarcities? Do they go without, broker uncomfortable deals with profiteers from the society intact, make their own from scratch, scavenge, or something else entirely? How do they prove themselves to be resourceful?

Dream Askew was directly inspired by *Apocalypse World*, by D. Vincent Baker and Meguey Baker. Apocalypse World is about sexy badasses who have complicated histories with one another, trying to figure out how to live after the collapse. A psychic maelstrom whirls just outside their perception. Dream Askew started as a remix of Apocalypse World, and slowly took its own shape.

There are two books which together perfectly capture the spirit of Dream Askew: *Station Eleven*, a post-apocalyptic novel which remains intimately human in scale, about what it means to build culture up out of the rubble, about how we never really escape one another's legacies; and *Black Wave*, about what it means to be queer and heartbroken when the world is crumbling all around you, about how break-ups and apocalypse aren't dissimilar.

The movies that most inspired Dream Askew are the works of Gregg Araki. His carousel of irreverent, cynical, campy, satirical, and at times painfully earnest storytelling has always hit me really hard and been super thought-provoking. I watched the Teen Apocalypse trilogy as I was figuring out my own sexuality and identity, and *Nowhere* and *The Doom Generation* are both inspirations. 2010's *Kaboom!* is another on the list, a movie about how it takes more than a mystery cult and overwhelming existential dread to keep college students from acting dumb and horny.

The game is also inspired by fiery, radical, queer community-building in the real world. I'm looking to groups like *STAR*, *Radical Faeries*, *Gay Shame*, the *Bash Back!* network, and *The Degenderettes*.

Dream Askew frames the apocalypse as a perpetual process, and the queer enclave as a contemporary artifact, and that's because it's a truth about the world as far as I understand it. The AIDS crisis was a queer apocalypse, with enclaves formed – and obliterated – as a result of it. That's not the first or only time. From Radical Faerie communes to post-war dockside communities struggling to keep alive the queer connections people found in the service, from STAR House to tentatively-staked gayborhoods everywhere, the enclave is more than just a speculative device. We are constantly falling outside of the society intact. And so while Dream Askew is a work of strange fiction, it's also a reflection on what precarity means for actual queer people.

Mediography

Movies: Kaboom!. Pride. Mouth-to-Mouth. How to Survive a Plague. Nowhere. Beats Per Minute. Pose.

Books: Station Eleven (Emily St. John Mandel). Black Wave (Michelle Tea). The Dispossessed (Ursula K. LeGuin). Year of the Flood (Margaret Atwood). The Marrow Thieves (Cherie Dimaline). Emergent Strategy (adrienne maree brown).

Games: Apocalypse World. Queers in Love at the End of the World. Who We Are Now. The Next World Tarot.

Design Notes

I first wrote Dream Askew in 2013. There was a handful of pages to explain the game, and plenty of open space to figure it out yourself. Returning to the design and continuing to develop it four years later has been wild.

The biggest difference about Dream Askew now is that the world around it has changed. Or maybe it's just that I'm less sheltered, having watched more of my community fall out of the society intact. It doesn't feel as speculative any more.

In 2013, I waffled on whether it made sense to include the digital realm as a setting element. Since then? Dear friends have suffered through years of Gamergate harassment. Doxxing and swatting have become familiar terms. Meme-fueled hashtag nazis have broken electoral systems. Silicon Valley has used the language of disruption to digitize and exploit our relationship to food, romance, travel, and neighbourhood. We now know that the digital realm factors into the collapse, and that it won't go away quietly.

Dream Askew feels more timely and relevant every day. These are the stories I want to be telling with my friends. And it's because they're stories about the collapse of civilization that don't wallow in suffering, terror, and militarization. They're about figuring out what comes next if we work together. About making community even when we're all sick, crazy, and afraid of each other. About finding abundance in the rubble. About playing to find out what happens next, in a fictional world but also in our own.

ACKNOWLEDGEMENTS
dave ring

So much gratitude to everyone who helped bring *Glitter +
Ashes: Queer Tales of a World That Wouldn't Die* into this challenging
reality.

That starts with the folks who backed and amplified the
kickstarter. Putting together projects like this require more capital
that a brand new small press has lying around, and getting that
financial support from backers was a gamechanger. Thanks as
well to the folks who signed up for Club Serpentine, and didn't
know what they might be in for!

To the contributors who signed up from jump: Christopher
Caldwell-Kelly, Cherae Clark, Marianne Kirby, Jordan Kurella,
LeKesha Lewis, and Brendan Williams-Childs. Doubly so to
Marianne, who tolerated all manner of other questions and
provided innumerable thoughtful suggestions. To Molly, for
sharing her thoughts on many of the early stories to come in. To
Charles Payseur, for hosting a post-apocalyptic conversation at
Quick Sip Reviews.

To the writers who added their voices to discussions on
Twitter about queer community and disability in the apocalypse:
R J Theodore, Nibedita Sen, Andi C. Buchanan, Christopher
Caldwell-Kelly, Morgan Swim, Juliet Kemp, Ada Hoffman, V.
Medina, and Jordan Kurella.

To Avery Alder, who graciously allowed me to include her game *Dream Askew* in these pages. Time and again, I'm struck by Avery's reminder that there are folks experiencing collapse *now*, every day, even before the world experienced a global pandemic. I hope those of you who haven't played a tabletop game before will consider telling stories together through Avery's beautiful system.

To Grace, for your stunning cover. I'm so grateful for the thought and detail you put into every aspect of it. I'll confess, I've never been drawn to rainbow flags, but the tattered colors you hung over this ragged crew speak to me.

To Michael and Ian and the Mason Jar Press crew. I'd never be here without *Broken Metropolis*.

To Bobby, always.

And to all the other friends, family, and queers in the pub who cheered me on along the way.

ABOUT

Saida Agostini is a queer Afro-Guyanese poet whose work explores the ways that Black folks harness mythology to enter the fantastic. Saida's poetry can be found in *Barrelhouse Magazine*, the Black Ladies Brunch Collective's anthology, *Not Without Our Laughter,* and her first collection, *just let the dead in.* Saida is a Cave Canem Graduate Fellow and has been awarded honors and support for her work by the Watering Hole and Blue Mountain Center, as well as a 2018 Rubys Grant.

Avery Alder is a queer roleplaying game designer hailing from Sinixt territory. She's the designer of Monsterhearts, The Quiet Year, Dream Askew, Ribbon Drive, and a host of smaller, scrappier projects. Avery's work blends facilitation, design, and play—bringing keen curiosity and visionary imagination to how we create together. In her design and play, she gravitates toward the moody, the personal, and the transformative.

Elly Bangs is a queer trans woman who was raised in a new-age cult, had six wisdom teeth, and once rode her bicycle alone from Seattle to the Panama Canal. Her short fiction has appeared in *Clarkesworld Magazine, Beneath Ceasless Skies, Escape Pod, Fireside Quarterly*, and elsewhere -- and her debut apocalyptic cyberpunk novel, *Unity*, comes out in Spring 2021. She's a 2017 graduate of Clarion West.

Phoebe Barton is a queer trans science fiction writer. Her short fiction has appeared in venues such as *Analog, On Spec,* and *Kaleidotrope*, and anthologies from Bundoran Press and Alliteration Ink. She serves as an Associate Editor at *Escape Pod*, and is a 2019 graduate of the Clarion West Writers Workshop. She lives with a robot in the sky above Toronto. You can connect with her on Twitter at @aphoebebarton or her website www.phoebebartonsf.com.

Christopher Caldwell is a queer, Black American living abroad in Glasgow, Scotland. His work has appeared in *Strange Horizons*, *FIYAH*, and *Uncanny Magazine*. He is @seraph76 on twitter.

Josie Columbus is a trans woman who strives to use her writing to normalize and celebrate the queer experience through the lens of speculative fiction. She started making up stories before she actually knew how to write, and since then writing has become both her passion and her favorite pastime. Her work has also appeared in the magazines *Eldritch Lake* and *Trouble Among the Stars*, and she is currently working toward publishing her first novel.

C.L. Clark graduated from Indiana University's creative writing MFA. She's been a personal trainer, an English teacher, and an editor, and is some combination thereof as she travels the world. When she's not writing or working, she's learning languages, doing P90something, or reading about war and [post-]colonial history. Her work has appeared or is forthcoming in *FIYAH*, *PodCastle*, *Uncanny* and *Beneath Ceaseless Skies*. Now she's one of the co-editors at *PodCastle*.

Trip Galey is a writer, a PhD student, and a researcher of all things pursuant to bargains, exchanges, and compacts of a faery nature. It is inadvisable to attempt to make a deal with him. He has been, in the past, a reluctant cowboy, an Ivy League collegian, and an itinerant marketing professional. Mostly harmless. Find him at www.tripgaley.com.

Blake Jessop is a Canadian author of sci-fi, fantasy and horror stories with a master's degree in creative writing from the University of Adelaide. You can read more of his queer speculative fiction in *Grimm, Grit, and Gasoline* from World Weaver Press, or follow him on Twitter @everydayjisei.

Marianne Kirby writes about bodies both real and imagined. She plays with the liminal space between vanishing and visibility. She authored *Dust Bath Revival* and its sequel *Hogtown Market;* she co-authored *Lessons from the Fatosphere: Quit Dieting and Declare a Truce with Your Body.* Marianne has contributed to women's interest publications, news outlets, and tv shows that require people to have opinions. She has been published by the *Guardian, xoJane, the Daily Dot, Bitch Magazine, Time,* and others.

Jordan Kurella is a queer and disabled author who has lived all over the world (including Moscow and Manhattan). In their past lives, they were a barista, radio DJ, and social worker. Their work has been featured in *Apex, Beneath Ceaseless Skies,* and *Strange Horizons Magazines.* Find them on Twitter (@jskurella), or at jordankurella.com.

L.D. Lewis is an award-winning SF/F writer and editor, and serves as a founding creator, Art Director, and Project Manager for the World Fantasy Award-winning and Hugo Award-nominated *FIYAH Literary Magazine.* She is the author of *A Ruin of Shadows* (Dancing Star Press, 2018) and her published short fiction includes appearances in *FIYAH, PodCastle, Anathema: Spec from the Margins, Strange Horizons,* and *Fireside Magazine,* among others. She lives in Georgia with her coffee habit and an impressive Funko Pop! collection. Visit her website at ldlewiswrites.com and follow her on Twitter @ellethevillain.

Otter Lieffe is a working class, femme, trans woman and the author of three trans feminist novels. A grassroots community organiser for over two decades, Otter has worked and organised in Europe, the Middle East and Latin America with a particular focus on the intersection of gender, queerness and environmental struggles. If you fall in love with Dee and Rob, the characters from this story, you can read more of their adventures in Otter's new novel, *Dignity.* www.otterlieffe.com

Darcie Little Badger is a Lipan Apache writer with a PhD in oceanography. Her debut novel, *Elatsoe*, will publish with Levine Querido in August 2020. Darcie co-wrote *Strangelands*, a comic series in the Humanoids H1 universe. Her short fiction, nonfiction and comics have appeared in multiple places, including *Nightmare Magazine, Strange Horizons,* and *The Dark*. She is engaged to a veterinarian who cosplays as both Cassandra Pentaghast and Luke Skywalker.

A.Z. Louise is a civil engineer-turned-writer of speculative things, whose conure keeps them company during the writing process. When not reading or writing, they can be found playing folk harp, knitting, or weaving. Their work has been published in *Strange Horizons, FIYAH,* and *NightLight Podcast*.

V. Medina is a queer, nonbinary, disabled, mixed-race author and occasional creative corvid who lives in lower Kentucky. Their stories are anything from sweet to strange and they delight in showing the world the odd things that live in their brain. They can be found on twitter @howsweettheword and their website is at www.howsweetthewords.com

Michael Milne is a writer and teacher originally from Canada, now largely from nowhere. He has tried the patience of cafe owners and baristas worldwide. He writes sad stories about spaceships, ghosts, and spaceship ghosts. Find him online at www.michaelmilne.ca or on Twitter @ironcardigan.

Anthony Moll is a Queer writer and educator. Their debut memoir, *Out of Step*, won a 2018 Lambda Literary Award and the 2017 Non/Fiction Prize. Anthony holds an MFA in creative writing & publishing arts, and they are a PhD candidate at Morgan State University. Their work has appeared in a variety of publications, including the *Times Literary Supplement, the Baltimore Sun, Hobart, Assaracus, jubilat* and more.

Mari Ness spent much of her life wandering the world and reading. This, naturally, trained her to do just one thing: write. Her short fiction and poetry have appeared in multiple publications, including *Tor.com*, *Clarkesworld Magazine*, *Lightspeed*, *Uncanny*, *Nightmare*, *Fireside*, *Strange Horizons* and *Apex*. Her poetry novella, *Through Immortal Shadows Singing*, is available from Papaveria Press, and a collection of essays, *Resistance and Transformation: On Fairy Tales*, is forthcoming soon from Aqueduct Press. She lives in central Florida, with a scraggly garden, large trees harbouring demented squirrels, and numerous books. For more, visit her occasionally updated website at marikness.wordpress.com, or follow her on Twitter at @mari_ness.

Aun-Juli Riddle is a writer and illustrator who lives in Baltimore, Maryland with her partner and trio of cats. She runs an online tea shoppe and enjoys traveling the country to sell magical wares and collect souvenir magnets. Find her online at www.aunjuli.art and on Twitter as @aunjuli.

Lauren Ring (she/her) is a perpetually tired Jewish lesbian who writes about possible futures, for better or for worse. Her other short fiction can be found in or is forthcoming from *Pseudopod*, *Helios Quarterly*, and the *Recognize Fascism* anthology by World Weaver Press. When she isn't writing speculative fiction, she is pursuing her career in UX design or attending to the many needs of her cat Moomin. You can see her latest work at laurenmring.com.

Adam R. Shannon is a career firefighter/paramedic, Sturgeon Award-nominated writer, aspiring cook, and steadfast companion of dogs. His work has appeared in Apex, Nightmare, The Best American Science Fiction and Fantasy 2019, and other magazines and anthologies. He's a graduate of Clarion West 2017.

A.P. Thayer is a Mexican-American author based out of Los Angeles. He writes grimdark fantasy, latino-futuristic magic-punk, and cosmic horror. His work has appeared in *Made in LA volume 3, Five on the Fifth,* and *Murder Park After Dark.* When he's not writing speculative fiction, he can be found cooking for his friends, DMing a tabletop game, or hunting down street tacos. Find him at www.apthayer.com or on Twitter @apthayer

R.J. Theodore is a creative magpie whose published work includes the Phantom Traveler series (self-published) and the Peridot Shift series (Parvus Press). They are co-host of the We Make Books podcast (@wmbcast). "A Future in Color" is R.J. Theodore's first published short story. For more information, please visit rjtheodore.com.

Izzy Wasserstein is a queer, trans woman who teaches writing and literature at a midwestern university and writes poetry and fiction. Her work has appeared in *Clarkesworld Magazine, Apex Magazine, Fireside Magazine,* and elsewhere. She shares a home with her spouse, Nora E. Derrington, and their animal companions. She's an enthusiastic member of the 2017 class of Clarion West.

Brendan Williams-Childs is a writer from Laramie, Wyoming who now lives elsewhere. His work has previously appeared in *Meanwhile Elsewhere: Science Fiction and Fantasy from Transgender Writers, Nat. Brut,* and *Catapult.*

About the Editor

dave ring is the publisher and managing editor of Neon Hemlock Press, as well as the co-editor of *Baffling Magazine*. The first anthology he edited, *Broken Metropolis: Queer Tales of a City That Never Was,* was published in 2018 by Mason Jar Press. His short fiction has been featured in numerous publications, including *Fireside Fiction, The Disconnect*, and *A Punk Rock Future.*

More info at www.dave-ring.com. Follow him at @slickhop.

About the Press

Neon Hemlock is an emerging purveyor of zines, novellas, queer chapbooks, and speculative fiction. Learn more at www.neonhemlock.com and on Twitter at @neonhemlock.